SHOWTIME

I pad into the bedroom, just too damned provocative-looking in my ultra-sexy *Say No To Crack* oversized T-shirt—which features a photo of a fat guy with his butt crack showing—worn to obscure the unmistakable perma-pooch of a childbearing gut that I hope is neither exposed nor touched in the upcoming process. Of course Jack isn't doing much better with his Lord & Taylor all-cotton pin-striped Ward Cleaver look-alike pajamas. All he needs is a cravat and a billowing pipe to make the picture complete.

I settle under the blanket, feeling about as relaxed as a Christian in the Colosseum after noticing the lions creeping stealthily toward him. As a stalling tactic, I grab the remote and flick on the television.

"Mmmmm," Jack purrs.

Ugh.

JENNY GARDINER

Sleeping With Ward Cleaver

LOVE SPELL NEW YORK CITY

To my wonderful family, for putting up with me during this wild ride.

LOVE SPELL®

Februrary 2008

Published by

Dorchester Publishing Co., Inc.
200 Madison Avenue
New York, NY 10016

ISBN 10: 0-505-52747-2
ISBN 13: 978-0-505-52747-9

The name "Love Spell" and its logo are trademarks of Dorchester Publishing Co., Inc.

Printed in the United States of America.

10 9 8 7 6 5 4 3 2 1

Visit us on the web at www.dorchesterpub.com.

Acknowledgements

This book might never have come to fruition without the collaboration of far more people than I could ever thank enough; I hope that I don't forget to mention anyone—if so, please forgive the oversight. It has, to say the least, been an unusual confluence of circumstances that has led me to publication. I hope you all are pleased with the results, despite the unconventional manner in which I got here.

First off, many thanks to Renaissance Man Peter Skinner at whose behest I got off my butt and started writing again. Also to Suzanne Macpherson who was the first industry professional to believe in me. Her continued support helped me through many dark spots (and Rejection Fridays) in my early quest for publication. Thank you so much to Claire Harrelson, who patiently read everything I wrote, even the really bad stuff, and to Sonjia Smith, for her unadulterated positive feedback and willingness to read version after version of my books. To fellow writers Donna Rosenbloom—such a sweetheart and so encouraging— and Kim Stagliano, who cracks me up all the time: thanks for being there. To my fabulous agent, Erin Cartwright-Niumata: thanks for taking a chance on me. To my fantastic publicists Elizabeth Middaugh and Nancy Berland, for wanting to make this book a success. And of course, deepest gratitude to my wonderful editor, Chris Keeslar, who believed in this book and also took a huge chance on me, and everyone at Dorchester who has been awesome, including Erin Galloway, Brooke Borneman, and the patient Julianne Levine (and the art department for that groovin' *I Dream of Jeannie*-ish cover!). Thanks so much to Kathryn Falk at RT, for co-sponsoring the American Title contest, and Liz French, who kept me laughing throughout (with each e-mail from her I hoped I would not be revealed to be the weakest link). To the fabulous Meg Cabot, whose voice I adore and always makes me laugh: thank you so much for taking the time to read (and like!) my book. Same goes to Jane Porter, Lauren Baratz-Logsted, Bev Rosenbaum (and for her wonderful input), Kristy Kiernan, Eileen Cook and all of my fellow Debs.

I can't begin to thank enough uber-agent Jeff Kleinman, who gave me such early encouragement and has put up with my being a real nudge at times. Jenny Bent, for a Very Positive Rejection with suggestions early on, and Virginia Barber for taking the time to read and comment on my first-ever submission. And to the fabulous Diane Salvatore at *Ladies Home Journal*, who gave me a wonderful break —thanks for paying it forward.

Many thanks to my countless friends and family members who not only supported me but endured me during this contest. Thanks go to the entire city of Charlottesville, and my immediate neighbors in particular (what a great place to live!), my terrific friends in the 6 a.m. cross-training class (especially my PR manager, Mo Gaffney, and my ardent supporter Bill Howard). Can't forget my favorite "mayor," Joey LeVaca and his lovely wife, Elizabeth. Enormous thanks go to my fellow sisters of Delta Delta Delta sorority (Alpha Phi's at PSU), especially Linda Wolf McLinden (and my Collegian buddy Pete Waldron for pointing me to her) and my many friends and supporters at the greatest school, Penn State, particularly Peggy McMullin, who came along at a perfect time, and Mike Poorman, another Collegian buddy who helped so much (along with Steve Sampsell). Thanks so much to various Greek organizations at UVA (especially Caitlin Deans!) and throughout Virginia; corgi breeders along the East coast (thanks Peggy Kessler!); lawyers in North Carolina and my mom's wonderful colleagues; I think there's a submarine full of sailors out there to whom I owe a debt of gratitude (!); the fabulous Rona, Mike, Todd, Lynn, etc. and the many well-coifed patrons of Moxie; Quilters Unlimited in Northern Virginia (special nod to Barb Tricarico who went the extra mile for me!); Bryan McKenzie from the *Daily Progress* who kindly humored me month in and month out; Sean Tubbs who took time out of his busy day to help plug me; Kathy Kildea, for including me in her Soup to Nuts menu each week (what a chef!); Judi Fennell—a really fun fellow Penn Stater who let slip her alumni chapter support; the selfless volunteers at Purrin' at Pantops who took time out of helping abandoned kitties to help this aspiring author; my high school buddy Rob Hamilton, who, I'm sure, had half the state of Florida voting for me; Rachelle Chase who sent me the most encouraging e-mail after I entered her contest last year; my friends at Backspace (what a great Internet home, and Stella, you rock!); the many writing loops and message boards who have backed me and provided guidance, including the Chick Litters, VRW and WRW; Elinor and Steve at my favorite wine shop, In Vino Veritas (yahoo for the wino vote!); people from my kids' many schools, sports teams, extracurricular ventures, and school activities; Anna Sass for her great marathon experience (better you than me!); Lynne Therese Gilardi, my old Barbie buddy, for alpha reading; the *Daily Progress* and WVTF-FM for giving me the freedom to write freely; Hawes Spencer for providing me with the delusional impression that getting published was going to be a breeze (thank goodness for that drought, which relaunched my writing career); Janis Jaquith for taking me under her wing early on; Bella Stander (BookPromotion101.com), who has been a guardian angel along the way; Kristy Kiernan and the Debs for anointing me as an '08 Deb (visit us at www.thedebutanteball.com); Ellen Silva at NPR for her professional encouragement; Rose Jacobius at the *Washington Post*; the Ladies Literary Lunch (now appearing in Charlottesville and Denver); my fellow Edgewood High School alums (at least those I was able to track down!); my mom, for the writing gene, and for generously investing in my career with the gift of a laptop when I needed it most; bCreative.com, who helped me a lot when I had to get manuscripts out (and all those votes!); Ron Baellow, my late-stage PR man, who hooked me up with the folks at WINA (what a fun interview!); Sue Haden for her faith in me; the Piranhas swim team in Menlo Park, CA, who still don't know me; Rod Stewart, whose Great American Songbook CDs provided the audio backdrop (and household noise escape) for writing this book; Mark and Victoria at Milano, where much of this book was written—if I can't be in Italy, then at least I can be at Milano!; Christina Ball, fellow writer and lover of all things Italian, and all my buddies in Italian class who followed the contest closely (and to Gianni G. for letting me pick his brain, unsolicited)—*mille grazie*!; Gerri Russell, who was a saint and as kind as can be; Ruth Kaufman, whose counsel was lovely; Lois Winston, whose very early support I am so grateful for; Gina Black for great advice; and to Jane at Chico's who's got such style and grace—stay healthy, my friend!

Lastly, it's been an added bonus to have forged friendships with my fellow American Title contestants, who all have shown great class and character: Kate, Judi, Kim, Raz, Linda, Cathy, Sally, Lindsey, and Meretta: no doubt soon to appear in print as well.

To all those who warmly embraced my cause and became huge proponents for me, I greatly appreciate your kindness. I love to hear from readers—please visit my Web site or blog: www.jennygardiner.net and www.thedebutanteball.com.

Chapter One

In roughly four hours, I'm scheduled to have sex with Ward Cleaver.

Ward Cleaver? you ask?

You know the guy: bland gray cardigan with leather-patched elbows, perma-press slacks, stern countenance. Stick up his ass.

Of course, it's not *the* Ward Cleaver, of black-and-white sitcom fame. The one married to June, that doyenne of conjugal perfection (by contrast with whom I could well be considered the Antichrist). Father of the Beav and all-around curmudgeon. No, no, no. Heavens, no. He's probably dead, for all I know.

Instead, I can stake my claim as being doomed to yet another Sunday-night roll in the hay with my very own version of Ward Cleaver: my husband, Jack Doolittle, a guy who once wooed me with sweet words and kind actions, but who now is content to deluge me with *do-this*es, *don't-do-that*s, and *do-you-understand*s? Somewhere along the line he morphed from gentle lover into bossy father, and I didn't even see it happen.

Yep. Years ago I went to bed with the man of my dreams. Now I find myself sleeping with Ward Cleaver.

It's six o'clock on a Sunday night, and I'm staring Ward in the face. The pork roast is fresh from the oven, the potatoes tender and hot, the beans steamed to crisp green perfection, and Ward—I mean my husband Jack—is hard at work hollering at one of the kids for some minor infraction. Great. Another dinner ruined because old Wardy-boy is on the warpath.

"Cameron, I asked you to rake the leaves four days in a row, and again you haven't done it," he nags. "So now I'm grounding you for a week."

Granted, Cameron would sooner march off to war than perform expected chores around this household, but the time to inflict extreme punitive measures isn't after I've spent three hours toiling over this picture-perfect dinner that no one but Jack will even eat. I'm lucky enough to have dragged these kids to the table at the same time; I don't need unwanted contention to flush this happy family meal in a swirling rush down the commode of filial resentment.

"If I told you once I've told you a thousand times, don't play with your food."

He's yelling at Chrissy now, who is stuffing green beans into her nostrils so that she looks like a walrus. I think it's kind of funny and let out a laugh despite myself. Jack glares at me.

"Young lady, if I have to pull those green beans out of your nose—and Lindsay, get your elbows off the table. You're old enough to eat like a lady."

We interrupt this lovely family dinner for a one-man bitchfest, brought to you by Ward Cleaver. . . . Our pleasant Sunday-night supper, which began with happily chattering children, has now devolved into a behavioral sermon conducted by the high priest of killjoy.

"And, Claire, do you suppose you might *someday* choose to remember not to disturb me on my cell phone when I'm out golfing?"

Out golfing while I'm home dealing with the kids and those to-do lists they aren't to-doing.

"Jack," I say through gritted teeth. I absolutely detest strife and will do most anything to avoid it. Even sleep with Ward Cleaver. "If you-know-who wants you-know-what, then you-know-who had better *back off.* Now."

Yes, it's Sunday night. Mandatory-sex night. Fuck. No wonder I hate Sundays so damned much. After a week of serving as mistress to house, husband, children, and career, the last thing I want is to have Jack point that gun at my temple.

I don't know when sex went from being the most glorious thing imaginable to being a loathsome necessity, ranking up there alongside trench warfare or changing bedpans at a nursing home, but somewhere along the line sex went from self-serving to servitude, and nowadays I find my mood worsening the closer I get to Sunday night.

Don't get me wrong. I still love Jack. And it's not that I think Ward's such a bad guy. After all, he's probably the one I'd count on to bring home a steady income, or to set the kids straight if we found a bong or a gun or a creepy snuff film in one of their dresser drawers.

But sex? With Ward Cleaver? Spare me. Or maybe send Ward's young nemesis, Eddie Haskell, my way. Maybe what I really need is a bad boy to save the day.

Ten o'clock. All the kids are tucked into bed, though it's guaranteed that at least three of them will waft unwelcome into the room like the aroma of overripe Brie during the next half hour.

Jack keeps eyeing me salaciously; he's a young boy on Christmas morn coveting the twinkling tree and its pile of colorful gifts sheltered beneath its limbs. If you could consider me a twinkling tree, as weary and out of shape as I've become. I'm more like the tree after the Twelve Days of Christmas have drawn to a close, the relatives have all gone home, the credit card bills have come due, and every last hint of life has evaporated from the poor thing and the naked limbs are surrounded by its exhausted needles littering the ground.

Sometimes I wonder how Jack can even look forward to this weekly venture, as I freely admit that sex with me has become about as much fun as getting it on with a week-old cadaver. Trust me, this body sure isn't hot, and in fact could barely qualify as tepid. I've tried to suggest to Jack that God gave him hands for a reason, but he just doesn't seem to take the hint.

The first child to return to the fold tonight is five-year-old Matthew, whose grimy baseball cap, worn backward, has become a permanent fixture on the boy's head. Jack calls him Bubba because he thinks he looks like a truck driver in the hat.

"Bubba, what are you doing up?" I snap, dismayed he's not asleep. Clearly bedtime is considered optional around here.

He squints his eyes at me, the bright light scorching his dark-adjusted retinas. "My nose."

I take a quick glance at his nose, see no blood, and dismiss him readily. "Sweetie, there's *nothing* wrong with your nose. Now get back to bed."

Matthew starts to cry. "My *nose!*" He sticks the stubby tip of his pointer finger up his left nostril.

I glance over at Jack, who lies in bed without a care in the world, not even bothering to lift his eyes off the page he's reading, despite his son's plaintive sobs. Where are his Ward Cleaverish authoritative ways when I need them?

I notice that Bubba's clutching something in his

right hand, and I peel open his fingers to uncover his cache. Resting in his sweaty palm is an elegant elbow-length lavender Barbie glove, the kind Barbie might wear to a state dinner. My son is staring at the glove and crying, all the while pointing at his nostril. I've always hated mimes; perhaps it's because I can't figure out what the hell they're trying to tell me. And I'm growing impatient with my little miming son.

I hear a soft knock on the door and look up to see Cameron silhouetted against the hallway light.

"Didja tell Mom yet, dopey?" Cameron enters the room and takes a tug at the sandy brown hair that's protruding from the adjustable strap of Bubba's cap. Bubba's eyes, as damp and dark as a tide pool at dusk, well up with tears of frustration.

"It is *not* okay to call your brother names," I say in a stern voice rich with unspoken threats. Then I realize Cam knows what's going on with his sibling. "All right. Confess. What's wrong with your brother?"

Cameron laughs above Matthew's wailing. "I'll give you a hint. You need pliers."

I see that Jack has donned a set of headphones, deliberately tuning out from this emerging crisis. His toe is tapping to the beat of whatever song he's escaped into. Probably Guy Lombardo. I could kill him.

"You two had better tell me what is going on before I count to ten," I say, then pull Matthew's hand into mine and drag him into the bathroom. I grab his chin and tip his head backward, using the light from the bathroom vanity to peer up the boy's nose, yet I see nothing.

"My nose, my nose," Bubba insists, tears wetting my hands that are still clutching his face.

I rifle through my Drawer of Excess in the bathroom, the clatter of inhabitants contained therein mocking me, reminding me of the complete disorganization that is a hallmark of my life. Finally I find the flashlight I'm searching for, buried behind the stash of condoms (long past their recommended shelf life), Band-Aid wrappers (which the kids refuse to dispose of properly), Vaseline, rusted safety pins, fingernail scissors, dental floss, wheat pennies, sullied cotton balls, and old tweezers, the ones I just can't throw away even though their tips no longer meet. I lean Bubba's head back again, shining the light up his nose.

"Aha, now I get it," I say, finally in on the secret.

Wedged deep into the recesses of the boy's tiny nostril is a lavender blob reminiscent of its mate, the one awaiting Barbie's White House dinner invitation in my son's tiny palm. Now that I've gotten to the bottom of this, I'm really angry.

"Matthew Joseph Doolittle. What in the hell are you doing with a Barbie glove up your nose?" I have this little problem with angry-mother-gutter-mouth syndrome. One time Cameron's teacher reprimanded him for saying the word *darn* in class, and he nonchalantly told her that his mother said far worse than that at home. It's a wonder Child Protective Services hasn't knocked on my door.

I turn to Cam. "And Cameron: A) How did you know that your brother stuck this up his nose? And B) Why did I have to discover this on my own while you insisted on playing twenty questions with me?"

His boyishly innocent pale blue eyes tug at my weak-willed heart. "Well, he was supposed to be asleep—"

"Yeah, and so were you."

"I went into his room to find the cat, and I found Bubba crying in the dark," he says.

"I want Dolly Llama," Matthew pipes in, sobbing now about the damned cat. Everyone fights over sleeping rights with that cat, who I'm convinced has mystical powers far beyond those of any normal household pet. How else would she know to run from me the minute she coughs up a hairball or pees on the living room carpet?

"So, let me get this straight," I say, then pause to peer out the bathroom door and again look at Jack, buried obliviously in some no doubt extremely engrossing biography, and want to smack him one. As horny as he might be, he'd rather check himself out of daddy duties and relax for a few minutes than help resolve this bedtime headache, even if his own sexual gratification is in the offing.

"Jack, do you think you could reenter the world of parentdom?" I ask.

"Huh?" He looks over at me, peering above his half-moon reading glasses. My God, he couldn't look more Ward Cleaver if he were sternly lecturing Wally and the Beaver right now. "D'you say something, dear?"

I roll my eyes in frustration and instead snap at the children in a cruel reversal of the old phrase, *Love the one you're with:* a sort of anger paradox.

Shining the flashlight up Matthew's nostril again, I can tell the glove is shoved deeply enough up there that it isn't going to easily just blow out, so I decide to resort to plan B.

"Grrrrrrr." I reach into the Drawer of Excess and dig for the random tweezers stash. I knew they would come in handy one day. I find an individual alcohol swab, clean the tip of a pair of blunted tweezers, and lean Bubba's head back yet again.

"Oooh, Mom, can I do that?" Cameron loves blood and gore. Once, when one of his sisters got stitches, he stood just inches away from the surgeon's needle, staring in awe as her forehead was sewn shut. The chance for permanent injury enchants him all the more.

"Dammit, Cameron, hold the flashlight, and not another word out of you." I reach precariously up

Matthew's nose—I never realized how small those little booger alleys can be—and gingerly guide the tweezers northward.

"Ooooooowwwwww," Bubba yells as I whip the tweezers back out, hoping I didn't pierce his brain or anything. I'm not so up on human anatomy as to know where the nose ends and the brain begins.

"Hold still and let me try again." This time I'm successful, and extract the gummed-up and slightly bloodied glove from the recesses of his nasal cavity.

"Hurrah for Mommy!" Matthew jumps up and down as Cameron leans in to inspect the surgical remains.

"Now, boys," I snarl. "I want those damn butts of yours in bed by the count of three—"

They flee before I can get the threat of punishment out. But all of a sudden I shut up as I realize the sad truth: I am just as much June as Jack is Ward. I am June goddamned Cleaver with a sailor's mouth. I'm no longer sweet young Claire Doolittle, Pan Am flight attendant. I am not Claire Mooney, cheerful and peppy former college cheerleader. I am not Claire anybody. I'm a cookie-cutter nagging, middle-aged mother-slash–sexless housewife, fighting a date with destiny: sex with Ward Cleaver and eventual death and burial as a washed-up has-been of a woman. How depressing.

Chapter Two

I brush and floss my teeth and blow a straggling strand of blond but graying hair up onto my head with my lower lip, about to settle into bed. I glance in dread over at Ward, much as I'd look at my gynecologist before my annual Pap smear, and brace myself. I hear a knock on my bedroom door and realize I'm about to get another momentary stay of execution.

"Mommy?"

"Chrissy?"

"My tummy hurts." She tiptoes into the room, pouting.

"Oh, honey. What's wrong?" I open my arms as Chrissy jumps into my lap where I sit on the bed.

"I don't feel so good," she says. She doesn't look so great, either.

I reach my hand to her forehead, which feels hot. "Sweetie, do you think you're going to throw up?" She begins to nod her head, then makes a dash toward the bathroom.

I'm sprinting in her wake, grabbing her long blond hair to keep it free of the flow of impending, uh, emissions. She makes it to the toilet with no time to spare, and I arrive behind her, pulling her hair back all the way and stroking her back supportively. After several violent heaves, Chrissy wipes her mouth and says she's feeling much better. I grab a washcloth from the linen closet and run some cold water on it, pressing it onto her forehead.

"Are you sure?" I know sometimes stomach bouts come and go fast, but other times you aren't so lucky.

"I think so, Mommy. I'm sleepy." She cozies up beside me on the cold bathroom tile; her body feels limp from the effort.

"Come on, baby doll. Let me get you back to bed. We'll get your teeth brushed, and I'll set a trash can by your bed in case this happens again and you can't make it to my room, okay?"

I can tell it's going to be a long night.

When I reenter our bedroom, the warm glow of the bedside lamp beckons mockingly. For a second I'm excited to fall into bed. Then I remember the task at hand. I'm furious with Jack for his failure to coparent this evening, which promises to make the Chore even worse. At least if he'd offered up a little help with the whining, tears, and throw-up, maybe he'd have redeemed himself a bit in my mind. Maybe then I would be feeling a touch more amorous right now. Then again, who am I fooling?

Jack looks up at me with that dopey primeval grin with which libidinous men are often afflicted. I realize I need to just ride the horse in the direction it's galloping, so I make my way to the bathroom to prepare for battle.

I remember years ago reading Erica Jong's *Fear of Flying*. Her concept of the "zipless fuck"— unencumbered by fumbling, stumbling, and psychological roadblocks—was merely a vague notion in my naive and carefree youth. Back then every fuck was zipless.

But now I have to be so certain I am zipped, sealed, locked, shuttered, and any other way assured that some rogue sperm doesn't find its way uninvited into my overzealous womb, that readying myself for sex is akin to prepping for major surgery. I'd fit right in at one of those highly sanitized Pentium-processor-chip factories, dressed from head to toe in hazmat gear. Or in lockdown mode at a maximum-security prison.

You see, I am one of the last holdouts who refuses to just deal with the Pill. Not only do I not trust it, but I also don't want to get fat, hairy, or otherwise chemically altered just so my husband can have a good time.

Instead, I tend to prefer the double-hulled oil tanker approach: protection on my end and protection on his end. That way if one system fails, we have backup measures in place. What this means is that preparing for sex is much like readying for battle, or attempting to ward off some dreadful communicable disease— also known as another baby. Not that I view my children as ailments, mind you. Yet, after five kids, another pregnancy would be akin to a chronic condition with which I might not want to be again afflicted. Plus, my organizational skills—or lack thereof—couldn't take such a hit. It's hard enough running seven lives as it is.

It takes me five minutes to ready the preventive measures, another few to jam that confoundedly slippery spermicided Frisbee up my crotch, and five more to drum up my libido enough to charge forth on this mission.

I pad into the bedroom, just too damned provocative-looking in my ultrasexy SAY NO TO CRACK oversize T-shirt—which features a photo of a fat guy with his butt crack showing—worn to obscure the unmistakable perma-pooch of a childbearing gut that I hope is neither exposed nor touched in the upcoming process. Of course, Jack isn't doing much better with his Lord & Taylor all-cotton pin-striped Ward Cleaver look-alike pajamas. All he needs is a cravat and a billowing pipe to make the picture complete.

I settle under the blanket, feeling about as relaxed as a Christian in the Roman Coliseum after noticing the lions stealthily creeping toward him. As a stalling tactic, I grab the remote and flick on the television. The only thing that reassures me my life is not too out of control is seeing how messed-up everyone else's lives are on the nightly news.

I'm just starting to get engrossed in a story about some country bumpkin whose pack of hunting dogs erroneously ate his newly dead mother's corpse when I feel Jack's hand inching along my flabby waist. I grind my teeth, hoping I haven't just cracked a molar. I gotta give the guy credit—coursing along the terrain of my midsection poses plenty of unwelcome challenges and can't be terribly appealing. Surely his fantasyometer must be in overdrive just to achieve an erection.

"Mmmmm," Jack purrs.

Ugh.

It is such a turnoff when he purrs. Not *because* he purrs. But because the *only* time the man purrs is when he wants to get laid. There's something so suspect about someone who makes carnal noises only while in pursuit of self-gratification.

There are no such sounds of pleasure coming from him when I've put in overtime at work. No purrs of delight when I've nursed three sick kids through the flu while he's been out of town wining and dining clients. No hum of contentment when I've fixed dinner for the seven of us—make that *four different* dinners for the selective eaters among the seven of us—or when he has a last-minute client he brings home unannounced to entertain.

Instead, the only time the man purrs is at moments like this. I think he's purring now because he erroneously believes *I* want to hear it or something, when nothing could be further from the truth.

But I fake it and purr back. I'm such a pussy. And I don't mean a cute little kitty cat, either. I mean spineless wimp of a woman, someone even *I* can't respect any longer.

Ward's hand is doing its cursory exploration of my left breast. Only the left one, because the right one is farther away from his reach and thus out of the plan of action. Which is just as well, because there's very little stimulation going on anyhow. After having nursed five children, I could probably have a Komodo dragon clamping down on those babies and I wouldn't notice it. Rub, rub, pinch, pinch, yeah, get it over with.

I close my eyes and try to relax. Try to fantasize about something. Anything. Sex with . . . hmmm. I can't think of anyone I'm particularly interested in having sex with right now. Oh, my God—I can't think of anyone in the entire universe I'd like to have sex with. What is wrong with me?

There must be someone. George Clooney? Well, it would probably be pretty one-sided with him. I've seen the women he dates, and trust me, I look *nothing* like them, unfortunately. Besides, I get the impression that the man drinks enough to make the entire act less than likely to come to fruition. I guess I could always *try* to imagine it; he does have those adorable nutmeg eyes and the crinkly laugh lines. And that million-dollar smile. Oh, and the vacation home in Italy.

What about Brad Pitt? Nah, not even remotely my

type. Plus he's got a thing for scraggly facial hair. His own, that is.

Matthew McConaughey? Hmm, that man is pretty hot. But even he isn't doing it for me. Christ, I'm a lost cause. Barely approaching my forties and thoroughly devoid of sexual desire.

Jack's hand has slipped beneath my aged underwear. I'm not talking a thong, here. More like the thong from the alternate universe: industrial-strength, buy-one-get-six-free, all-white, one-size-fits-all, full-of-holes underwear. This stuff couldn't turn on a faucet, let alone a person of the opposite sex. But I guess Jack doesn't care, judging by the forward thrust of his hand into my nether regions.

Okay, I need to start thinking of something to put me in the mood here. For lack of imaginative alternatives, I ponder having sex with the real Ward Cleaver. Somebody out there has sex with Ward Cleaver types. There *must* be *some* attraction to it, right?

I tighten my eyelids and try to visualize a sexier version of Ward Cleaver before me. Sexy Ward Cleaver. Now there's an oxymoron. Truth is, that concept is only making my stomach churn. It's actually making me claustrophobic. I feel like I'm trapped in a world of domestic horror and I can't get out. The doors and windows in this vinyl-sided rambler are sealed shut. As Ward bears down on me, all I can see is his big, domineering face peering judgmentally at me, his bob-nose and meat-loaf breath bearing down oppressively.

"Now, Beaver," he intones as he enters me. I think I'm getting Indian rug burns, I'm so dry. How *could* I be anything but, with the eminently paternal Ward Cleaver pummeling into me? I'm ready for him to yell at me for climbing up on the billboard and falling into the steaming cup of soup. Or for losing my lucky rabbit's foot, or because Miss Landers gave me a D on my grammar test. Or, or, or . . .

As my bad fantasy morphs back into reality, all of a sudden my stomach is feeling really queasy, but not just in my warped mind. I think I'm going to be sick. I must be coming down with whatever Chrissy has. I give Jack three final thrusts, allowing the deed to be done, dislodge him immediately, roll over, and rush like hell to the bathroom.

After throwing up for several grueling minutes, expelling every last one of my green beans from dinner, then cleaning up afterward, I return to the bedroom. Jack is sound asleep. I swear I see a smile of peaceful contentment spread across his slumbering countenance. The fucker.

Chapter Three

I'm wide-awake in bed, my stomach still unsettled, and my brain even more so. Reeling from the aftermath of that little Teddy Pendergrass moment, I wonder when exactly things took this precipitous downward turn. Here I am, awake at midnight in bed on my mandatory sex night—the Bataan freaking Sex March, for God's sake—and all I can wonder is how the ever-loving hell I got to this point. With all due respect to the esteemed soul singer Mr. Pendergrass, this doesn't look like another "Love TKO."

Jack and I met on a blind date. It's not that either of us was such a total loser that we had to resort to back-door dating, because we weren't. We both had jobs that kept us on the road a lot, and we rarely had the chance to meet people except in passing. My friend Kat was dating some guy, Tony, who knew Jack from work, so we all went out one night for dinner.

I was taken at first by Jack's intoxicating good looks. He wasn't just handsome; he was *handsome*.

Smoldering brown eyes flecked with bits of gold, as warm and inviting as a grizzly bear's pelt, long inky lashes, a devilish look on his face, and dimples. It was as if he came ready-made from the ideal-boyfriend factory. With several shooters and a few frozen margaritas under my belt I knew I wanted to get to know him better, and fast. As the night progressed, I was smitten by his clever repartee, his impressive résumé, and his obvious intelligence. And his broad shoulders, faded-Levi's-clad tight ass, and confident swagger.

We agreed to another date that night—just the two of us—before I hopped a cab back to my Adams Morgan apartment in DC. Back then I liked to tell everyone I lived in Adams Morgan, which was a hip, gentrifying neighborhood that had such cachet to it. In reality I was far closer to the Shaw District, which eventually became known for its nightly gang-related drive-by shootings. Luckily I was well out of there by then.

Anyhow, for our first "real" date, not only did Jack pick me up in my somewhat seedy neighborhood, risking his Saab convertible on the closest parking space two blocks away, but he also brought me a bunch of lilies-of-the-valley, my favorite flower.

How, you ask, did he know that? More than likely by the heavy dose of the floral-scented perfume I was sporting on our previous meeting. (What can I say? It was an '80s thing.) Nevertheless, I was impressed that he was savvy enough to recognize the aroma and surmise that I liked it enough to drown my own body in it. Or maybe he just asked Kat. With that simple gesture, Jack set a precedent for doing sweet things. Well, at least until we were married.

As we headed out for dinner, I was mortified to reach his car and see that the roof had been slashed and his stereo nabbed.

"Welcome to the neighborhood." I groaned, feeling totally responsible for the theft.

Instead of getting mad, he just smiled at me. "No big deal. Happens all the time. Besides, you're worth at least a tape deck."

Considering I was used to the kind of lame guys who said they'd call after a date, then maybe possibly actually did so ten months down the road, after having gone through five other women in the meantime, I wasn't quite sure how to handle such a courtly comment.

We shared a couple of bottles of Bordeaux at the Willard Room, and a meal that put my usual airline fare to deep shame. I figured the best response would be to encourage him on for more. As we left the restaurant and waited for the valet to deliver the damaged Saab, Jack asked if I was ready to go home.

"Not if you're not."

"So, then, if it's not your place next, where to?"

As I mulled this over for a moment or two, knowing full well I wasn't going home empty-handed, yet unwilling to dare ask the man to park his car outside my apartment all night—he'd be left with only a few bolts and an axle by morning—I made the executive decision to be a total slut and yield to my primitive yearnings. After all, this guy was the holy trinity of eligible men: gorgeous, intelligent, *and* nice.

"How about you show me your place?"

"You sure?" He arched a hopeful eyebrow my way.

"I'd love to go slumming in suburbia. And I don't have to fly tomorrow, so I don't even turn into a pumpkin at midnight."

With that, Jack slipped his hand in mine and led me to the car, safe in the knowledge that, barring unforeseen circumstances, he was gonna get lucky.

Jack lived just over the river in Arlington, in one of those posh high-rises that made you wonder who the fortunate bastards were who got to live there. He had a balcony that allowed a pretty obscured but nonetheless somewhat visible view of the Iwo Jima Memorial. You had to lean far off the left railing—six stories up—which was a little bit dangerous, but I figured I was living on the edge already that night, so I didn't hesitate to check it out.

"Jack?" He was in the kitchen fixing coffee or something. For all I knew he was rifling around in his nightstand for that box of condoms he'd picked up at People's Drug Store that afternoon, banking on an immediate need for them.

"Yeah?"

"Um, I can't exactly see this memorial, like you said. Do you have some binoculars or something?"

He didn't answer me, but a few minutes later I felt him grab me from behind, and I damned near jumped out of my skin. I screamed as loud as my lungs and larynx would allow—so much so that a neighbor popped his head out to be sure nothing untoward was going on.

"Oh, hi, there, Mr. Jacobs. Just having a little fun with my girlfriend out here." Jack winked at me.

Mr. Jacobs looked less than amused, standing there in his bathrobe, but was obviously assured that Jack wasn't a murderer trying to hoist me over the edge, so he retreated into his apartment, presumably to mind his own business.

My heart was pounding in my throat, and I smacked Jack on the arm. "You scared the bejesus out of me!" But he'd also referred to me as his girlfriend, so how could I stay mad?

He pulled me closer and landed a kiss on my mouth that left me swooning.

Sweet Jesus, I was so horny I was practically hyperventilating.

"You okay?" he asked.

I panted a little and wiped my razor-burned lips.

"Are you kidding? I'm a mess. Save me from myself." I pulled him back in for a little more where that came from, and within minutes we were wrestling each other on a chaise longue on the balcony, scrabbling to remove each other's vital articles of clothing, knocking over the glass coffee table and creating quite a ruckus.

Mr. Jacobs peered around his sliding glass door again, and I will say I was a touch embarrassed that this stranger was catching us in the throes of such heated passion. Good thing I didn't know the guy; I could tell by his repeated throat clearing that he felt we should take our behavior to a less public venue inside.

Normally I wasn't so, well, forward with a guy. But there was something about Jack that just made me behave recklessly. I knew I was violating all of those rules of propriety—buying cows versus free milk and all that nonsense—but there was this electricity that ran between us, and I knew that if the power were switched off, the world would become too dull. So I charged forward and took my chances.

"Listen, Claire. I'll completely understand if you're not ready to take this any further—"

I placed my hand over his mouth. "Shut up and keep doing what you're doing."

I'm sure Jack figured he'd scored the jackpot with me: Easy Ellie, right to bed on the first real date. But he was such a gentleman, and, oh, my God, did he smell divine. He stood up, grabbed me by the hand, and pulled me impatiently into his apartment and toward the bedroom, bits of our outerwear strewn across his balcony, my bra half-cocked on my arm, his unzipped pants falling down with the weight of his belt buckle.

I was pleased to see that he hadn't actually placed an industrial-size gross of condoms on the nightstand—that would have displayed a bit too much confidence in my bedability. We spent the next fourteen hours in our own little horizontal tango, coming up for air a few times and resting in between to replenish our exhausted energy stores. But still, that electricity was there.

After that, Jack and I became inseparable. When not traveling for work we were together constantly, and spent the vast majority of our waking hours in pursuit of each other.

Now I try to remember those days: having sex like a couple of minks—is it true that minks are prolific that way?—and just generally behaving like two people whose passion for each other was inextinguishable.

Damn. Whatever happened to that passion?

BZZZZZZZZZZZZZZZZZZZZZZZNNNNNNNNNNNNNNNNN NNNNNNKKKKKKKKKKKKK.

I peel apart one glued eyelid and try to focus on the LED display on Jack's clock. Five fifteen—a.m. I barely nodded off to sleep finally a few short hours ago, my stomach continuing to perform its unhappy gymnastics throughout the night.

I jab Jack in the ribs. It's his damned alarm going off. Were it not for this blaring aural intrusion, I could have been guaranteed at least an extra hour and a half of sleep. Normally this early morning reveille is bad enough, but I deal with it; today it promises to be my death knell.

Jack scrambles out of bed, unnaturally alert, neglecting to sustain a polite level of silence for the ostensibly slumbering partner beside him. Jack gets up this early so that he can squeeze in a long run before he has to get ready for work. He's recently begun training for a marathon—a truly selfless venture for a father of five, don't you think?

Marathon man lumbers into the bathroom and hits the light, casting a beacon of brilliance that stabs in my direction, piercing through the protective shield of my eyelids. The illumination is so bright I feel like I'm the subject of a police interrogation. Which I could well be, if I acted upon the current urge I'm feeling to kill the man. Finally he shuts the bathroom door—with a resounding thunk rather than gingerly twisting the knob and closing it delicately.

Nevertheless, through the closed door I can hear his five-minute stream of all-night urine hitting the toilet bowl. How the man's bladder can endure six-plus hours without evacuation escapes me. I can barely hold it in for two hours, tops. But then again, he hasn't had five babies pressed against his internal organs for a grand total of forty-five months of his adult life. No bloody damned wonder my bladder retention isn't like his.

Next Jack runs the electric toothbrush. Even with two pillows firmly lodged over my head I cannot escape the eternal buzzing coming from the bathroom. Two full minutes of brushing—dentist's orders—then gargling.

"Aaaaaaaaaaaazzzzzzzzzzzzzzzzhhhhhhhhhhhhhhhhhh-hhhhhhhhhhhrrrrrrrrrrrrrrrrrgggggggggggggggggghhhhhhhhhhhh-hhhhhhhhhhhhh." He expectorates loudly into the sink. From a distance I can hear our parrot, RePete, downstairs, imitating that same grotesque grinding, rising-from-the-gullet phlegm-removal sound. Lovely. Why would I *ever* think I'd get back to sleep at this point?

I get up and trudge into the bathroom, scaring Jack in the process, causing him to drop his can of deodorant on the ground, the clattering noise guaranteed to wake at least one kid up.

"Good morning," he says pleasantly enough. I don't dare start off the week accusing him of being an inconsiderate oaf.

"Mmmmph," I say through a mental haze.

Because I am before him in body, he assumes I'm there in spirit, and so begins ticking off chores and duties that need to be attended to over the next several days. My arms are crossed against my chest, and I'm leaning against the door frame in the hopes that it might keep me from falling down. My eyelids are at half-mast, and I nod out of obligation, completely oblivious to what the man is saying.

"Do you understand?" His voice sounds stern, and he looks at me as if I wasn't listening to him or something.

"Huh?"

"What I was saying. *Do you understand* everything I told you?" Uh-oh. He seems annoyed. The Ward Cleaver metamorphosis has begun.

"Um, yeah, sure, yeah," I lie.

"Well, then, tell me—what did I say?"

"Oh, something about the cat being inspected, and Charlotte needing a replacement part, and Cameron has to cut the dog's hair—"

My attempt at humor has fallen short. "See, I *knew* you weren't listening to me. Dammit, Claire, can't you just focus for once in your life?"

Deep inside of me, the Claire-that-used-to-be is screaming, *Listen, buddy. I wouldn't even be standing in front of you if it weren't for the amazingly, unbelievably, outrageously, selfishly inconsiderate manner in which you arise each morning. Just because you want to drag your goddamned butt out of bed at the obscene hour of five a.m. doesn't mean that I do. If you had one lick of courtesy left in that miserable fucking body of yours—*

But instead I say, "Look, Jack, I'm tired and I don't feel well. We'll talk about it later."

Of course, the Claire-that-used-to-be would also not be in this situation. Rather, she would be grabbing Jack by the still-tight ass and pulling him into her, burying her mouth in his, making him forget all about his run.

I remind myself that things are the way they are. I should just be grateful that Jack, now temporarily placated, settles into his prerun stretching routine, which I guess means I've been formally dismissed. I pretend not to notice his complete lack of concern about my not feeling well.

When Jack and I first met, I was working for Pan Am, based in Washington, DC, and flying mostly domestic routes but taking on an occasional transcontinental route as well. The pay sucked, but it was marvelous seeing the country, flying around the world during my free time, having not a care in the world.

Jack was working with a high-powered architectural firm in DC; he was considered a young lion in his field, and his professional future looked bright. He often commuted between Washington and New York working on large building projects. He'd been out of college for a couple of years and was no longer subjected to the hazing type hours required of a newbie architect.

I had come out of college entrenched in a long-term relationship with a guy I thought I was going to marry. His name was Todd, and as far as I knew we were marching our way toward wedded bliss; we'd talked about honeymoons, discussed names for our children, what city we wanted to settle in, even shopped for engagement rings. Imagine my surprise when he came home one night to tell me he met someone at work named Vanna and he was getting married. Vanna Black. I was supplanted by a girl named Vanna fucking Black. No doubt the evil twin to that infamous dim-witted letter turner. You can understand why I could never again watch *Wheel of Fortune* without grimacing.

I wallowed in misery for a while, then plunged myself into my work—as much as you can when you're a glorified midair babysitter. More like I plunged myself into having fun traveling and being commitment-free.

My friend Kat liked to call me the Sky Slut, although, truthfully, I wasn't morally loose or anything. Well, not much. Besides, she was picking up more men on the flights we worked than I was. And yes, because I know you're wondering, the Mile-high Club *is* way overrated.

By the time Jack entered my life, I was ready for a little stability in my fly-by-night world. Someone to look forward to coming home to every now and then. And he certainly was someone great to come home to. He was a phenomenal cook, and when I flew in from a shift he'd have a gourmet meal waiting for me, a bottle of wine open and breathing, and a warm body to snuggle up to at night.

When I was on call and had to sit by the phone— these were the days before pagers and cell phones— Jack knew how to fill my once-vacant hours with plenty of diversions. And whenever possible, he and I would go on long runs on the bike trails along the Potomac River, sometimes throwing a picnic into a backpack, which we'd share while sitting by the Reflecting Pool on the Mall in DC.

We'd been together about seven or eight months when Jack asked me to fly to the islands with him for a long weekend. He'd booked us into a small resort in the Bahamas for a romantic getaway. To my great surprise, Jack proposed to me under the stars as we strolled along a deserted crescent of beach, just me,

Jack, a bottle of Veuve Clicquot, and a sheet he had appropriated from our cabana room. Oh, and the two-carat emerald-and-diamond ring he'd managed to secure in his carry-on bag without my finding it.

We celebrated the occasion by making love on the beach for hours, until the predawn fishermen could be heard in the distance, at which point we scurried back to the room to carry on.

Times sure have changed. In fact, it's almost painful for me to recall those strife-free, I-could-just-devour-you-in-one-sitting days, as it serves only to remind me that we're so far removed from that now. It seems that now we're living in the I-could-just-chew-you-up-and-spit-you-out-on-the-pavement days. It's as if I'm suffering from phantom-limb syndrome: the hint of its previous existence gnaws at me tauntingly, serving only to remind me how wonderful it was by comparison and how very much I miss it.

Since I can't get to sleep I tiptoe downstairs to my desk, flick on the kitchen light, and sit down at my laptop: the electronic god of cyberspace beckons. With a little luck I'll get caught up on some work before dawn nudges me unceremoniously into mommy mode.

I no sooner wake the computer up than I hear my e-mail alert ding. Odd; I wonder who would be sending something to me at this obscene hour? I scan my inbox rapidly, a sniper on a mission, intent on finding work-related e-mails I can delete and pretend I never received.

I scroll down the thirty-two e-mails I've received since Friday afternoon when I cut out of work early to meet Kat for a drink. I swear, I'm finding any excuse in the book to get out of work these days.

Seventeen e-mails from my boss, Robert, a man with a penchant for electronically issued mandates. I randomly delete several of his, then tick down the list.

Sarah, Melinda, Amazon.com, the Company Store, MAC Cosmetics, the *New York Times* online. Penile implants. Breast augmentation. Viagra. Delete, delete, delete. My finger is trigger-happy with the kill button. Kat—save that one. Rodney from accounting? Delete. Mom—save that one. My sister, Sydney. Syd and I were always very close. And although she's only a few years younger than me, the chasm between us has expanded exponentially over the years because she's never married. While I've slogged on in the trenches of marital warfare, Sydney has remained starry-eyed in her determination to find Mr. Right, even as she's seen me become less and less enchanted with the state of my own union. I hate to be her shining example of how not to proceed in holy matrimony, but I'm afraid it's my legacy at this point.

Well, I'd better see what's up with her.

Hi, Claire!
Guess what? I went out with that new guy from my office on a real date Saturday night. He was awesome! So cute, so charming, so wonderful. I decided to employ the Claire Mooney "How to Land a Guy in One Easy (note emphasis on the word *easy*) Step" method.

I laugh.

I know, stop laughing. So I slept with him. Nothing you wouldn't—or didn't—do, right? It was definitely worth the sacrifice ☺. Not that we got much sleep. Amazingly, we had brunch on Sunday. (Can you believe it—he stayed for brunch? Hell, we're practically engaged!) We're going out again on Wednesday night (a midweek date—is this good or bad?). Until then I'll just have to rely

on my memories from Saturday night to keep me
going. <Sigh>. Call or write back if you want me to
fill you in on all the dirty details.

Sigh is right! Only it's my sigh, not hers. My little sister's getting laid. And in a good way, lucky duck. No
wham-bam-no-thank-you-Ward sex for Sydney, that's
for sure. I guess that makes it official: I am now relegated to living my sex life vicariously through my little
sister. The only way I get to relive those glory days is
through the telling of her sordid tales of slutdom. I can
only hope her sex life doesn't devolve into the nihilist
act of passive aggression that mine has become. I'm
actually thinking about calling her and waking her up
to get the lowdown when my eyes graze over an unfamiliar listing in my in-box, from Toddster@USD.com.

Who the heck is Toddster? I click on the name,
opening up a lengthy epistle. I scroll to the bottom,
and my heart does a double beat in my throat. Todd.
Todd Sterodnik. AKA the one who got away.

It's true, he did get away, fled from me faster than an
evacuee from a natural disaster. But upon further consideration, Sterodnik? I could never have married the
guy, not with that name. Claire Sterodnik? I should
have known from the get-go that we were not meant to
be. What misery it would be living life with a name
like that.

I look at the e-mail address again. Toddster. What in
the hell kind of e-mail name is *that*? Toddster? Did the
man fall that far off the pedestal that he's turned into a
complete doofus? Well, I guess it's better than him becoming an overly confident lothario: ToddtheRod, for
example. That would be skeevy.

I break into a cold sweat, and I don't think it's fever-
induced, even if I am sick.

Okay, Claire, get a grip. After all, the man can't actually *see* me. As far as he knows, I am still the gorgeous vixen he got rid of like a bad case of acne lo those many years ago.

Who knows? Maybe he's thought it over and doesn't want Vanna after all. Yeah, right.

Oh, Christ, Claire, that was nearly twenty years ago. I take a look at my reflection in the mullioned glass of my kitchen cabinet. Hardly the clearest image of myself, but pretty shoddy nonetheless.

My paranoid imagination takes over. What if there were no Internet? What if Todd—no, pardon me, Toddster—wanted to find me, but the only way to track me down was by pounding on doors until eventually he arrived here?

What if right now, at this very minute, Toddster was parking his Buick—no, make that his Lexus—in front of my house, and was adjusting his Brooks Brothers tie and straightening out the creases in his impeccably tailored Saville Row suit, and striding confidently up the walkway of this house—this very house—then ringing the doorbell, and of course then my dog, Tripod, would bark mercilessly and the children would wake up demanding attention, and RePete would start squawking and maybe burp really loudly just like Jack, and Todd would peer through the peephole and see the distorted me that he left behind, and I'd be forced to open the door looking like a hausfrau gone mad.

Oh, imagine the humiliation. I'd stand there as he stared at a very neglected me, from the bottom of my unpedicured feet to the badly-needs-a-foil-job tips of my doll-stuffing hair (which is standing on end in a most unattractive manner), and he'd get a whiff of my sour throw-up-residue breath, take note of my less-than-come-hither appearance, and open his mouth to speak, giving a quick shake of his head, rethinking his words, only to finally say, "Oh, I'm so very sorry, ma'am; I *must* have the wrong address. I'm looking for a beautiful young woman named Claire. I obviously must have gotten my information wrong."

At which point I would be forced to nod in bewildered agreement and say, "Yes, you must have gotten the wrong person."

Then I would turn and walk, shamefaced, back into the house, close the door then realize that not only am I a complete and utter failure, but I'm also not even June fucking Cleaver, as I feared, because at least that woman took good care of herself.

The truth is, June would've had a nicely pressed shirtdress on, and a patent-leather belt cinching that impossibly thin waistline of hers, a starched apron, and stiletto heels. And her hair would have been coiffed and her bright red (or was it black? Hard to tell in black and white) lipstick would be neatly applied, and she probably would've had an apple pie to greet him at the door, even right now, at five in the morning, and, and, and . . .

Suddenly I remember that Toddster isn't actually at my door. My panic subsides. I breathe a sigh of relief and begin to read his missive:

Dear Claire, he writes.

Well, by "Dear Claire," does he mean that I *am* dear, or that I *was* dear? Does he want me to be dear again? Or am I reading too much into this salutation?

Dear Claire,

I know this will surprise you after all of these years. Probably the last person you ever expected to hear from again was me. And chances are good that you don't even ever want to hear from me again, as I was such a cad to you and ended things so abruptly with no explanation.

The man's a damned rocket scientist. What was his first clue?

Of course, you were always too much of a lady to hold a grudge against anyone, so you probably forgot about me long ago and found someone better suited to you anyhow. First of all, please accept my most belated apologies for being such a shit. No matter what my excuses, no one has the right to be so inconsiderate toward another person, particularly one with whom I shared so many important moments, not to mention a great deal of love, and even better sex.

Oh, my God. A man other than my husband is talking to me about sex I once had. *I* once had sex! And I enjoyed it, didn't I? I did? Hell, I can't even remember it anymore. It's all a well-forgotten deposit in my long-term memory bank. I must've lost my ATM card for that account. I wonder how I can access that information. Do I have to apply, deep within my brain? I'll need to know my mother's maiden name. The banks always ask that question.

Oh, shut up, Claire, and keep reading.

So, if you are willing to imagine me on bended knee, I truly am sorry for the heartless behavior of a confused young man, and hope that you have long since abandoned your justifiable bitterness toward me.

I'm not quite sure what has motivated me to write this letter to you. I guess it's hard to forever put to bed (excuse the pun) past loves, and so even though our lives have marched on over the

years, somewhere tucked inside my memory bank
are many fond thoughts of you.

He has a memory bank too! Maybe Todd is the key
to my own locked bank account. *Oh, yeah, sure,
Claire. Why don't you just call him up and ask him for
details.* "Hello? Todd? Yeah, remember me, Claire? . . .
Uh-huh . . . Yeah, that's the one. Yeah. So, uh, I was
kind of wondering, uh, can you give me a little information about you and me and sex and having fun?
'Cause I kind of forgot, and all of a sudden it dawned
on me that I used to have sex. And enjoy it. It wasn't
like sleeping with Ward Cleaver. So I'm trying to remember when it was fun; then maybe I can figure out
when it went from that to being a burdensome chore,
like taking out the trash, and . . ." I shake my head out
of my stupid fantasy and continue reading his e-mail.

I got your e-mail address from a fraternity
brother of mine who married Kat's friend Elizabeth's sister Sarah. You're probably wondering
why Kat didn't warn you that I would be sending
you an e-mail, but not to worry. Sarah simply
pulled it off some mass e-mail she got from Elizabeth, who got it from Kat, who got it from you. I
think it was a dirty joke about a priest, a rabbi,
and a flight attendant. (Way to go, Claire—glad
to see you still have that bawdy sense of humor.)
    Anyhow, I guess what I'm trying to say is that
I just e-mailed to see how life's treating you. To
see where life finds you at this middle point. I
heard that you're married, but I don't know if you
have any kids, a job, special interests. Are you a
homebody, or do you still love to travel, like in the
old days?

I'll understand completely if you don't want to respond to my e-mail, but I'll hold my breath in anticipation that you are at least a little bit curious about me after all of these years. With fondest regards, I hope to hear from you.
Todd.

Whoa, Betty. That's one way to start my day. I read the e-mail about four more times to dissect it for deeper meaning. Finally I close my laptop, my hands actually trembling, and stealthily climb back upstairs and into bed before Ward can return home to disrupt my old-boyfriend-reunion fantasy I'm about to fall asleep to.

Chapter Four

"Mommy, wake up." I feel a small hand jiggling my shoulder. I open an eye to see Lindsay, my seven-year-old, staring at me with her big brown puppy-dog eyes and her pixie-short brown hair. She smells of sick.

I look at the clock. I must have miraculously fallen back asleep. For twenty-three minutes. Just long enough for thoughts of Todd to start revving up my engine. That very same engine I thought had completely seized from lack of proper maintenance.

"Mommy, I threw up in my bed."

Nothing like that pronouncement to wake me from my slumberous safe haven, floating as I was through an erotic dream involving Todd, me, and a banana split. So much for that purrin' motor.

"Oh, my poor LuLu," I say. We sometimes call Lindsay LuLu because she had a hard time pronouncing her name when she was little. "Let's get you cleaned up, then, and back into bed. Looks like there'll be no school for you *or* Chrissy today."

Twenty minutes later I'm pondering my options.

Two kids home sick; looks like I won't be making it to work today. Work is a relative concept anyhow. More like mind-numbingly dull tedium that could qualify as virtually unpaid serfdom. So's motherhood on occasion, for that matter. I'm a serf at home and a serf at work. I'm a little serfer girl.

I work part-time at a public relations firm. Hardly the world's most gratifying profession, but I needed something in my life that didn't suck the lifeblood out of me, and I erroneously thought my career choice was that. I was wrong. But now I'm used to the extra mad money coming in and the hint of independence it suggests, and so I don't have the courage to give it up.

I reach for the phone and dial up my boss's extension. Thank goodness he won't be in yet.

"Hi, Robert? It's Claire. I'm really, really, really sorry, but I've got two kids home throwing up right now, not to mention I spent half the night hurling myself, so I don't think you want me in the office today. I promise I'll work at my computer, and you can just let me know if you need me."

At least now I don't have to wrestle with whether I should stay home to take care of myself versus doing the "right" thing and suffering at the office with the rest of the miserable slobs there. Instead I'll get to stay home sick with the sick.

One of the things they never warn you about concerning parenting when you're still in the healthy glow of that first pregnancy—once the morning sickness subsides, before the hemorrhoids take over—is how brutal it is to be sick when your kids are sick. At least now the kids are a little bit older and can be somewhat self-sufficient. But with two at home, if they start to rebound then I'll be forced to deal with the inevitable bickering that will ensue. Oh, boy, with a little luck, that'll leave me hunkering over the toilet (which probably hasn't been scrubbed in weeks, a fact that further unsettles my tumultuous stomach) while the girls go at it. Lovely.

Nevertheless, I can't belabor that issue, because I now must wake the rest of the children and get them off to their various schools.

First I approach fourteen-year-old Cameron. I open his bedroom door and am bowled over by the aroma of teenage boy. It seems like only yesterday I was imbibing the intoxicating scent of newborn baby's breath from my firstborn, and now I am scrambling for a clean sock lying somewhere on the floor—because all of Cameron's laundry, clean or dirty, is strewn about the ground—to mask the assault on my acute olfactory system. I find a pair of clean boxers, which will have to suffice, and flatten them over my mouth and nose.

"Cameron, love, time to get up," I say in a muffled manner. Now I know how hard it must be for a bank robber to communicate the stickup commands.

"Your money or your life," I joke, but Cameron's too tired to get my joke, and he rolls back over and begins to snore.

I pull the covers down from the top and up from the bottom, leaving the important extremities exposed to the cold morning air. That works, and he pops up, hollering.

"Mooooooooooom," he moans. "You didn't have to do *that!*"

"Hurry up, or you won't have time for your complete breakfast," I tell him. I love to sound like one of those ridiculous commercial moms. I picture myself holding up a jar of Jif peanut butter or something. Quite the parody, me in my wrinkly old T-shirt sporting a bad case of bed head.

"Mom, will you drive me to school today so I can sleep longer?" he begs.

"Nope, sorry. Lindsay and Chrissy are home sick, so I have to stay here with them."

He grumbles but stirs enough that I know he's well on his way to motivating. His brother's next. By the time I have Cameron going, Matthew's motor is fully stuck in the "on" position and he's buzzing about like an oversexed mosquito. I rarely have to wake that boy; he has some internal timepiece set much like the universal-happy-hours clock.

For Matthew, the theory is, "It must be time to wake up somewhere in the world." I much prefer the old, "It must be five o'clock somewhere in the world." That saying seems to blend better with the lifestyle of my fantasies rather than my lifestyle of choice.

Charlotte has arisen, unable to sleep through Matthew's racket. The other two girls appear to be in an illness-induced coma for the time being. While I'd prefer they slept later on rather than now so that I could get a few more hours of shut-eye myself, it will simplify my morning ritual if they don't choose just this moment to demand my attention.

Jack is pitter-pattering into the house now; he still thinks he's in jog mode, but he won't get far inside like that. He's soaking wet, and he shakes off like a dog all over the kitchen tile. It must be raining, because he never sweats when he runs, or at least not like that. Sure enough, I peer outside to see rain slanting down on the garage roof. This day looks just as dismal as it already feels.

"What's for breakfast?" he asks. I heave a sigh because, pity the man, he really *doesn't* get it.

"How about a bowl of warmed-over puke with a side order of green bile?"

He never enjoys my jokes as much as I do.

"Ha, ha."

"As you have clearly not deciphered on your own, Mr. Hardy Boy detective, a good thirty percent of this household is waylaid with a stomach bug, so breakfast is going to be catch-as-catch-can."

"You're not going to fix me *anything*?" he whines with open palms.

"I'll be happy to fix *you*," I grumble under my breath, and thrust a box of Cap'n Crunch into his waiting hands.

Jack departs to shower and shave, and I successfully get the remaining three kids fed and lunches prepared. I'm just returning from the bus stop—Jack's oversize trench coat the only thing between my pathetic nightshirt and the watchful gaze of my neighbors—when I realize that Matthew forgot his lunch box.

"Dammit," I mutter. Someone is *always* forgetting his lunch around here. But then I realize Jack is perfectly capable of providing transportation for his youngest son's wayward meal.

Jack rises from the table, leaving behind his half-empty orange juice glass and the cereal bowl with the telltale yellowish milk and spoon encrusted with Cap'n Crunch crumbs. He assumes the maid is going to clean up after him. Except that we haven't got a maid.

"Ah, ah, ah," I remind him. "You, too, are perfectly capable of rinsing and loading your bowl. And here." I hand him Bubba's Polly Pocket (a hand-me-down, poor-boy) lunch box.

"I've got an important meeting in town. I don't have time for that," he objects.

"You have five minutes to divert to school so the poor child has his peanut butter and jelly!"

"Oh, fine." He grabs it despite himself, delivers a cursory kiss, and departs.

I plop myself down on the couch and flick on *Live with Regis and Kelly* to see what I, too, could have looked like if I were really rich and didn't have quite so many children and were the toast of Manhattan.

The contrast between Kelly and me is especially glaring this morning, considering I've already cleaned up after two sick kids, I'm still in my pj's, my once-bountiful soft blond curls are graying and looking a bit like the gnarled stuffing spilling out of this sofa cushion, and, oh, God, I totally forgot to pull out that diaphragm that is now giving me childbirthlike cramps somewhere in the vicinity of my uterus. Ugh. That thing will be ripe.

I glance down at my calloused feet, spread my hands to examine my splintered fingernails, and I realize that I have become a parody of the perfect house-wife. Jesus, Mary, and Joseph, where on Earth did Claire Doolittle disappear to? And is she gone for good, or is she just away for a long winter's rest?

I decide to humor myself, just to find something positive about my day so far. Walking into the bathroom, I heave out a deep breath (wisely expelling any extra unwanted weight) and quickly hoist myself delicately onto the scale. Surely, after my activity level of the past twelve hours, I must have shed a couple of pounds.

To my dismay I've gained two, despite losing last night's dinner. Can nothing go right today? I return to the kitchen and fix myself a cup of tea and nibble on a few saltines, hoping to settle my stomach.

Alas, my little Folgers moment is cut abruptly short by cries from upstairs. Tripod starts barking relentlessly, that shrill canine alarm that makes me want to reach down his esophagus and extract his vocal cords strand by strand. The dog is dancing around on his remaining three legs—we don't know how he lost the one; he came that way from the pound—happily alerting me to noise I can ably hear without his assistance.

"Tripod, shhh, be quiet," RePete hollers at the dog. For all the work that parrot creates for me, cleaning up the myriad feathers, shredded paper, and bird crap he strews about my house, his chatterfests make up for it.

"That's one, two, time-out," he yells in an exact replica of my voice putting my own kids in time-out. I take comfort in knowing that I am probably the only person on the face of this Earth who has a bird who puts the dog in time-outs for bad behavior.

I toss Tripod out the back door, where he is guaranteed to dig puddly holes in the red soil and come back inside through the dog door with a filth-encrusted snout and ankle boots of mud. I take the stairs two by two and find Chrissy on the landing, looking green around the gills.

"How ya feeling, baby doll?" I wrap my arms around her and scratch her head.

"Not good." She pouts.

"Do you feel like you're going to be sick?"

She just shakes her head and points toward the bedroom. Sure enough, I'm greeted with more cleanup. I pop Chrissy into the shower and head off to find a bucket and scrub brush; the carpet looks like it took a pretty big hit. All in a day's work.

At eleven thirty I get a call from Matthew's school. Jack forgot to drop off his lunch.

"Is there any money in the account for a hot lunch?" I ask the school secretary. I know there can't be, because my kids hate cafeteria food and we've been packing lunches every day since Cameron was in first grade.

"It looks like your account still has money in it from a few years ago," she says. I hesitate to tell her it's been nearly a decade. Thank goodness they don't have a statute of limitations on school lunch accounts. "Yes, it appears that you have over twenty dollars still in here."

It's a good thing I can't keep track of much in my life; otherwise I'd have taken that cash out ages ago and used it for some illicit three-martini lunch with Kat or something. Claire's dirty little secret: the main reason I can't give up my miserable job is that it gets me away from my household so that I can have drinking lunches with my friends and not worry about where my kids are.

"Oh, thank goodness, Mrs. Martin," I say, relieved. The last thing I want to do is have to dive in to the shower, gussy up my sick girls, and hightail it down to the school just to deliver the second lunch I'd have made for Bubba today. I don't even bother to tell her that Matthew will probably turn his nose up at everything offered on the menu. But at least I know he won't technically starve to death—food options do exist for the child.

The next phone call I get is from Kat. Kat is a party planner in Washington. She is thrice divorced, with one child who splits her time between her parents. Kat lives the high life, going from party to party when she doesn't have Tallulah with her. Nevertheless, my dear friend can relate to my state of mind, because she's been through it all—which is why she's no longer married.

"Claire, you didn't return my e-mails this morning, so I called your office and they said you were home sick!"

"Please don't tell me you talked to Robert."

"None other."

"How'd he sound?"

"About you, or toward me?" Robert has the hots for Kat, one of the few things going in my favor at my place of work.

"Kat, tell me," I implore.

"Well, he said something to the effect of, 'Claire is absent *once again.*'" She laughs. "I can't imagine he's thrilled to tears, but he'll get over it."

In some perverse way, even though Robert is a total wanker, Kat is intrigued by the man. They play this silly little telephone cat-and-mouse game all the time.

"So, he didn't say anything about wanting to fire me or pour boiling oil over my head or maybe torture me on the rack? Of course, I could use a couple of hours of stretching—a few inches taller and I wouldn't have to worry about losing the weight I've put on lately," I joke.

"Oh, stop it! You look wonderful." It's great having a best friend who will lie to you just to boost your self-esteem.

"Oh, man, if only you could see me now, you'd re-think that little piece of propaganda. Actually, I'm really glad you called. You are never going to believe the e-mail I got this morning."

"You've got me on pins and needles—go on!"

"Are you ready? I opened an e-mail from Toddster@USD.com. Do you know who Toddster might be?"

"No way."

"Yes, way."

"Get out of town."

"Would I lie to you about something of this magnitude?"

"Todd *Sterodnik* sent *you*, Claire—née Mooney, now Doolittle—an e-mail?"

"I swear to God. Can you believe it?"

"Well? What'd it say? He pledges his undying love, a

few years too late? He wants you to be the mother of his children? He found an overdue library book you'd checked out twenty years ago on his card and he wants you to pay the fine? And by the way—Toddster? He *is* kidding, right?"

"I guess old Toddster thought that was a clever little moniker, what with his useless appendage of a last name and all."

"Yeah, I can't see that one looking too professional in the corporate in-box, though. Can you? I mean, *Toddster*?"

"All right, enough about his bad choice of e-mail names. Let me fill you in on the important stuff. It wasn't exactly anything earth-shattering, per se, but he did stir up the old libido for a minute. That is, if I *had* a libido left it would have been stirred up. Make that shaken, not stirred. God, I could go for a martini right about now, except it probably wouldn't sit too well in my stomach. Actually, I could go for James Bond right about now. Except I'd forget what to do with him."

"Yoo-hoo! Claire! You're veering off topic here. He talked *sex* with you? Online?"

"No, not exactly, but he made reference to us having shared great sex."

"Did he mention the two of you in that glassed-in elevator in that hotel up on Capitol Hill?"

"I had sex in a glassed-in elevator?"

"Or so you told me. You don't remember?"

"Not exactly."

"Jesus, Claire. How can you not remember having elevator sex? *Glassed-in*-elevator sex?"

"I told you already, Kat, my sex life has taken the elevator down to the basement. Better yet, to the subterranean parking garage. Not only does my sex life suck—and not in a good way—but I can't even remember what it was like when it *was* good."

I hear Kat on the other end of the line making those admonitory noises all mothers love to make. "Tsk, tsk, tsk, tsk, tsk," she clucks. "You have fallen prey to the worst disaster known to modern woman. Claire, we need to fix this problem. You're thirty-nine years old, for crying out loud. You're about to reach your sexual prime. You cannot be neutered for the rest of your adult life!"

"Well, what can I say? I married someone who has morphed into a bad version of President Eisenhower or something. I can hardly *have* sex with the man, let alone *enjoy* it. I think I have just blocked the whole damned chore out of my brain as a coping tool!"

Kat gasps. "Chore?"

"I know, I know, 'How can the words *chore* and *sex* be uttered in the same breath? Sex is an act of love, of intimacy, of bonding souls with your chosen partner,' blah, blah, blah," I mock Kat. "But somewhere along the line that stopped being true, you know? And I found I didn't really need it. Or at least, I didn't think I did, but now that I'm actually starting to think about it, I think I *do* need it. Bad. But meanwhile, Jack being a member of that alien species known as men, he always needs it, and so I dole it out to him sparingly, like kibble to a mongrel who will take as much as he's given, even if it's rancid, or if it makes his stomach explode from overconsumption."

"Claire, Claire, Claire, Claire, Claire!" My elegant friend is no doubt waggling her perfectly manicured crimson fingernail at me. "There is no such thing on this great Earth as overconsumption of sex. *Au contraire*, my dear, there is only underconsumption. And clearly you are suffering from that. You are undernourished sexually. Sexual malnutrition—a ghastly yet perfectly curable condition."

I heave a sigh of exasperation. I know she's speaking the truth. And as painful as it is for me to hear it, I know I need to listen. I mean, the way things are right now isn't doing Jack much good, and it certainly isn't helping matters for me.

"Okay, teacher, so what do you propose I do about this?" I ask her, afraid to hear her response.

"That's right, your teacher is going to take you under her wing and figure out how to fix this terrible situation. After all, Jack is a very handsome man."

"Yeah, yeah, I know. But it's not the looks. It's how he *is*. He's so serious, so stern. So somber. So *blah*. So engrossed in his Ward Cleaver ways. I mean, come on, Kat, even *you* wouldn't have sex with Ward Cleaver."

"Of course not. That's why I unloaded that last ex-husband of mine. But for you it's different," she says. "Like I said, Jack is still a very handsome man. But on top of that he's a good guy, Claire. He's a good father; he loves his family. He's a great provider. Maybe you need to figure out how to ring his bell again."

"Oh, yeah, right. Ring his bell. I think his bell has a big old crack running through it, just like the Liberty Bell, so it won't ring no more."

"Well, in that case, you'd better figure out how to ring your own damn bell, honey, and I'd say the best way to start is to backtrack in your sexual history. If you don't want to discuss this with Jack, then perhaps you should consider discussing this with Todd. After all, Jack was the first big romance in your life after Todd left. Maybe that holds some key to something."

"What are you, Nancy Drew or something? We're living *The Mystery of the Old Goat's Libido*?"

When not TV sitcoms, my point of reference often tends to be children's books, being that they're all I ever get to read.

"No, I'm just saying that you'll be a lot happier if you start getting laid, rather than being had. Come on, Claire, your life is full of lots of *have-to*s: your kids, your husband, your pets, your work. But what are you doing for yourself? Having an occasional drink with friends? That hardly counts. Why don't you start doing what *you* want to do? Not what you *think* you should do. And not what *Jack* thinks you should do. What is your passion? What stirs your pot? What gets your juices really flowing? Claire, for too long you have been an appendage to someone else in your life—first Todd, then Jack, then, of course, your little football team of a family. You lost the 'you' in you. Matthew is in school now; it's time for you to really start dabbling in the rest of your life."

Christ, I had no idea that Kat was a soothsayer. "I didn't realize I was on the phone with the Dionne Warwick Psychic Hotline. How much are you charging me per minute for this advice?"

"Claire?"

"I know, I know, I'm being a smart-ass. But that's the last remaining thing I'm good at that doesn't suck the life force from me."

"Claire?"

"Okay, okay, you are making valid points here. It is time I capitalize on all that I have to offer not just everyone else, but me. You're right. I am going to carpe diem or whatever that is, and the first thing I'm gonna do is e-mail old Toddster and take a stroll down memory lane for real."

"Good girl. And you'll report back to me on your progress?"

"Aye-aye, Captain."

"Oh—and by the way, Claire?"

"Yeah?"

"Do you mind if I meet Robert for drinks tomorrow night?"

"Please tell me you aren't planning to fuck my boss."

"I'm just going for drinks!"

"Have you ever just gone for drinks with a man?"

"Well, no, but that's not because I sleep with anybody, you know." She sounds a little defensive. "It's because I've already vetted out the good ones. By the time I get to the actual date, I have a game plan in mind and I'm ready to advance the troops."

"I don't care what you do, just as long as you're careful and you have fun and you don't jeopardize my job. I need it to keep me away from my home. And whatever you do, don't get pregnant!"

"Ta-ta!" Kat hangs up, and I feel a little less cranky than I did twenty minutes ago.

The rest of the day is relatively uneventful, except when I find Lindsay on the sofa engrossed in a sordid little scene of *All My Children*. The last time I'd looked she was watching PBS! Jack calls to say he's staying in town for a meeting and dinner; which leaves me the delightful option of breakfast for dinner; a mom's best friend in the kitchen.

Chrissy and Lindsay are by now both ready to stomach some pancakes, which is a good sign. I bypass my usual dinner-preparing glass of wine, even though my stomach has felt fine since this morning; I don't dare take a chance of relapse, although the stomach-purge diet could come in handy.

Homework, baths, and bedtime come and go without incident, and amazingly I find myself at my computer, ready to catch up on some work, by nine thirty. But as I sit down at the desk I grudgingly admit to myself that I have no intention of working on some stupid damned press release for Jerry's Ford's end-of-the-month clearance sale, and instead go right to my e-mail.

Dear Todd, I begin to write.

I delete that.

Hi, there!

No, too trite.

Hey, Todd!

Christ, that sounds like Annette Funicello inviting Todd to a Beach Blanket Bingo.

Well, well, well, I begin.

Perfect. Just the right amount of cynicism in that introduction.

I never thought I'd see the day: Todd "love-'em-and-leave-'em" Sterodnik coming to me on bended computer screen. A full-fledged apology? To what do I owe that moment of crow eating?

I don't want to give you the impression that I haven't gotten over you, because truthfully I have, but I just couldn't resist a fleeting moment of retribution. I'm not that mature of a person that I'm able to bypass a caustic swipe for old times' sake ☺.

So, what is going on in your life after all this time? I see your e-mail has something to do with USD.com. What exactly is it? What do you do? Are you still married to—oh, sorry, I tried to type the name but my keyboard must have locked up. Oops, another caustic swipe. Meow. You always did say I was very feline. But I think you were referring to my flexibility, not my cattiness.

Are you married or single? Kids or free? Plastic or paper?

I am married to the man of my dreams (although, granted, sometimes you wake up from your dreams and things aren't quite as rosy)

Delete, delete, delete.

I am married to a wonderful man, Jack Doolittle, and we have five marvelous children. They really are terrific kids, and we are very blessed with them.

I had to give up my Sky Slut career when my oldest, Cameron, came along. But it was just as well. While I loved the freedom to travel, that was cut off at the knees with a baby anyhow.

Delete, delete, delete.

While I loved the freedom to travel, I got sick and tired of being cooped up in those big old leper colonies in the sky. I was always catching some godforsaken illness from some hacking passenger, so it was just as well that I grounded myself. At least now I only catch local diseases ☺.

We live in the suburbs outside of DC now. I know: it is shocking to learn I gave up on city life. Another of those things that you abandon once children come along. But life's all about trade-offs. You of all people should know that.

Delete, delete, delete.

Life's all about trade-offs, and my kids are absolutely worth every sacrifice I've made.

Delete delete delete.

After all, life is about change and taking chances, isn't it?

So we live in Fairfax now. The kids are in good schools. Jack is a partner in an architectural firm downtown and has to turn down work, he's so busy. So, life is good.

I hope you will write back and let me know more about what you've been doing. I'm glad you had the courage to contact me. Take care.

Claire.

Before I have a chance to reconsider, I push the send button, throwing the gauntlet into cyberspace to good old Todd the Rod. Now, let's see if he's up to the challenge.

chapter Five

There's something I should explain about Jack's background, because ultimately I think it provides insight into how Jack became Ward. Because our romance was a bit whirlwind, at the time of our engagement neither of us had actually met each other's families yet. Jack had talked endlessly about his older brother, Colin, who was so close in age to Jack—twelve months separated them—that they were practically twins.

Colin was a writer living in San Francisco. Following our engagement we decided to fly out so that Colin and I could get acquainted. But first Jack decided to come clean with some information he'd chosen to withhold.

"I need to tell you something about my brother."

"He's a serial killer?" I joked.

"Ha, ha. No, he's not a serial killer."

"He's a cocaine runner for a Columbian drug cartel?"

"Stop it! He's not that either."

"Well, quit being so cryptic and tell me what he *is*, then," I demanded.

"My brother is gay." Jack looked at me as if he thought I would storm from the room right then and there and never return.

"And so?"

"Well, he's gay. I just thought you should know that."

"Jack, it doesn't bother me that he's gay. There are lots of great people who are gay. I'm glad that he's comfortable enough with it to have told you."

Jack looked relieved, as if I'd spared him unnecessary surgery or a proctology exam or something.

"You mean it doesn't bother you at all?"

"Jesus, Jack. I'm an enlightened human being. I don't think there's anything wrong with someone being a homosexual. If you're gay, you're gay. It's not a perverted lifestyle choice; it's just the way you're made."

Jack scooped me up into his arms, delighted that he no longer felt the need to hide what must have been a tender topic. In fact, it surprised me that my attitude about something like this hadn't come up sooner. Perhaps because Jack and I spent so much of our time wrapped in our own world, we hadn't concerned ourselves much with others.

In San Francisco, Colin met us at the airport with his partner, Roger. Both men were strikingly handsome—Ken dolls with pulses. Roger looked almost unnaturally thin, however.

"It's wonderful to finally meet the woman who has captured my little brother's heart." Colin hugged me as if we were old friends. I would soon learn that he had an engaging way of making one feel that way.

"Hey, I'm hardly your *little* brother," Jack joked, puffing out his chest and shoulders and trying to appear manly next to Colin, who was the more diminutive of the two.

I rolled my eyes at Jack. "I'm so happy to get to meet

Jack's *bigger* brother, the one he speaks so highly of all the time."

"If I had known he held me in such reverence, perhaps I'd live a little closer to him so I could soak up the adulation."

Later, when Jack got me alone, he expressed some concern.

"Do you think that Roger looks unhealthy?"

"I have no basis by which to compare him."

"Don't you think he looks a bit gaunt, and almost weary or weathered?"

"Well, yeah. He looks awfully thin, if that's what you mean."

"The last time I saw him was about a year ago, and he was buff—I mean, he was a strapping dude, like the guy who might beat up the ninety-pound weakling on the beach. Now *he* looks like the ninety-pound weakling."

"Hmmmm," I pondered. "Let's just feel things out and see if we can decipher this." I gave him a hug. "In the meantime, I'm so excited to meet your brother."

"Colin means the world to me. Thanks for being so open-minded. I couldn't share my life with someone who couldn't understand Colin's lifestyle."

"It's not something that is even relevant—you know that. It's Colin's business, and Roger's. Not anybody else's."

We spent the rest of the afternoon touring China-town and Fisherman's Wharf. It was one of those gorgeous afternoons that makes you want to drop everything and move to San Francisco. We had a phenomenal Italian meal in North Beach.

"So, tomorrow we'll spend the day in Sausalito," Colin said over tiramisu.

"Then on Saturday we'll drive up to Sonoma and

visit some of our favorite vineyards," Roger added, coughing into his napkin.

"That's some cough you've got going," Jack pointed out.

"Yeah, I've had this nasty cold and can't seem to shake the cough."

"You ought to check it out—you might have pneumonia," I said. "That happened to my cousin one time, and they almost had to cut out part of her lung by the time they diagnosed it."

"Lovely after-dinner conversation," Jack joked. "But really, Roger, you should get a doctor to listen to your lungs."

Colin and Roger exchanged solemn glances; then Colin changed the subject.

"So, when are you two planning to be married?"

"We haven't even really discussed timing with Claire's folks—or with Mom, for that matter," Jack said. Jack's dad had died of a heart attack when he was only forty-seven.

"Just give us plenty of warning so we can get time off work," Roger said.

"Don't worry; we couldn't get married without you two there," Jack assured them. "Plus, Colin, you're my best man. I guarantee you'll be the first to know."

Unfortunately, it wouldn't be long before we were the first to know some unpleasant news from the two of them.

Chapter Six

Today starts out much more agreeably than yesterday. All the kids are off to school, Jack is toiling in the coal mines (figuratively), and I can spend the day making up for yesterday's lost time. While I'm catching up on my laundry mountain, my mother calls.

"Hi, sweetie! I just thought I'd let you know that Daddy and I might stop by for a visit next week. We're going to a wedding in Reston—the Taylors' oldest daughter is getting married."

"Great, Mom, we'd love to see you. Why don't you guys stay here?"

"Oh, you know your father." She sighs. "The older he gets the more he refuses to stay overnight anywhere. It doesn't matter that we'll end up in the car for eight whole hours and be exhausted from the traveling. I guess men just get more set in their ways the older they get."

This is a very discouraging revelation.

"Hell, Jack's so set in his ways in his forties—what is he going to be like when he's Daddy's age?"

"Jack? Set in his ways?"

"Uh, this is my husband we're talking about. Don't sound so surprised. Life is so mundane and regimented with him around, I feel like I've been sentenced to a chain gang sometimes."

"Honey, that doesn't sound like something you'd say about Jack!"

"Oh, Mom, forget I said anything."

"Why don't you tell me what's going on?"

I take a gulp of air, feeling my emotions on the edge. All of a sudden everything about my marriage is weighing heavily on my mind.

"It's nothing, really." I begin to sort through the waist-high pile of dirty clothes that has materialized in my laundry room.

"If it were nothing, you wouldn't have said a word to me, Bear." Mom still sometimes refers to me by my childhood nickname, Claire Bear.

"It's just that . . ." I'm at a loss as to how to explain that my former sex-god husband has become warped into someone too much like my dad. "Jack just isn't . . . well, *fun* anymore."

My mom lets out a howl of laughter that would probably beckon home coyotes for the night. "Fun? *That's* the problem? He's not *fun?*"

"Look, you just don't understand." My anxiety is turning to tension. "*Fun* isn't exactly the word I mean. It's just that at one time Jack was my friend and lover, and now he's more like my boss or my father. Sort of like Ward Cleaver."

My mother releases another gale of laughter. "Ward Cleaver? You mean that handsome man from the old sitcom *Leave It to Beaver?* What's so bad about that?"

"First off, Ward Cleaver was hardly handsome. Well, if he was, then I could never get over his patronizing paternal mannerisms to see that. But secondly—

ewww. It's like having sex with your father!" I knew I ran the danger of seriously insulting my dad. I mean, I love my father and all. And it's not like I want to pick apart Mom's choice of a partner, but sheesh, he's not exactly heartthrob material. He's my dad, after all. Nobody can look at their father in *that* way without getting seriously grossed out. Or maybe I'm just painfully immature.

"See, Mom, everything about Jack is so serious and all-business now. He's incapable of getting past his stern exterior to be the fun man he once was." I cradle the phone to my ear and reach into the pile to separate the smelly clothes, avoiding excessive skin contact with the fouler-smelling bits, like Jack's soiled running clothes and Cameron's gym trunks.

"Now everything's about errands and duties and chores and punishments and stuff. It's like someone went inside of his brain and flicked off the happy switch or something. But then when I least expect it—and least desire it—the little Amorous Andy switch goes on in his gray matter and he thinks that just because *he's* feeling frisky that I can set aside the stern-taskmaster stuff and just pretend he's someone he's not!" I'm sobbing now, all the while surprised I can confess this information to my mother, of all people.

"Then, on top of it, I got an e-mail from Todd yesterday, and it has reopened wounds I thought had scarred over long ago. And I've been sick and so have some of the kids, and I'm tired, and no one helps around here, and the damned dog won't stop barking, and if I have to wipe up one more glob of bird shit off my kitchen floor I think I will roast that parrot for tonight's dinner."

"Wow, I see we have a bad case of the sniveling mommy syndrome," my mother says in that maternal way that implies I have a lesson coming. "And honestly,

Claire, I can't for the life of me imagine why you would even respond to an e-mail from that Todd person. You were well finished with him years ago. If you ask me, he is bad news with a capital B. Don't let yourself be tempted by some fantasy version of someone just because things aren't feeling quite so perfect right now."

"I am *not* sniveling, Mother. This is serious. I'm halfway through my life, and I don't understand how I got to the point where my husband is more of an adversary than a partner. That's serious. Besides, maybe Todd's not as bad as he used to be. At least *he's* interested in me."

"Wow. You must be hallucinating. Do you have a fever? I think you need a little break to clear your head. I'd have wagered money on your hating Todd till the day he died. Probably with good reason. If that man is interested in you, then look out. He's got something up his sleeve; I guarantee it. Listen, honey, why don't you take a little time off from everything and come up here to visit for a few days? The break will do you good. You'll have a fresh perspective on things."

"Thanks, Mom. But there's no such thing as a break from things with five young children." I smile a tepid smile, realizing that in a way I have become a prisoner of sorts. Except my captors are those I love most dearly in the world. Sort of like Stockholm syndrome, only not.

"Well, Bear, the offer stands. Your father and I would love to have you. You could sleep in your old bed; I can cook you some nice meals. It'll be good for you. Listen to your mother."

Yeah, right. Sleep restlessly on top of a thirty-year-old twin mattress, eat those horrid senior-citizen meals of theirs that have no fat, no salt, and no pleasure, and be grilled by my mother for a few days about the stability of my psyche.

I pile the whites into the washer, pour the detergent in, close the lid, and turn the machine on. I reconsider and open the lid again, adding bleach to the dispenser. Bleaching is good for things every so often. Maybe I need to douse my own life with some bleach.

"Thanks, Mom. I'll keep it in mind. In the meantime I'll look forward to seeing you next week, and you know the offer still stands. The guest bedroom is ready and waiting."

"I'll try to work on your father. And maybe we can get Sydney to come help you with the kids for a few days."

Oh, just what my sister would like—a few days hanging around a germ-infested group of banshees. Sydney has a thing with catching disease. She opens bathroom doors with her elbows to avoid other people's cooties. I shudder to imagine how she'd handle a family outbreak of a stomach bug.

"Sure, Mom, I'll ask her," I lie.

At dinner Jack mentions that he might have to go out of town next weekend.

"But it's your birthday. Where are you going?"

"Hmm?" His nose is buried in the *Washington Post*. Bad enough that he spent breakfast devouring one section, but he's returned with another section for a command performance.

"Where are you going?"

"Miami. A big convention. I wasn't going to go, but two of the other partners had to back out at the last minute. I've got a few important clients I'm meeting with there." He tells me this without looking up.

Miami, huh? Land of tight asses and bogus tits. He goes to Miami, and I get to stay here as the serfer girl. Damn, sometimes life's not fair. And *I'm* the one who needs the vacation.

"I know! Why don't you bring me along? It'll be a fun birthday thing to do."

He looks up at me and laughs a half laugh. "Yeah, right, and we'd put the kids on autopilot?"

"I was thinking maybe we could install a Velcro wall and just secure them to it with feed bags before we left. Surely they'd be okay for a few days? Or maybe I could get Sydney to come take over." He knows I am reaching with that idea. Besides which, Sydney is too busy having really good sex with someone who is most certainly *not* Ward Cleaver to compromise her fun quotient by coming here.

Jack just grunts.

"Well, when do *I* get to go somewhere and be a grown-up?" I whine. Since I failed in my escape-mission strategy, I'm resorting to pouting. It works for the kids; why can't it work for me?

"You can go away whenever you want," Jack says.

Only, he and I both know that's a crock of pure, unfiltered bullshit.

"What? *You* gonna use the Velcro wall?" I get up from the table, simmering with resentment and not fully knowing why.

When Jack and I announced the news to my folks about our engagement, my mother couldn't have been more delighted. She thought that Todd was beneath me, and rarely failed to point that out to me.

"Claire, you are too good for that boy," she'd say.

"I know, I know: 'You were practically a debutante. You could do way better than that Todd fellow,' " I would reply, mimicking her mantra to me. Of course, I was nowhere near a debutante, unless you count that ridiculous dancing school my mother made me attend in junior high school. Sometimes I wonder where my mother gets her crackpot notions.

The thing was that Todd and I kind of grew into adults together; we spent most of college as an item, and even into our first jobs out of school. He was comfortable, like an old pair of slippers. Sometimes you just can't bear to throw out those old slippers, even when they've got holes in them and no longer function well.

When I brought Jack home, heralding news of our engagement, the champagne flowed. Mother adored him, Dad thought he was a class act, and so there was celebration to go around. My parents planned a grandiose wedding at the country club back home in Philadelphia where Daddy golfed. It would be a springtime affair; the lilacs would be in bloom, the air succulent with their perfume.

My mother took charge of the planning and orchestrated it like a drum major with a marching band. Since I was traveling so much for work, I was happy to yield to her on most occasions. Plus, I had never really entertained any particular notion about my wedding. I had a friend who subscribed to *Bride* magazine when she was seventeen, just to provide fodder for her already vivid wedding-obsessed imagination. Maybe I just never anticipated someone actually wanting to marry me, I don't know, but visions of the big day were never something to occupy my idle mind.

Then we got the call from Colin. Early morning phone calls are most often the emissaries of unwanted news, and this was no exception.

"Hello?" I answered the phone in Jack's apartment.

"Claire? It's Colin. Is Jack there?"

"Yeah, sure." I handed the phone to Jack. "It's your brother."

"Hey, man. Is everything all right?"

"It's Roger."

"What do you mean?"

"Roger is dying. He's in San Francisco General right now. They sent me away because I'm not a member of his family, they say."

"What happened to him? Was there an accident?"

"Roger has AIDS. He was diagnosed a while back, but took very sick a few weeks ago. I got him to the hospital last night because he was throwing up blood. They took him in, then wouldn't let me see him."

Jack's face blanched. Being a seasoned eavesdropper—it was something I loved doing on those long flights—I kept an ear pinned to the earpiece of the phone, straining to glean what information I could.

"What can we do?"

"Not a whole hell of a lot," his brother said with an air of resignation. "This is a disease that only the freaks of society get, Jack. We don't get treated like other people. You know that."

"And you're telling me there's no way that you can get in there to at least hold Roger's hand?"

"Not unless I have authorization from his parents."

"And are they coming?"

"Nope. They washed their hands of Roger years ago."

"So your partner will die alone in a hospital bed, being treated like he's got the plague, with no love or comfort to coax him through his dying breaths?"

Colin broke down into heaving sobs. Jack had tears streaming down his face as well.

"Listen, Colin, I'm on the next plane out there. Just sit tight. I'll meet you at the hospital."

It certainly helped that I could get us on the first available flight. We arrived to find Colin virtually unrecognizable. He too had lost a tremendous amount of weight. His face looked gaunt, hollowed out. I noticed a few telltale sores on his arms and knew right away that Colin was grieving not only for Roger, but for himself.

The next several days were insufferable. Coming to terms with Colin's fate was an unfathomable thing, even without the impending death of Roger. Jack seemed to take on a supernatural calm, this logical automaton clicking into overdrive. He was able to sweet-talk his way into Roger's ward, and to get Colin in to provide support. A lot of good it did, as Roger was unconscious anyhow.

Five days later Roger passed away. Jack and I took care of funeral arrangements, and the cast of attendees at Roger's funeral was a testimonial that this disease was ravaging an entire population of people. A gray rain battered the fog-enshrouded mourners at the grave site, reminding us why we chose not to live in a place like San Francisco.

We tried to convince Jack's brother to come back east with us, where we could help take care of him, but he wouldn't hear of it. He wanted to continue to work for as long as he could, and he had other friends he needed to nurse through their own untimely deaths. All we could do was move up the wedding so that Jack's best friend—his brother—would be able to attend. We contacted my family and his mom and flew everyone out to San Francisco. This was back in the days when I could've readily flown my third cousins twice removed for free without corporate objection. The wedding was a bittersweet event, knowing as we did that it was heralding the impending death of Colin Doolittle.

Through it all, Jack was the Rock of Gibraltar. I could not believe how stoic he was. This man who was so full of light and laughter and vitality had transformed into the guiding beacon for the rest of us, the one to make the decisions, to stanch the flow of tears, to reassure the weak-willed among us.

Following the wedding we both took a few weeks off work and stayed in San Francisco to spend some time with Colin and to help him get his affairs in order. It was not quite the honeymoon we'd imagined, but we managed to steal off to Napa for a day here and there, and had some lovely meals in the city as well.

When we said good-bye to Colin at the airport, we knew our chances of seeing him healthy again were slim. It was strange how the reality of the situation imposed an eerie calm upon us all.

As Jack and I walked up to the door at the gate, I heard Colin call out to me, "You make sure to take good care of my little brother, okay?"

I bit back the tears and promised Colin that Jack would forever be safe in my hands. At that point Jack didn't shed a tear.

I think the rest of the light went out in Jack the day we buried Colin. We mourned his loss at a quiet memorial service held near Jack's boyhood home in Baltimore, where Colin was interred alongside their father, Randall Doolittle. In hindsight I suspect that somehow those two tombstones, silently sitting side by side, evoked a fear and angst in Jack far deeper than I could have imagined at the time. Throughout much of the graveside service Jack just stared, rarely blinking, at his father's and brother's graves. He didn't say a word. And when I tried to hold his hand, to lend him what little support I could, he merely flinched and turned away. And so crept in unbidden a new and far more sober phase to Jack Doolittle.

chapter seven

One side effect resulting from years of motherhood is the strange things you hear even when you don't hear them. Not like you're hearing satanic voices or anything that might send you running to a shrink. More like babies crying when the vacuum is running. Or the telephone ringing when the hair dryer is on.

I'm in my bathroom blow-drying my hair, and I'm convinced the phone keeps ringing. Each time I turn off the blasted dryer, however, I hear nothing. The problem is that it could be one of three things: a false alarm, part of my vivid overactive imagination; an actual phone ringing somewhere in the house; or RePete making the sound of the phone ringing.

This time it must have been RePete, and it's now taken me twice as long to dry my hair because of it. I'm racing to get to work on time. All of the kids are off to school, and I'm putting the final touches on my hair. Jack scootches by me in the bathroom and tweaks my breast.

I don't know why that once would have been such a sweet little affectionate gesture to me but now feels like he's violating my personal bubble. Like some strange pervert trying to cop an illicit feel. I throw him a dirty look and smack his hand away, and he gets the message and skulks off.

A few minutes later the garage door opens and closes, so I know he has left for the office.

I hear a cacophony downstairs and race down to see what has happened. How much commotion could there be with everyone gone already? Then I see RePete, *clickety-click*ing his black talons across the kitchen tile, dragging his red tail plumage in his wake, and Tripod skidding into the wall from an obviously unsuccessful hunting attempt. Tripod must have some bird dog in him.

"No! No! No! No! No! Tripod! You're a bad, bad boy!" RePete is yelling at the dog, who looks a little confused. The crazy bird must've been flapping his wings for some exercise and fallen off his perch. The loud sound no doubt sent Tripod running. He still doesn't understand that this bird is a family member. A family member who shits all over the floor without compunction.

Amazing—I can't even get a moment's peace when everyone's out of the house. As I drag Tripod by the collar into the mudroom, then rescue the bird from his imminent demise, my eyes scan the kitchen and I'm dismayed at the host of dirty breakfast dishes sitting right where everyone left them. Over on the counter closest to the back door I see Lindsay's Power Rangers lunch box (another hand-me-down), waiting expectantly to be carried off to school. That means I have ten fewer minutes to get to work.

I hear a ding on my computer and take a quick peek to see whom it's from. Toddster.

I open the e-mail quickly, promising myself I'll take only five minutes to read his reply. Since Kat had her "drinks" with Robert last night, my boss should be in a fine mood this morning anyhow, no doubt having consumed more than just cocktails with my raven-haired friend.

I click on the e-mail and read:

> Claire Mooney. You did not let me down, you feisty little wench! If you had sent a purely innocent little response to me I would have been worried about you. But your retaliatory skills have clearly held you in good stead over the years. So with a feint, a flick, and a parry, I freely admit you won that match. Touché.
>
> It gets my juices flowing again just reading your loaded words. That tongue has worked wonders on many a person over the years, both figuratively and literally. I can vouch for that. If I recall correctly, you gave new meaning to the term *tongue-lashing*.

My eyes read the words but my mind interprets the dual meaning. My tongue? Did *that*? Willingly?

> I miss going head-to-head with you ☺.

Oh, my God. Is he talking about what I think he's talking about?

> Well, Claire. I'll give you a brief synopsis of my life over the past umpteen years. You'll be pleased to know that things did not work out long-term between Vanna and me. We lasted a few short years and one child; then she divorced me. I can't say I was sorry about it. She forced the kid on me in the first place, then couldn't understand when I didn't want to have to share the burden.
>
> So she took the boy and moved out to Wyoming,

where I hear she married some cowboy who is one of those Promise Keepers. She's gone so far off my radar screen that I no longer even hear from her at all.

I remarried a few years later. Her name is Tina. We get along fine, though I travel a lot on business. She's starting to make noises about wanting a baby, which seems to be my cue to exit stage left.

What a shit. He has a child with whom he has no contact, nor does he desire such. Then he marries another woman, and once she wants a baby, he bolts?

Anyhow, I've climbed the corporate ladder at USD and am in a high-level managerial sales position (selling real exciting things like cogs and bolts), and spend most of my time on airplanes (sound familiar?), at trade shows, and on uncomfortable hotel mattresses. But I guess you could say I got what I wanted, so I can't complain.

Tina and I met through a scuba club, and we have a time-share in Aruba, where you'll usually find us if we're together. I guess I'm most at peace with the world when I'm submerged beneath the ocean exploring a coral reef.

I've moved repeatedly over the years—been in ten cities in thirteen years—and the latest place of residence is Bloomington, Indiana. Hardly the kind of place you'd ever want to live in, so it's probably best that we didn't end up marrying. Plus, all those kids . . . Well, they're giving my final boarding call, and I can't miss this plane. Just one more thing I'm dying to know. Do you miss me at all?

I look at my watch. I'm already ten minutes late leaving the house, and I have that lunch-box stop to make. I want to reply while it's fresh in my head and no one's here to bother me, but I have to run.

As I back the car out of the driveway, I ponder that odd question: Do I miss him? *Do* I miss him? God, no. Not really. Do I miss the promise of what we once had? Sure. How could I not? The road not taken is a tempting one to peer down. You never see the potholes or detours on that road. It's just a clear, straight, smooth stretch of pavement that goes endlessly into the sunshine-flooded horizon.

If I'd ended up as Mrs. Todd Sterodnik, would I now be alone with a passel of kids, fighting Todd for child-support payments? Or worse yet, would I be home-schooling those kids on some ranch in Wyoming, remarried to a Promise Keeper named Jedediah or Ezekiel?

Or would I have used my feminine wiles to keep Todd from ever wanting to leave me, trapping him in a web of sexual nirvana from which he could not escape? Well, hardly likely, considering I haven't even done that with my *actual* husband, let alone my what-if one.

After dropping Lindsay's lunch box off, I head to the office. I stop at a traffic light, and the elderly man sitting at the bus stop nearby leers and winks at me, catching me off guard.

Christ, there was a time in my life when I turned heads. When men—boys, even—would actually walk by and gawk at me. Then, all of a sudden, one day I realized I was virtually invisible to the other sex.

No longer do men gaze longingly at me. Instead I'm left with decrepit old men at bus stops being the last of my dying fan club. Maybe I should wink at him and sensuously run my tongue along my upper lip, appreciative that at least *someone* is looking.

Clearly I've sunk to a new low.

I smile courteously and move on when the light turns green. After contending with the remaining dregs of rush-hour traffic, I pull into my parking spot, race to the elevator, and arrive at work precisely twenty-two minutes late. Shit.

I look around for Robert, who is nowhere to be found. Phew, I think I'm in the clear. I grab a cup of coffee and sit down at my computer and boot it up. There's an e-mail from Kat from this morning.

Claire, darling,
Hi, sweetie! Just thought I'd send you a quick note of apology.

Oh, great, I know what this means.

But he was irresistible, honey. Really, he was. We went out for drinks, then ate at this romantic little French bistro in Old Town, and we had such a magical time, and the food was sublime, and you know he lives really near there, and so he offered for me to go to his place, and how could I turn that down? By the way, he has a bitching penthouse apartment; you can see some of the monuments from his balcony if you strain to look.

I chuckle. We all know where those balconies with great views lead.

So in case you were wondering, your boss is fantastic in the sack. He has the stamina of a team of Clydesdales, and I can make some other draft-horse comparisons. . . .

This is getting far more gruesome than I can stand. We're well past the need-to-know basis.

> *Well, I know you don't want to know those details, since it's your boss and all, but let's just say I had a really great workout and I think at the very least you'll have a good day at the office, judging by the mood he was in when I left him this morning ☺. I've gotta run—I have the Indian ambassador's wife coming in to discuss plans for some garden party or something. Ta ta!*
>
> *K*

So now even my wanker boss and my best friend are getting it on with great sex. Is this some sort of communicable condition? And if so, can I catch it? Or do I want to? I notice an e-mail from Robert, so I click to open it.

Claire: I'm taking a personal day today, so please make sure you take care of the press releases for the National Paint and Tint Association that we discussed via e-mail yesterday morning. You can send copies of them to my e-mail account and I will go over them at home later on. You can call if you have any questions. Robert.

Short, sweet, and to the point. Jackpot! The cat's away, the mouse will play. To hell with writing tedious press releases suggesting that a fresh coat of paint can improve productivity in the workplace. I can knock off those pieces of fiction in no time, but meanwhile I'm going to kick back and enjoy my day at the office.

I take a sip of coffee and settle my fingers on the keyboard.

Todd, Todd, Todd. Feisty little wench? Well, at least you didn't write "saucy" wench, as I am definitely not saucy. Feisty? I plead the Fifth. Wench? You decide. Now, if you ask my husband, he'd say I was more like a wrench, or some other lifeless tool—

Delete, delete, delete.

Wench? One can always hope—

Delete, delete, delete.

Wench? Well, that's the first time I've heard that description applied to me in quite a while. . . . I must admit, I forgot how you used to like to call me names like that. And about that tongue thing . . . I hate to say it, but this tongue has atrophied for lack of use—

Delete, delete, delete.

—this tongue serves one purpose and one purpose only: it's an instrument with which I scream at my kids—

Delete, delete, delete.

And about that tongue thing . . . perhaps you can clarify what you mean by "tongue-lashing"? My memory seems to fail me at this late date, so I beg you for more information. I don't recall my tongue working wonders on anything, but maybe you can enlighten me.

Now, with regard to that ex-wife, she-who-shall-not-be-named situation of yours: Todd, while I can't say I'm saddened that she had hers in the end, I have to say I am shocked that you have chosen to not participate in your only son's (that you know of!) life! That doesn't seem like the Todd Sterodnik I once knew (and loved?).

I wouldn't have pegged you for a heartless cad (that is, until you unceremoniously dumped me out of the blue). I should say, at least not a cad toward small children, particularly your own! Todd—you shouldn't even do that to a household pet, let alone a child. What is up with that deal? And with your current wife, Tina: did you two not discuss your procreating options, or lack thereof? Did this Tina chick not realize what went down with wifey number one?

You know what I think? I think there's a reason that you have contacted me at this point in your life. I think there's a reason that I have been contacted by you at this point in my life. I think that in some perverse way, you and I need to fix things in each other's lives.

I know this sounds crazy, and your pointer finger is probably hovering over the delete button right now, thinking that I am a certifiable whack job, but I am not kidding you—I can read between the lines and tell that you are crying out for help—

Delete, delete, delete.

You know what I think? I think you should reconsider trying to have a relationship with your son, Todd. I can't emphasize enough how important it is for a child to have loving parents.

Why don't you call him, have him come to visit you, do something, go on vacation together, something, and just give it a try. I don't mean to beat you over the head about this, but I think you'll be surprised by the gift of fatherhood once you decide to accept it.

Just think about it, Todd—this boy is just waiting for his father to realize what a great kid he is; he's just waiting for what has been due to him since you brought him into this world: his father's love.

I know I sound like Penelope Leach or Captain Kangaroo or something, and really I don't want to, but maybe you can think about it just a little bit. Who knows? Maybe someday you'll be so appreciative that I nagged you about this that you'll let me have use of that time-share in Aruba!

Okay, okay, okay, so I don't want you to think I'm bashing you for nothing. I have to admit to you, maybe things aren't altogether perfect in my life either. But that's all the more reason I want to help you. I know that I am very blessed with a wonderful family and a loving husband; it's just that sometimes I wonder if things couldn't be better—

Delete, delete, delete.

Sometimes I wonder how I got to where I am right now, and maybe it's helpful for me to go back and probe into our relationship to better understand my own current relationship. Does that make sense? Well, I'd better go work on some media releases right now. Take care! Claire.

Oh, and P.S.—Do I miss you? That is the most loaded question I can think of, coming from you. And I'll let you know when I have a loaded answer for it.

Ciao—Claire

Chapter Eight

Another thing for which I was ill prepared as a child rearer: sleep deprivation. I wish I knew during college that those sleep-till-two-in-the-afternoon days would soon be a ghost haunting my withering psyche.

I really *liked* sleeping in. It suited me. But I haven't slept in since Cameron was conceived in a blur of passion and a broken condom over fourteen years ago. Who knew the sponge wasn't quite as effective a backup contraceptive as we'd assumed?

Nowadays, sleeping in on a Saturday morning means that if I'm really lucky, no one wakes me until seven fifteen. So today is a real treat when I open one eye slightly to see that it's already going on eight o'clock without a word from any of the kids. I roll over, fall back into a deep sleep . . . until now, when the blare of the telephone jars me abruptly awake. Jack is sleeping like a wintering bear.

"Yeah?" I rasp.

"Claire? It's me, Candace."

Jack's mom. Imagine someone of her advanced age

named Candace. I just didn't realize that anyone older than my contemporaries had names that could be shortened into edibles. It seems sort of bimbo-ish for an older woman.

"Oh, hi, Candy. To what do we owe this pleasure?" My voice is gritty with sleep.

"Did I wake you?"

"Uh, well, not exactly," I lie. Candace is a sweetheart, so I don't want her to feel bad, even if she did destroy the best sleep-in I've had in a decade and a half.

"Well, I was talking to Dick the other day—"

Candace is now married to a guy named Dick. I swear to God, she's been married to the guy for almost as long as Jack and I have been married, but still I cannot say or hear his name without sniggering like a pubescent boy. Pity all the Dicks in the world. How could their parents have known that their son's name would become a common slang reference for every man's most treasured anatomical feature?

"—and Dick and I thought maybe we could visit you all next weekend, if that is convenient."

My mind tries to compute our active (ha, ha) social calendar and the heady demands of my kids' athletic schedules. Then I remember: Jack is going to Miami Beach, land of the thong—for his birthday, no less. And I am relegated to my own little beachhead of despair, having not punched out on my maternal time clock since well before Matthew came along, half a decade ago. Of course, I can't imagine life without my little Bubba, but damn, I could use a break.

Wait a minute. I *could* use a break. I could use a *break*. If Jack can do it, then, dammit, so can I.

"Gee, I'd dearly love to see you and Dick." I bite back my laugh as I say his name. Poor Dick. "And I know the kids would adore spending time with you. But Jack has to travel to Miami Beach for work next weekend. I had really hoped to find a sitter so that maybe I could join him, but no one's available."

There's silence on the other end of the line as Candace takes a nibble on my bait.

"I have an idea. Why don't we come and stay with the kids for a few days; it'll give you and Jack a chance to have some time alone together."

I thought she'd never ask.

"That's an awful lot to throw on you!" I slather the false resistance on thick. Although, truthfully, I wouldn't even impose my brood on my *own* mom, they've such strength in their numbers against any invading force. I'm almost certain my mother would cut me out of the inheritance if she had to keep my kids for more than an hour. Not that my kids are bad or anything, but I can barely corral them and their lives myself, so would never expect a substitute to be able to do so. But I *am* feeling desperate.

"No, really. We'd be happy to help out. I know you could use a break, anyhow." The woman is a freaking clairvoyant. Too bad that gene wasn't passed on to her son.

"If you're sure about that, I would love to take you up on your generous offer."

Now I'm finally awake. Awake with the prospect of a few short days of freedom. Halle-bloody-lujah.

Yippee!!!!!!!! I'm freeeeeeeeeeeeeeeeeeeeeeeeeeeeeeeee, I want to scream. But, of course, that would be in poor taste.

"You're such an angel, Candace," I say instead. "When can I expect you?"

"Why don't we arrive late Thursday afternoon? You'll be able to fly out by dinnertime."

"Thank you so much. You don't know how much I appreciate this!" I hang up the phone, basking in the afterglow of her generosity.

My thoughts are swarming with fantasy images of Jack and me frolicking on the beach, a barely there bikini covering just what needs to be obscured on my lustrously tanned torso. Jack, burnished by the near-tropical sun, looks healthy and relaxed. We revel in our cocktails poolside, converse convivially over elegant dinners al fresco, and drown in our lovemaking morning, noon, and night. Ah, bliss.

But then my thoughts are jarred into reality by the snoring presence next to me and a quick glance into the mirror above my dresser, which reveals the flaccid reality of me as I truly am, rather than the fantasy me as I once might have been.

A deflated zeppelin, that's what I am. Well, better that than a zeppelin that's exploded in a blistering conflagration. But that's okay. Instead of my being Annette Funicello and Jack being Frankie Avalon, having our own little Beach Blanket Bingo, I'll be a quasi-corpulent June Cleaver to Jack's still fit but nevertheless humdrum Ward. At least I'm getting away from Wally and the Beav for a few days, I think gloomily—with just a hint of hope.

We make pancakes for breakfast after Jack departs for his morning run. Charlotte and Chrissy decide to pour the batter into a squirt bottle, somewhat unsuccessfully trying to make pictures on the griddle with their pancakes. The kids are giggling and making a huge mess when Jack comes in through the breakfast room.

"Girls! What are you doing over the stove? You're spilling that stuff everywhere! Does your mother know you've been up to this?"

Well, what do you know? Jack went off to run and Ward came back in his place.

"Of course I know they're doing that, Jack. I helped them get started."

"If they're going to be irresponsible with their cooking then I will revoke the privilege," he growls.

"Lighten up, honey. They're having fun. It'll clean up."

In order to change the subject, I spring the great news on him.

"So, guess who's going to Miami with you next week? *Moi!* I can help you celebrate your forty-fourth birthday!"

Jack stares at me like I just told him I joined a cult.

"Excuse me?"

"Me! I'm going to Miami! Your mom offered to come spend the weekend with the kids! Isn't that great?"

Jack knits his brows in a Ward-like way. He doesn't look so much delighted as constipated.

"Christ, Claire. Don't you think you could ask me before you go making some grandiose plan to join me on a business trip?"

I turn toward him, hands on hips, and glare at him with pent-up fury.

"Tell me something, Jack. Did you sharpen that needle of yours before you plunged it into my happy balloon? Or would that somehow indicate that you actually *planned* to be an insensitive oaf, rather than it merely being an unintentional act of deeply entrenched ignorance? Because I'd like to believe that you're not actually a premeditated asshole, only one by happenstance."

I storm out of the room, the kids standing there aghast, and me furious that once again Jack has reinforced my fears that he's become an incurable prick. Jack, however, is hot on my heels.

"Perhaps you misinterpreted what I meant." I can tell by his conciliatory tone of voice that he's buffering his reaction in the hopes of not killing his chances for his upcoming Sunday-night fuck.

"Oh, noooooooooooooooo," I sneer. "No, way, fella.

The only thing I misinterpreted is what kind of man you would one day become."

"Look, I don't know what you're talking about. I just wish you had consulted with me first, as I have a very full schedule for this trip and won't have a moment for you."

"Not that you have a moment for me anyhow, Ward."

"Excuse me? Who's Ward?"

"No one. No one. Just . . . never mind. It's none of your business. You know what? I don't want to go with you anyhow. Instead I'm going to go somewhere on my own. I'm gonna take a weekend and go away for *me*. Just Claire. It'll be a Claire-filled getaway. I'm gonna go and have fun and maybe get my nails done, and maybe sit there and drink an entire bottle of champagne by the pool, and you can just go on to your little Miami Beach thing, and do whatever you architects do when you go to the beach—I don't know, build sand castles? Woo-hoo! Go to town, buster. Cause I'm gonna paint the town red. Blood-fucking-red."

Jack looks combustible all of a sudden. I don't think my little tirade appealed so much.

"I don't know what's gotten into you, Claire, I really don't," he snarls. "You act as if you are living some horrible existence here, like you're somehow suffering or something. Well, I'm sorry if that's what you think. But you have a loving husband, five wonderful children, and a fantastic home. What more do you want?"

Tears are beginning to descend. Loving husband? Yeah, right. If loving means critical, evasive, and anything but affectionate. How can I explain how I'm feeling to him without offending him deeply, and without making him realize how much I've grown to abhor the man he's become?

"You just don't get it, Jack. You just don't get it."

* * *

The rest of the weekend is played out on two levels. Level one: we aren't speaking to each other, and I'd sooner have unscheduled bowel irrigation than have contact—aural, oral, physical, or otherwise—with Jack. Level two: we attend a cocktail party and have to pretend that we're the happy, loving, simpatico couple that defines us to our mutual friends.

Under normal circumstances the party, hosted by the founder of Jack's firm at his sprawling contemporary home along the Potomac River, would be at least interesting. Elegantly attired women in über-overpriced couture clothing. The elite in the art-and-architecture community. Top-shelf drinks and premier catered food.

But circumstances aren't normal, and I'm stuck at Jack's side for lack of someone else's side to which I could adhere, forced to pretend I'm a perfectly happy little pig in shit with the man.

"Glass of wine?" he asks without looking at me.

"Please," I barely whisper, as if any higher a decibel level would signal to him an unintended reconciliation.

It's nearly as hard to force the niceties out of my mouth as it was expelling each of my five children from the birth canal. Something, I might add, that I did all on my own. Just like my little weekend getaway will be. On my own. Without Ward. Wardless.

I realize how similar Ward is to a warden. In my confining little marriage Jack has become my jailer, and now I've got the key for a weekend leave. I think about that, and finally I get it. I'm not sad that I won't have a weekend with Jack so much as sad that he rejected the notion without even a perfunctory consideration of my attending. As if the idea of me being there is so contraindicated that—

Hmmm. I wonder if he has more planned on the agenda than he's let on.

"Julia, I'd like you to meet my wife, Claire." I'm interrupted from my thoughts by Jack, whose chest has fluffed up like RePete when his feathers are ruffled. All of a sudden he's not looking as much like Ward Cleaver as he is a rutting male mountain goat in one of those science-class filmstrips about mating in the animal kingdom.

"Claire, this is my new colleague, Julia." Jack beams at Julia. I pointedly note to myself that there's no beaming directed my way.

Julia has naturally blond hair and heart-shaped lips. Who the fuck has naturally blond hair after the age of twelve? And heart-shaped lips? I thought those were found only on cartoon drawings of buxom women, like the secretary in Beetle Bailey. My lips are the flat line of a heart monitor still hooked up to a dead patient.

"Julia? Pleased to meet you."

Julia grabs my hand in a pandering, I'll-pretend-I'm-one-of-you-housewives wimpy half handshake, which I absolutely detest. I would sooner lick a dirty ashtray than shake hands with someone with a dead fish for a hand. I deliberately squeeze too hard.

"Claire, so wonderful to *finally* meet you!" she says with an energetic enthusiasm reserved only for the unmarried and childless in the world. She's a human exclamation point. Fucking bitch.

"Finally?" I wonder how long Julia's wanted to finally meet me. Or is that she wants to finally fuck my husband?

Jack interrupts. "Yes, Julia joined the firm a few months ago, and I've told her all about you."

"I *bet* you have."

Jack throws me a caustic look that could strip paint.

"So, Julia, what brings you to Kelley, Kelley, Goodman, and Doolittle?"

"Well, I finished up school a few years ago, but took some time off to travel, see the world. I got a little side-tracked by some personal things. Jack hired me on a few months back, which was so sweet of him, considering I hadn't had my hands in the trade for a while."

I wonder where her hands *have* been.

"Oh, that's so like Jack, so thoughtful and all," I say without a hint of warmth. "Always cutting other people slack." I mentally grind my stiletto heel into his groin.

Julia just smiles in agreement. I decide to chum my hook for a little fishing expedition.

"So, Julia, I bet you're looking forward to that trip to Miami next week."

"Oh, my God, am I! I even bought a new little bikini! I can't wait!"

I wonder if she's lined up the Brazilian wax just for the occasion. I glare subliminally at Jack as I smile politely at Julia.

"Why, I'm surprised you'll even have a chance to get to the beach, what with the *brimming schedule* you'll have."

I'm enjoying watching Jack begin to squirm before me. That glowing candle he was a few proud moments ago is turning into a puddle of melted wax, snuffed out by yours truly.

"Oh, gosh, I was under the impression that this was one of those perk weekend getaways, to make up for all of the late hours we put in." Julia twinkles a super-nova look at Jack. "I was told we only had a meeting or two and some nice dinners out."

I arch an accusatory brow toward Jack.

"The partners have a far more trying schedule lined up," he interjects.

"Oh, I'm sure you'll be trying a *lot* with your schedule."

Julia is not reading the subtext of our conversation, not that I'd care if she could.

"I'm sure Jack will be working far more than I will," she says.

"Yes, knowing my Jack, he will be working it. Uh, excuse me, I think I need to refresh my drink."

A waiter steps up to us with a tray filled with wine and champagne, but I scurry past him, intent on getting as far away from this mutual admiration society as possible.

So, Jack is committed to a real working weekend, is he?

Well, maybe he needs someone to supervise his work while he's in Miami. Maybe that's exactly what old Jacko needs.

chapter Nine

It's late when we return home, and I linger at my desk checking my e-mails in order not to tangle during the bedtime rituals with Ward. I'm of no mind to have any more contact with him at this point.

I scroll down my screen and see an e-mail from Kat.

Hi, Claire! Am just coming up for air and thought I'd send you a quick note to tell you what an absolutely divine time I'm having with your Robert. Really, I don't get what it is about him that you don't care for! My God, the man practically ravished me shortly after dinner the other night, and we've been inseparable since. He's the perfect gentleman, he's gorgeous, and he's insatiable. What's not to like?

I just have to knock off a quick reply to Kat while I'm thinking about it.

Kat, dear. You go right ahead and have intercourse with any old man you please. If you choose to have sex with Robert, it's not my place to comment on it. But for me, it's kind of like imagining your parents having sex together, you know? I've only seen Robert in a capacity as a boss, and he's awfully bossy, I might add. So, conceptually I'm having trouble with this notion. But really, honey, if you're having fun, then that's all that matters. I'll get over my little psychological hurdles in time. XOXO Claire.

As my eyes scan the list of e-mails, I see the one I'm hoping for.

Claire Mooney. Tsk, tsk, tsk. I can't believe you need a refresher course about that tongue! My God, woman. What has suburbia done to you?! Does Fort Lauderdale bring anything to mind? Or what about my twenty-first birthday? Or yours, for that matter? Jesus, Claire, your tongue was practically your best feature (well, after a lot of other aspects of you that stand out in my mind).

It saddens me to think that you can't remember the magic you worked with that thing. In fact, I'm a little worried about you, Claire. Perhaps it's fortuitous that we have renewed contact with each other at this late date, and we could each benefit from the other's unsolicited advice and observations. Maybe it's a sign—like we really are meant to somehow help fix things for each other. In fact, I'd like nothing better than to fix things for you ☺.

Speaking of unsolicited advice, regarding what you said about my failure as a father, I can only say ouch. You took me by surprise. The last thing I expected from you was a stinging rebuke of my superficial lifestyle! And there I was innocently spilling my shallow guts to you, not expecting you to splash it back in my face!

That said, you have a point. You hit the nail on the proverbial head. I am a shit, and I do feel bad about it. No child deserves to have an absentee parent. But things have gone on like this for so long, I haven't the faintest idea of how to fix them. I wouldn't know where to begin. I mean, what do I do, pick up the phone and say, "Hey, there, Sam, it's me, your deadbeat dad. Long time no see"? Hardly. So, what would you do if you were me?

And, Claire, although you dodged the answer to my question, I will tell you that no matter what has happened over the years, I do miss you. I've missed you ever since I left you. I just can't get around that. I know, I know, circumstances are different, and you're happily married now, and drowning in the lifestyle of the picture-perfect American family and all that.

But I just want you to know, I miss you. I miss your smiling face, I miss your knockout body, I miss your incisive wit, I miss that damned tongue. That husband of yours doesn't know how great he's got it. Uh-oh, I'd better run. Final boarding call for me, or I won't make it to LA tonight. Write back.
T

Holy shit. There is a man out there who fantasizes about me! Well, he didn't come out and say exactly that, but I can read between the lines. Somewhere, somehow, I have left my mark on a man, and he can't quite shake me. Wow. How's that for a little slice of ego boost?

I know this is not the time to write back to the man who was once my intended (or so I thought). I know all I'm going to do right now is confess my deepest, darkest secrets about the miserable state of my marriage. But with a few glasses of wine under my belt,

and an ache in my heart that refuses to be suppressed,
I neglect to follow my better judgment.

T: I enjoyed your e-mail. And you have piqued my cu-
riosity about this legendary tongue. Please enlighten. I think
I've blacked out about my life pre–the arrival of Generation
X (when was that? The eighties? The nineties? It's all a
blur). I have no other explanation as to how I cannot remember much of anything about my life back then. Well,
perhaps too much partying in my youth killed off memory
cells, but I don't think that's it. More likely the mundane
demands of a suburban housewife sapped my brain of
fond memories, supplanting it with vital information about
diapers, spit-up, toilet training, how to be a fry cook on a
budget, Lysol versus Formula 409, and the like.

Re: my husband not knowing how great he's got it.
Hmmm, I'm impressed by your ability to read into the
man's soul. Bravo. If by that you mean my husband takes
me for granted, then you're right. And if you think that he
doesn't know how lucky he is to have a bright, sexy, and
wonderful woman in his bed, well, I'd like to say you're
right. But I'm not so sure I'm bright and sexy and wonderful
anymore. It's more just like I am what I am. Whatever I am.
"What do you mean by that, Claire?" you ask. Well, I'll tell
you. Once upon a time there was a girl named Claire with
stars in her eyes. Claire who thought that every girl grew up
to be a princess, who would be swept off her feet and
permanently enamored with the prince of her dreams.

This girl Claire grew up one day, though. And she realized that life's not all that we expect it to be. And that the
prince might have a little more in common with a toad than
she ever realized. And by the time she realizes it, it's too
late to do something about it. Because then the toad is
mucking around the swamp of the enchanted forest with

other princesses, much younger and sexier and with naturally blond hair and heart-shaped lips—

Delete, delete, delete.

Oh, damn it, Todd. I don't know what I'm saying. Except that perhaps there is no such thing as a perfect anything. On paper I must look like perfection. But I can promise you, I have more flaws than your average diamond purchased at JCPenney.

Somewhere along the line I slipped from my pedestal, and now I just plug along and get to the end of the day, hoping that tomorrow I'll be a better mother, a better wife, a more compelling human being. Maybe I'll do something useful, like work for the environment, or help elderly people in nursing homes (oh, God, I couldn't do it. I'm too shallow; it's too depressing to do something like that). You know what I mean. Engage my spirit in something that will wake up my soul.

Don't get me wrong, Todd. I love my children dearly. They're wonderful, they're fabulous, I couldn't think of a life without them. But I guess everyone wakes up one day and realizes that they need to fix what's wrong in their lives, or embellish whatever it is that they do have, or maybe they need to make that mark they haven't yet made, or whatever. And I guess that is the crossroads at which I'm finding myself right now.

Todd, I have to say this to someone. And because I'm a little drunk and extremely angry, I'm going to confess this to you: I found out tonight at a cocktail party with my husband's firm that there's another—younger—woman. I could tell by the vibrant spring in Jack's step that he's enchanted by her. And I could tell by her dopey smile that she was intoxicated with his stature, his power, his, oh, I don't know, maybe his body?

I mean, he still looks pretty damned good. And she doesn't get to see the Jack that I get to see. She gets to see the manly, sexually alluring authority figure with the hint of mature gray at his temples, who still has a pretty nice ass in his expensive Brooks Brothers suit pants. I get to experience the annoying authority figure, who bears an eerily distinct similarity to a certain father figure from a fifties sitcom. The man who still has a nice ass because he's out there exercising while I take care of his children in his stead. While I sit there atrophying, a wilting flower on the vine, he's just thriving in his world of power and success and—

Oh, God, not for the first time this weekend the tears are streaming down my face. Should I really admit all this to Todd? Don't I just want to leave him with the permanent impression that I'm "the one who got away"? Do I want him to see I'm not the prize he still thinks I am?

And am I going to let some little homebuilding, home-wrecking bimbo take her turn with Jack? Do I really even give a shit if she does? Wouldn't that take the proverbial monkey off my back? Or does it simply piss me off that he thinks he can just gallivant around like some swinging single while I stay home and tend to his brood? His free babysitting service, his low-cost housekeeper, his cut-rate dinner-on-the-table-at-six-come-hell-or-high-water fry cook?

Is this all that I have come to represent to him? I'm no longer a great tongue, a great body, a great *anything* to the man? I'm just a service provider (including that one service that now makes my skin crawl—such a foreign concept to me I shudder to admit it).

I think about the fact that geese mate for life, and wonder if a female goose is any happier at midlife than I currently am. Does the gander help with the nest? Does he babysit the goslings so that goosey girl can go out with her friends every once in a while?

Does the gander invite the little goose missus along on an occasional business trip?

I hear a faint snickering sound and realize that RePete is still awake and imitating Jack's laugh. Impeccable timing. Makes me want to throttle the damn bird. It's like Jack's laughing at me and he's not even here.

I gaze at the screen, which glows up at me from the blanket of late-night darkness into which I'm cocooned. Truth or fiction. What do I tell the man?

I whisper almost inaudibly, "Ocka, bocka, soda crocka, ocka, bocka, boo, in comes Uncle Sam and out goes Y-O-U. He loves me, he loves me not, he loves me, he loves me not."

Oh, Christ, Claire, are you out, or in? Or is it Julia who's in? Does he love me? Do I love him? Is there actually still love there, somewhere, that's entombed in a coffin of ice, like some ancient explorer buried deep within the confines of an enormous iceberg, an iceberg that's been built up over years of stormy confrontation, harsh realities, and marital discord? Or is the love gone? Where? Where has the love gone? Christ, I'm sounding like the lyrics to a sappy love song now.

I return to my missive.

Todd, did you ever imagine that halfway through your life things would feel so unsettled, so tenuous? That despite how entrenched we are in our lives, things really are in such flux? Wasn't life supposed to be about happily-ever-afters? No one ever mentioned to me the "unhappily ever after" option, and dammit, I don't like it.

I heave a weighted sigh of dismay.

So, how about you divert my mind from the unhappily part. Regale me with tales of our glory days, would you? I need to know about a time during which things were cheerful and carefree. A little mental escapism never hurt anybody, right?

I apologize for dumping on you like this, Todd. And I will understand if you decide that you have no interest in being part of my rehab therapy. It does seem a little weird; you know what I mean?

But if you do want to enlighten me, then how about you start with this: Kat mentioned to me something about you and me in an elevator up on Capitol Hill—the one that's all glass and you can see outside when you're riding it. Did we really do it in a public elevator? Could I have been so bold? On that note, I'm signing off for now. Morning will come too soon for me, and there is no rest for the weary when you are the mother of five. Good night.

C

chapter Ten

The perspective of time is generous, granting you a farsightedness that is imperceptible when you're living through an event. Thus was the case with how Jack handled the death of his brother, Colin. Because at the time I didn't notice the paradigm shift that must have occurred as a result of this shocking and defining event in his life.

Granted, he became a bit more withdrawn, sullen, short-tempered. During the relatively brief period of our courtship, Jack had never even demonstrated a capacity for impatience with me. Hell, he gazed upon me with the adoration reserved for the Madonna.

When Colin died, I expected Jack to be off his mark, and I wasn't surprised when he was unnecessarily prickly toward me. I assumed it was a fait accompli that his mood would reflect that hardship with which he was struggling internally. I tried to be there to comfort him, but really, he hardly let on that he needed it.

"Are you okay?" I asked him one day about two months after Colin passed away.

"What do you mean, 'okay'?"

"You know." I hardly liked to even mention the situation. "Dealing with the aftermath of losing not only your brother but your best friend."

"Claire, I'm *fine*," he insisted, holding up his hand. "Just quit asking me. I don't want to discuss it."

Thus the conversation was stopped cold, his obstreperous tone of voice making it abundantly clear to me that the subject matter was entirely off-limits. After a while I just stopped asking. If he said he was fine, then I had to accept that he was fine.

But he wasn't. Something inside of Jack died with Colin, but I didn't realize then that it, like Colin, was never going to return. There would be no resurrection of Jack as he once was. As I said, outwardly it wasn't terribly obvious, but I knew, I guess, deep down, that Jack had lost his joie de vivre, that he had become quite sobersided. I guess back then I naively assumed that eventually that spark would be reignited in Jack's soul, but now I realize that I let the years get ahead of us while Jack's internal flame, his pilot light of sorts, remained extinguished.

At the time, I leaned heavily on my sister for comfort.

"Claire, this will pass," Syndey would reassure me. "Jack's a great guy. He's just going through a transition, you know?"

"I don't know, Syd," I'd say. "This seems like it's bigger than that, you know what I mean?"

"Look, do you remember Howdy?" Sydney asked.

Shit, she was breaking out the big guns by bringing up Howdy. His name was one that simply didn't come up in conversation anymore. Howdy was the man Sydney had wanted to marry. Howdy, who had a personality as big as his Rodeo Bob–sounding name. Howdy would come into a room and all focus would shift to him. Like, even if there was a cute little puppy in the room, it didn't matter. Howdy won out. And it was always all about him.

We all liked Howdy—I mean, you couldn't not like the guy. He had the kind of smile that spread from person to person, like a baton being passed in a relay race. He had this boyish freckled face, with reddish hair, and he called every woman he met *darlin'*. He was sort of a universal big brother.

Sydney and Howdy dated right out of college. Everything was going along fine for them. There was no doubt in anyone's mind that soon Howdy would propose to Sydney, there would be a gorgeous wedding and precious little flower girls and birdseed tossed for good luck, and life would be good. But then my sister got pregnant. To Sydney it wasn't quite how she'd planned it, but since she expected they'd be married anyhow, she figured it would just step up their plans a little bit. Hell, she wasn't even worried about telling Howdy. He was great with children—he even made balloon animals at parties, for God's sake; he'd always said he wanted them.

But when Sydney told Howdy that she was expecting his child, Howdy said adios faster than you could blink your eyes. He wanted nothing to do with any babies. He left her a few hundred bucks on her dresser to "take care of it," as he so kindly noted on the envelope, and just evaporated from her life. The bastard. I guess it was lucky for Sydney that before she had to figure out what to do about that baby she miscarried. Probably her five straight days of tears didn't help matters, all that stress and all. But once she miscarried, we all went back to life as we knew it, and not once did we ever bring up Howdy's name again. Until now.

"Couldn't quite forget Howdy," I said, a little hesitant. We were treading in a minefield, as far as I was concerned. I mean, after the Howdy episode ended, it was as if he'd never existed.

"Yeah, well, trust me, I tried," Sydney said. "And it's been long enough now that I think I can bring up Howdy without getting too worked up. But why I mention him is this: see, Howdy, he was a boy. He wasn't a man. And when the going got tough, Howdy checked out. He couldn't face his fate with any sort of maturity or good grace. Jack's not like Howdy. Jack *is* a man. I think you need to just give Jack a chance to work through his sorrow and his fears in his own way, Claire. Jack will come back to you. You just wait and see."

Only, Jack never did come back to me the way he once was.

It's Sunday night, and normally the countdown toward the inevitable would be commencing right about now. But tonight I am safe in the knowledge that I will not have to have Jack's fleeting amorous desire imposed upon an unreciprocating me. He knows that he is so far in the doghouse that sex is not an option. Not that he hasn't tried.

At dinner he complimented me on my hair. Lame attempt, considering I haven't done anything with it in weeks. In fact, I have a sort of reverse skunk look going on at the roots, my duplicitous mousy brown-gray hair revealing its ugly self like some pervert flashing his privates from beneath a trench coat, exposing my faux blond for the impostor it really is.

When Jack attempted to flatter me in such an obviously disingenuous manner, I just looked at him, a dead expression on my face. He knew then that he'd have a better chance of being accepted into MENSA than into my loving arms.

Loving arms. Ha.

* * *

"So. Are you just going to continue to give me the cold shoulder indefinitely?" Jack asks as I'm brushing my teeth.

I choose not to respond.

"Claire?"

Silence.

"For fuck's sake, Claire! Answer me!" Jack throws his toothbrush against the bathroom mirror for emphasis.

I look at him with hollow eyes. "Yes."

I spit my toothpaste into the sink and stare at the swirl of creamy blue-green effluence coursing into the drain. I pick up my hairbrush and begin my nightly ritual of one hundred strokes through my tangled tresses. One, two, three, four. It's one of those beauty tips I took under advisement from *Glamour* magazine back in probably about 1974; the editors insisted that it would assure glossy, bouncing, and behaving locks. I've known for years that they just pulled that nonsense out of thin air, but just like old marriages, old habits are hard to break. So I keep brushing. Seventy-eight, seventy-nine, eighty.

"Yes, what?"

"Yes, you bet your ass I'm going to continue giving you the cold shoulder."

"And when do you plan to abandon this childish endeavor?" And there we have it. I knew it was only a matter of time before Ward entered the room.

"Childish endeavor? *Childish endeavor?* How about *your* unseemly little childish endeavor—the pursuit of some young twinkie who's old enough to be your daughter? How's that for a childish endeavor?" I really can't believe I'm actually confronting him about this.

"Jesus H. Christ, Claire. What in the hell are you talking about?"

"Oh, please. Spare me. You know exactly what I

mean, little Mr. Twinkle Toes. I saw the spring in your step, the glee that alighted in your eyes when that Julia chick stepped into our little circle of love last night."

I look at Jack, and the only word I can think of to describe his appearance is *apoplectic*. It really is a great word, a very visual word, because you can instantly picture someone who is described as apoplectic: their eyes ready to erupt from the sockets, steam pouring from the nasal cavities, the ears, and the mouth. Fury on the scale of an angry Zeus. A fury capable of inciting natural disasters of biblical proportions.

"What is *wrong* with you? You seem to be living in some bizarre state of delusion. You think I have something for Julia Julliard? Are you out of your cotton-picking mind?"

Cotton-picking mind. So like Ward to use such a dated colloquialism. I smile at him, but it's not a smile with warmth, rather one overflowing with disdain.

"Ward," I begin. "I mean, Jack. You must think I was born yesterday." Jeez, I'm starting to sound just like June Cleaver. Life imitates art. And what's with the name Julia Julliard? That's almost as bad as Bob Roberts, Tom Thompson, Jim James. Why would someone choose redundancy when naming their offspring? Ease of committing the name to memory? I wonder if people with repetitive names tend to choose simple phone numbers: 555-5555, 242-2222. If that was the case, I don't doubt that old Julia Julliard would choose 666-6666, being the Antichrist I suspect her to be.

"Look, Jack, you can stop fooling me already." I sigh. "It was as plain as the nose on your face."

The aquiline nose on his face, the face I used to smother with kisses, those kisses proof of my undying love for and understanding of this once-magnificent man.

And now all I want to do with that miserable nose is slug it.

"You're nuts," he shouts as he slams the bathroom door on me.

"Don't you *dare* slam that door on me, you bastard." I am seething with rage now, following on his heels to the bed, where Jack and his crisp striped cotton Lord & Taylor Ward Cleaver pajamas have settled under the comforter, his back turned to me. "Who the *hell* do you think you are, feigning indifference with me toward that . . . that . . . that *child*, the same child with whom you no doubt plan to have a cozy little weekend in Miami Beach?"

"Oh, spare me, Claire. I'm not going to Miami for a cozy weekend with anyone. *Good night.*"

You know that thing you always read about successful couples who have celebrated their golden wedding anniversary, and everyone asks them the secret to their marriage's longevity?

No, it's not when the guy says he drinks a fat finger of whiskey every day (although I bet that helps). It's that they agreed from the beginning not to go to bed angry at each other. To stay up all night, if that was what it took, to resolve their differences.

Long ago I tried to impose that rule on our marriage, but Jack felt it was irrelevant, and so he refused to play along. Hence right now I have two choices: I start pounding maniacally on his back to try to break through that thick skull of his the fact that I am not happy and that this unchecked anger with which we seem to live continually is threatening to metastasize throughout the body of our marriage, and at some point will be declared inoperable. Or I can just internalize my wrath, allowing it to fester in my soul, sickening my insides with this toxic fluid of despair. Fuck.

* * *

Jack and I manage to avoid each other during the morning routine. Seems he took his running gear, gym bag, and a change of clothes along and left early for work. Good riddance to him. At breakfast the kids wonder where their father is.

"Why isn't Daddy down here reading the paper this morning?" Chrissy asks.

"Hmmm?" I figure if I pretend not to hear the question they'll move on to something else.

"Didn't you hear Mom and Dad screaming last night?" Cameron asks her as I pick my jaw up off the floor. I had no idea the walls were so thin.

"Honey, Daddy and I weren't screaming. We were having a discussion." I try to speak reassuringly, as I know children can get upset about these things.

"Yeah, well, if we had a discussion like that at school, we'd be shipped off to the principal's office so fast—"

I used to be so proud that my children were smart; now I'm thinking cluelessness isn't such a bad quality in a kid.

"Mommies and daddies are human beings, and human beings can't get along *all* the time—it's unnatural. Sometimes we disagree, and when we disagree we discuss it and come to a solution." It's so hard to lie to your own flesh and blood.

"Then how come when we disagree with each other you and Daddy always punish us?" Charlotte used to be such a sweet, unassuming child.

"That's different."

"Why?" Lindsay pipes in.

"Just because it is. The rules are different for grown-ups than for brothers and sisters who fight and punch and kick and pinch and all those things you're not allowed to do."

"Did you pinch Daddy?" Bubba asks, his forehead creased with worry.

I scruff his hair around his baseball cap. "Of course Mommy didn't pinch Daddy!" Though I'd have liked nothing better than to do at least that. "Mommies don't punch and kick and pinch daddies, honey."

"Yuh-huh," Cameron interjects. "I saw on the news just last week about this guy—"

"Zip it!" I glare at Cameron. How this conversation evolved into the topic of spousal abuse I'll never know.

"But—"

"Cameron, enough! Everyone: you have nothing to worry about. Mommy and Daddy are fine; we just had a little disagreement. Daddy simply had to leave early for work this morning because he had a meeting." I neglect to mention that if he really did have a meeting, it was probably with that home-wrecking home-builder I now loathe.

"Now let's go, kids. The bus will be here in a few minutes. Chop chop! Gather up all of your things. Chrissy? Don't forget your lunch box!"

Chapter Eleven

I finally get all of the kids off to school and return to the kitchen and put on a pot of coffee. Thank God caffeine is a legal drug in this country; otherwise I would spend most of my waking hours trolling squirrelly low-income neighborhoods in the District trying to score it from disreputable dealers.

I'm so glad I don't have work this morning; I could barely stand to see Robert, all sexually sated and looking like a snake that just ingested the neighbor's cat.

I sit down at my computer with my steaming cup of joe and sift through a mountain of e-mails. One from Mom, which can definitely wait. One from Sydney, two for better mortgage rates, seven for some supplement to increase sexual desire (could be a sign), one from a plastic surgeon selling me on implants, and the usual flurry of messages from my favorite online shopping wonderlands. Can't wait till the bills come due this month.

I decide to open up Syd's first.

Hi, Claire! I haven't heard from you in several days, so I thought I'd drop a quick e-mail to say hello. Now, don't be jealous or anything, but I just spent the most amazing weekend with Philip— you know, the guy from work? We had dinner Friday night, went out to a jazz bar, couldn't keep our hands off each other as we listened to some band playing Thelonious Monk, and finally left our martinis on the table with a tip and blew out of there in a, uh, hurry. Figure it out. I'm telling you, Claire, this guy is all that. I mean, I've been around the block a bit—how could I not? I'm thirty-four years old, for crying out loud—and this guy by far is the most incredible man I have known. Do you know that while I cooked breakfast, he composed a poem for me? Claire! He composed a freaking poem for me! Have you ever heard of such a thing in your life? And it wasn't some lame "roses are red, violets are blue" thing, either. It actually made me cry, it was so touching. Well, what else could we do after that but retreat back to bed, where we spent the vast majority of the weekend? I didn't even need food! And you know that's unlike me.

I think I'm going to vomit, right here and now. As I watched my world decompose before my very eyes this weekend, my sister got laid about sixty times and lived to brag about it. Life is so not fair. I mean, what did I do to deserve this? Meanwhile, as I percolate with envy, I have to write her back. She is my sister, after all.

Sydney: You bitch! Why do you get to have great sex all weekend long? I want to have great sex all weekend long. I want to have great sex and have poems written for me, and be wined and dined and treated like a princess and have the man of my life open the car door for me, and I might as well wish for world fucking peace. I'd probably settle for one day without acrimony at this point.

I'm sorry to dump on you. I'm happy for you, Syd; really I am. If there's anyone out there who truly deserves fervent, steam-up-the-car-windows, multiple-orgasmic, G-spot-hitting coitus happily-ever-afterus, it's you, honey. Really. Right on, sister. I hope you get enough for me to get a vicarious thrill. At the rate I'm going, it'll be the last exposure to good sex I'll ever have ☹. Maybe someday things will be like that for me again. But I doubt it.

Speaking of great sex . . . Guess who I heard from after lo these many years? None other than Todd the bod. Yes, I know it's hard to believe, but maybe it's true that dogs do find their way back home eventually. Although, not like I'm his home or anything.

He hinted at always holding a torch for me. Whatever. I haven't told him that not only do I not hold a torch for him, I don't hold a flashlight, a glow stick, or any other type of illuminating device. But I must admit, it's sure nice to get some attention lavished on me by someone, at least. Even if it is from some bizarre blast from the past who hasn't seen me in half a lifetime. Well, better run. Talk later!
Love, Claire

I hit the send button, knowing that as soon as Sydney reads this she will be on the phone with my mother to find out what's wrong with me. Won't that take Mom by surprise? And she thought I was so entrenched in wedded bliss. Well, actually, I guess she knows I'm suffering from "sniveling-mommy syndrome" or whatever the hell she called it.

I hear the familiar ding and rush to see who this e-mail is from. Aha! Just who I was hoping to hear from.

Hello, stranger . . . Do I detect trouble in paradise? A chink in the armor? Spoilage in the refrigerator of love? (Pitiful metaphor, don't you think?) Claire, I am honestly so sorry to hear that things aren't all they're cracked up to be. Having been in a similar boat, I can appreciate how hard it is to deal with.

Do you know for certain that there's some sort of liaison going on with your husband and this strumpet? (Ha, ha. I've always wanted to use the word *strumpet* in the appropriate context.) Or is this speculation on your part?

Speaking as a member of the male species, I should advise you that not all interest in the opposite sex implies sexual involvement. Not to defend your husband needlessly or anything, but we are guys. Guys get off looking at good-looking young women. Especially if they have great tits. Does she have a great rack? Sorry, it's just all part of that perpetuation-of-the-species thing. We are programmed to sniff out greener pastures. It doesn't mean we then graze there. We're just on the hunt. Does that make any sense to you?

Grrrrrr. I hate how men excuse away their groin-centered brain concept so readily. Like the Twinkie defense or something. *Gee, Officer, I couldn't help it! My dick made me do it!* Yeah, right.

I take a swig of coffee to bolster myself for more quasi-unsolicited advice from Todd. It is considerate of him to add his two cents. It's also somewhat pathetic that I am paying even a moment's attention to the counsel of a man who not only ditched me with no warning and no courtesy but also discarded his own kid in a similar manner. I mean, how wise could

Todd be? Although, probably the most interesting times I remember with Todd were when we engaged in deep philosophical discussions. Maybe he's wise about those other than himself. Sort of like the cobbler with no shoes of his own. Back to Todd's reflections . . .

Have you confronted him with this? If so, what does he say? If he is betraying you, then, Claire, you must do something about it. And if he won't admit it to you and you still suspect something, then become a private eye and figure it out. Go through the man's wallet when he's asleep, sift through his pile of suits waiting to go to the dry cleaners, empty every pocket. Smell him. What does he smell like? Someone else? Someone else's perfume? Or worse (God forbid)?! And you know what I'm talking about, Claire. Don't bury your head in the sand, honey; take control of this situation, so at least then you can decide how you're going to handle things, you understand?

Now, enough about your as-yet unfounded suspicions. Let's talk about you. First of all, that tongue of yours. Jesus, Claire, I swear I get hard just thinking about the things we did together. But I'm not just talking about that. I mean, even your kiss was so sensuous, it could melt the heart of the most hardened of men.

You kissed as if you were ingesting every sense of me: you devoured my taste, absorbed my touch, inhaled my scent, obscured my sight, deafened my hearing with the beating of your heart. You kissed as if it was the last sensation you were going to experience before you died, and you wanted to encapsulate a lifetime in that moment. That kiss, that spellbinding gesture. Christ, Claire. As I think about that now, I don't get what made me walk away from you. What the hell was I thinking? I had perfection in my lap, and I threw it away. For greener pastures? Fuck, I'm sorry, Claire. I'm really sorry. What a god-damned fool I was.

Jesus, I think my eyes are practically bugging out of my head. First off, is he asking me whether Jack smells like some other woman's snatch? Please, please, please, please, please tell me I am not contemplating this right now.

And second, how can it be that I was once sensuous? I'm about as sensuous as a diaper pail at this point in my life. I ingested the man? I *ingested* the man? When I think about inhaling the smell of Jack, I can only think of the perfunctory smells of him that I avoid like the plague: his casual flatulence, his uninvited burps, his wretched morning breath when he infrequently tries to kiss me in failed attempts to get amorous with me in the early morning hours. Christ, Jack knows that I'd cut off his balls if he woke me from sleep; it's *the most* precious commodity in my life. Apparently it's supplanted sex in that starring role.

I think back to when morning breath was a welcome aroma, as it indicated that the guy I'd just spent the night with cared enough about me to stay until dawn. "Prideless tramp," you're saying. But you know what I mean. Who can't recall those fleeting one-night stands? Those moments of lost self-control, when the desire for sex overrode your common sense, when you knew that what was about to happen was about two people seeking self-gratification and nothing else.

But then every blue moon, the man didn't slip out in the middle of the night, maybe even stayed for breakfast. Which gave you hope that there could be a future beyond ten a.m.

Not that this was a frequent occurrence in my jaded past (at least, I don't think so), but now that I think about it, it did happen. I realize there *was* a time when I would have consumed the mouth of a man as if it were my last drink of water, at five in the morning, despite his bad breath, despite the stale smell of sleep on his skin. The more that Jack has become a thorn in my side (as opposed to a rose in my vase?), the more his inadequacies have become amplified, almost unforgivable flaws. Now Jack's morning breath is about as welcome as a case of head lice. Besides which, I'm never inclined to be close enough to actually smell him. How could I ever have even detected the scent of another woman on him? I take a sip of my now-cold coffee and glance down at my computer screen.

Claire, I'm so saddened that the mundane grind of life has sucked the sparkle from you. That the rainbow landscape of all that is you has evolved into a monochrome still life. I cannot believe that you aren't still as sexy and brilliant as ever. If anything, it's just lurking beneath this now-insipid exterior you claim to suffer from.

And it sucks that your husband doesn't appreciate you. Speaking from firsthand experience (having worked my way into a second marriage, I'm probably more expert than some on this subject, I might add), it's awfully easy to become complacent with sameness. Whether it's with a spouse, a friendship, a job, a hobby, even the food you eat, or whatever, the rut of constancy can inure you to that

which was once so important and special. It's such
an unfortunate side effect of daily living. I guess
that's why all of those women's magazine head-
lines scream about trying to keep the spark in a relationship, striving for intimacy, and all that
blather. It really is work, isn't it?

I wonder when Todd became such a sage. It's not
just work. It's hard work. And who the hell has time for
hard work when you're drowning in diapers and spit-
up and temper tantrums and drool and carpools and
sibling rivalry and fevers and unexpected medical
emergencies and everything else that takes the "you
that once was" out of the equation?

The equation is overflowing with everyone else and
everything else; there's no more room for *you* in it. I
think about a little medical emergency I had last year.
One of those strange situations whereby, for the first
time in over a decade, I got to sit back and do nothing
but heal myself. The most self-indulgent act I performed in my recent adult life: recuperating from surgery. Ha. How's that for a cruel twist of fate?

Whew! Lost my train of thought there for a minute. I
take a swig of my coffee, spit it back into the cup, it's
so rank, and return to Todd's e-mail.

Re: old sitcom father figure gig. I'm trying to picture you hanging with some guy with burnished
sideburns and a pin-striped zoot suit and it's making me laugh. I don't think you'd be terribly com-
patible with a stern disciplinarian. In fact, you
used to kick my ass whenever I tried to pull anything bossy on you. When on Earth did you of all
people start to buckle when it came to a man's will?
Again, not to defend that cad of a husband

you've got, but just to give you the male perspective on things: Just as a man may perceive his wife as becoming such a bitch after they're married, the wife may too view this negative transformation in her spouse.

But you need to understand that the burden to provide for a family is indescribable, Claire, and trust me, it's capable of bringing out the worst in a man. At times it is like a vise crushing your chest. There's so much pressure to provide for everyone—financially, emotionally, you name it. It can instill in someone fear and an unnatural intensity heretofore unknown. It can make a happy-go-lucky man become a real dickhead. I'm speaking from experience, Claire. Lest you forget, I'm the guy who washed his hands of his own flesh and blood. You can't get much shittier than that.

Hmmm. It's true how we're so busily engrossed in our own problems and burdens that we lose perspective of the other partner. I hadn't thought about the intense sense of responsibility that Jack has encountered, having to feed and clothe and house a family of seven.

While he's been consumed with providing for them, I've been preoccupied with surviving them. And I don't mean outliving them; I mean making sure that not only do they live another day, but that they live it healthily, and they learn to grow as human beings, and treat one another with kindness and respect, and to love thy neighbor and do unto others as they would have others do unto them, and get their homework done, and brush their teeth and take their baths and eat their fruits and vegetables and not jump off a bridge even if their friends did, and to not take rides from strangers, and not take that first drink at the party when all the other kids are doing it, and say no to drugs, and, oh, Christ, I'm exhausted thinking about it all.

And that's not even taking into account keeping the house free of allergens, ensuring that clothes are washed, sheets changed, dishes cleared, meals cooked, schedules juggled, pets fed, phones charged, passwords remembered. Holy Mother of God, life is full of *have-tos*, isn't it?

But then I think about those poor African women who are impregnated—no, make that unwillingly circumcised, forced into a marriage, *then* impregnated—against their wills. And they toil in the fields until the very minute the baby drops from their womb into the cassava crop or whatever else they're harvesting. Not an hour later, after the blood and afterbirth are wiped up, they're back carrying a hundred pounds of firewood or enormous jugs of water atop their colorfully scarved heads, for miles on end, with a wailing baby strapped across them.

And the men are sitting around the village getting drunk on banana wine, just waiting for dusk to force themselves upon the women all over again. I suddenly realize I haven't got one bloody damned thing to truly complain about in my life. I have it *great*. Five fantastic children, a beautiful home, sweet pets—even if they do mess my house up—friends and family I love, a husband I love who at least wants me to a certain degree, I guess. So what's my problem then? What's wrong with me?

I think I've answered my own question. I've allowed myself to be buried under life's gargantuan avalanche. When it all toppled onto me, I just couldn't figure out which end was up, how to find fresh air and comfort before being paralyzed by the onslaught. I suppose I've been waiting for the spring thaw, hoping that then

I'll be able to start anew, get my act together, fail everyone a little less (including myself). Hell, maybe even learn to like my husband again. As if.

I shake my head to clear the burgeoning and burdensome thoughts swimming through my brain, and start to read some more.

Claire—you cannot allow yourself to wither and die. That isn't the Claire I once knew and loved (!). You would have stood up to the adversity and overcome it, as you must now. At the risk of sounding like Dr. Phil, I'm going to lay it on the line. I was just reading this whole thing, written by some life-coach-to-the-stars, in an airline magazine recently, and it made sense. And here's what she said: Life is composed of stages. Even substages.

Our lives are woven in and out of these various stages, and one day you'll find the tapestry of your life is this beautiful and incomplete work of woven majesty. Parts of it will be brilliantly colorful, perhaps blindingly so. And other parts will be dull, drab, and indifferent. But perhaps in those areas, upon further inspection, you will see the most amazing weaving-work imaginable.

Hidden in the mundane you will see extraordinary beauty buried deep within. That's the thing about life, Claire. It comes at you, and who you are is defined by how you handle it. Ha. I sound like the fucking yogi atop the mountain or something. Some goddamned peyote-smoking shaman. Like I'm so wise and worldly.

I guess the thing is, Claire, it's easier to see the truth in others than it is to see the truth within yourself. Maybe this is because we're too close to our own situations to gain the perspective needed for entrenched honesty. Because then we would see the real warts and the ugly spots that we want to hide from.

Don't get me wrong: I'm not saying your life is full of warts. I'm just saying that maybe it's easier for me to give you this pep talk than it is for you to give it to yourself. So here it is, for what it's worth, Claire: carpe diem, girl. Don't allow yourself to drown in the drab colors of your today. Learn to appreciate the intricate weaving, honey. Then start adding your own color.

Once you do that, you might find that this tapestry of yours can be both colorful and beautifully worked. But until then it's an underappreciated work in progress, just waiting for a little TLC. And in that, Claire, is where you will truly find your happily-ever-after. You have to have a hand in it; you can't expect it to come on its own without hard work on your part.

Hard work. Who the hell has time for hard work in life? My whole daily schedule is hard work. And now I have to add to the list? Shoot, I don't even have time for a haircut or a manicure, but I have to find time for myself? Ha!

Claire, I want you to know that I'm honored you've asked me to help cheer you up and get your mind off your current reality. Though I will at the same time urge you to work to repair things, rather then let it fester. But start by working on you. What makes you happy, Claire? Is it anything that you actually do? Or are you spending your life with *have-tos*? Remember, all work and no play makes Claire a dull girl!

All work and no play makes Jack a dull boy, too. Although, who knows? Maybe he's playing to his heart's content while I'm hard at work on this family. And hard at work not playing. And not using my once-sensual tongue, and not kissing as if my life depended upon it.

Please don't ever think you are dumping on me. It's a privilege to be able to be your sounding board; really it is. And by the way, Claire, I am taking your suggestions to heart. I contacted Vanna and told her I was interested in opening up a relationship with our son. You could have heard light waves traveling in the deafening silence that ensued after I dropped that bombshell on her.

But she said that she'd think about it. In fact, scarily enough, I think she said something to the effect that she'd "pray about it"—can you believe that? I haven't got a prayer. Excuse the pun ☺. Anyhow, I await her decision, and now realize that the fate of my fatherhood lies in her hands. Her hands clasped in prayer, I guess.

Okay, abrupt subject-matter change. Now, on to the great elevator caper. Sheesh, you really have lost your memory, haven't you? You honestly mean to tell me you have no recollection of me taking you up against the glass window of the exterior elevator at that hotel on Capitol Hill? Was I that forgettable? I can promise you that you weren't. You, my dear, were a veritable vixen. Thank goodness no one needed a lift that night.

Actually, if you'll recall, we'd attended a big New Year's Eve bash at the hotel. And it got late, and at some point neither of us could find our room keys. With that slinky dress of yours, no wonder you had nowhere to stash a key. But I must have dropped my key somewhere along the line.

   And time was ticking along, and we were getting awfully horny, and we roamed the hallway searching for my key to see if I'd dropped it in one of those corridors; then we got in the elevator to go back downstairs and see if we could get another key at the front desk; then the lust just overtook us in the elevator, and— Oh, shit, I have to run, Claire; they just called final boarding for my flight to Atlanta. Listen, I'm really sorry that your soul has become dormant, Claire. It's such a beautiful, vibrant aspect of you. I want to help awaken it from its slumber, so just think about what I said. Uh-oh, gotta go.

T

Damn, just when things were heating up. That man is always boarding a plane to somewhere. He must never see his wife.

The phone rings.

"Hello? . . . Uh-huh . . . Chrissy's lunch box? Again? . . . And she doesn't want the creamed chicken over rice? Okay, yeah, sure, I'll bring it right by . . . Sure, bye-bye."

I look to the counter, and sure enough there's Chrissy's Strawberry Shortcake lunch box. I run upstairs, throw on some sweats, grab my purse, and get into the car.

Amazingly, I hardly give a second thought to showing up at my kids' schools dressed like some insane aunt you'd usually keep hidden in the cellar: drab, oversize sweats, hair not even brushed since I went to bed last night (although those hundred strokes must have worked overtime for this morning), not a hint of makeup. My eyelashes are so straight (God, I'm a slave to my eyelash curler) you can't even tell that I have any in this state.

Nevertheless, through the now-pouring rain I run into the office, drop off the forgotten meal, then scoot back to the car, unobserved by anyone but the school secretary, who isn't looking much better than me, thank goodness.

I decide to swing by the grocery store to pick up a few things for dinner while I'm out. The rain intensifies as I veer toward the Giant shopping center. By the time I get to the store water is pummeling the pavement. I cruise the lot, trying to get a close space. Not like it matters if I get wet. I play a little game of cat and mouse with some woman in a mega-SUV with fogged-up windows who looks determined to trump me in her mission of getting the best available parking spot. Just because of this I dog her, wending my way through the Monday-morning grocery shoppers' cavalcade, jockeying my way around their carts in an effort to get a better space than my competitor. I cleverly maneuver around an old fellow supported by a cane, and slide into a space just as the other woman turns the curve into my aisle. Ha! All hail the conquering hero! Clearly I need to get a life.

I get out of the car, cold rain slicing down on my skin, and I'm feeling quite smug at my little victory. But as I revel in my stupid little moment of type-A Northern Virginia–competitive-driver glory, a car whips by me going far too fast for a parking lot, and I'm hit with a wave from a newly formed trench of muddy water. My sweatpants are drenched, and I am so darned irate I could just chase after that driver and give him a piece of my mind, except that he'd probably whip out a semiautomatic and gun me down.

I seek the cover of the grocery store, wishing I could shake off like Tripod—one of those ear-to-tail shakes

that rids one of all but the most stubborn of clinging
water, a wave of skin moving like a tsunami from one
end to the other.

Instead, I practically waddle into the store like the
drowned duck I look like. And the first person I encounter is Talia Sortini, whose husband, Mario, works at
the same firm as Jack. Talia Sortini, who drives a large
black SUV just like the one I beat out for a good parking
space. I absolutely detest Talia Sortini, and would rather
run into Satan or Dick Cheney—sometimes I think
they're one and the same—especially when I look like
this.

"Why, Claire, *look* at you, darling."

The way she says *darling*, like she's Eva fucking Gabor
or something, makes me want to pull on those perfectly
tweezed eyebrows of hers and twist till she screams. I
can barely conceal my distaste for the woman.

"Talia."

"Well, Claire, don't *you* look like the worm washed
down the storm drain?" If she is trying to endear herself to me, she's not succeeding.

"Ha, ha. Funny, Talia. I just had to run out quickly
and wasn't expecting the Spanish Inquisition."

"So. Interesting party the other night, *n'est-ce pas?*"

"And what do you mean by that?" I can tell she's
driving at something.

"Oh, I just happened to notice that little chickie-poo
who was clinging like Saran Wrap to that handsome
husband of yours."

I look at her sculpted scarlet nails that are vividly
displayed across her Angela Bassett–like biceps
(which make me so damned jealous, the bitch) and
wonder whose type-O positive was used to color them.
Surely she's made it a blood sport to plunge those
talons into some sacrificial mammal or another on a
regular basis, just to stain her claws the right color.

"Whatever are you talking about?" I am not about to give her the pleasure of my shame.

"Oh, please, Claire. Don't tell me you didn't notice that cute young thing who was gazing so longingly at Jack? Or that quaint paternal gaze it seemed that Jack had reserved exclusively for her?"

I wonder if anyone has ever been beaten to death in the produce section of the Giant, or if Talia is about to be the first.

"First of all, Talia, Julia is Jack's protégé. And second of all, I find it compelling that you are so concerned with what others are up to when your own husband was looking awfully cozy with that young man who delivers the pastries to the office last week when I was there."

Of course, I haven't been to Jack's office in forever, so I haven't a clue as to whether Mario has been sniffing around gay young men. But he does seem to have an unnatural affinity for personal grooming, so it doesn't bother me to plant the seed of fear in Talia's small mind.

Talia looks offended. "My husband has had no interaction with anyone who delivers pastries. He's on a no-carb diet."

"Well, think what you will, but the wife is always the last to know." I turn my cart with a flourish and wheel away, my own seeds of trepidation, which had been sown just a few short evenings ago, now sprouting roots and unfurling leaves like one of those time-lapse videos you see on a Discovery Channel science show.

The first thing I do when I get home is park my anxious butt in front of my computer and book an over-priced plane ticket to Miami.

It seems I am off on an unexpected sleuthing mission. That's okay. After all, I'm sure I can combine a few mojitos poolside with a little subterfuge over my mini holiday weekend. And while I'm there, I'll find out exactly what Ward is up to with his little protégé.

Chapter Twelve

I'm finishing the dinner dishes when the phone rings. As I set a crystal wineglass (a cherished wedding gift from my grandmother—who, I might add, was happily married for fifty-six years) on top of the dish drainer, it smacks into the pasta pot and snaps cleanly at the stem, slicing silently into my palm. A fresh stream of blood trickles from the heel of my hand. I suck the blood into my mouth and grab the phone before it stops ringing.

"Claire?" It's my mother.

"Hey! Why are you calling so late?" I ask, squeezing my hand to stanch the flow of blood. Usually by now my parents are both fast asleep, fueled by their late-day high-octane martinis, something they call their "sundowners" with good reason.

"I have something to tell you that I knew you'd want to know about." Sounds cryptic. My mother loves to dish gossip, to scoop it out like ice cream for the dessert-famished, like me.

"Geez, Mom. It's almost eleven o'clock on a weeknight. It must be some serious news to keep you up this late."

"I spoke with Angela Marbury about an hour ago." Angela is the mother of Tina Gray, a girl I was a cheerleader with in high school and college who married what I considered at the time to be the near-perfect man. Angela and my mom used to do Jack La Lanne exercises together three mornings a week in my living room when Tina and I were children, and they keep in touch periodically.

My mind flashes back to picture Mom and Angela in their royal blue leotards and footless leggings, both wearing shimmery coral lipstick and false eyelashes, hands on their hips, struggling awkwardly through Jack La Lanne's televised calisthenics while Tina and I ate Froot Loops by the gross. Angela sported the unfortunate postpartum shape of an ostrich, and try as she might, she never seemed to be able to shake that skinny-legged, round body figure that wasn't particularly flattering in stretch wear.

"Tina and Mark are getting a divorce," my mother says, interrupting my train of thought.

Like that fleeting moment of quiet after glass shatters, I stand silent with the phone in the crook of my neck, awaiting the delayed response from my lips.

"You must have misunderstood her," I say. "There's no way that Teeny and Mark are splitting up. They have the perfect marriage. Three children. Two dogs, for God's sake. He's a partner in her dad's law firm. It's a match made in litigation, if nothing else."

"I'm not kidding you," Mom insists. "Her mother is sick about it."

Teeny and I were friends during childhood, but when we went to college we sort of parted ways. It was a weird coincidence that she married a fraternity brother of Jack's, this guy Mark whom I've always considered to be one of the nicest men on the face of the Earth. Poor Mark got a real full plate with Teeny, as she was always a hand-feeder.

Jack and I sort of split up the world of women into two camps: the foragers and the hand-feeders. I most definitely am a forager: I can survive long stretches of time without emotional nurturing and feeding, and if need be I'll dig and scrape and fight to survive. The hand-feeders need round-the-clock TLC and intensive attention lest they starve of neediness. They tend to attract the overnurturers, men like Mark, who treat them like wounded baby birds and scoop them up into their solid, warm chests, feeding them a steady diet of love and affection—worshipping them.

I always marveled at Mark's stamina, as Teeny completely exhausted me to the point that I could remain only a peripheral friend of hers.

"How do I look?" she'd ask ten times a day, knowing full well that even with greasy hair and no makeup she'd outshine ninety-nine percent of the girls at Walt Whitman High. After I lavished her with flattery and reassured her of her stunning natural beauty, she'd reply, "Oh, I look terrible," and I'd want to shake her senseless and tell her to shut the ever-loving fuck up. Especially during those acne-laden hormonal teen years that she seemed to gracefully bypass, but in which I seemed to be inextricably mired.

Women like this can be quite depleting to be around, and were it not for her positive attributes (some of which I'm struggling to recall right now) I would have abandoned her long ago. Well, actually, I did abandon her long ago. Thus I think many of us felt especially grateful that Mark took her needy little self off our laps, because she was so trying at times.

Mark was the perfect foil for Teeny because he was one of those guys who planted trees on Earth Day. I mean, what kind of optimist is that? Who the hell even takes Earth Day seriously? Unlike the rest of us, who in college were drinking ourselves into a blind stupor or inhaling residual bong water by accident, the Marks of the world were doing something decent and respectable and caring for the needy, planting trees on Earth Day and such.

Not that Mark wasn't somewhat self-serving. He wasn't caring for the needy in, say, Bangladesh. Rather, he was caring for the type of needy who sported a healthy bustline and a Certs-with-Retsin smile, one who was reputed to be the queen of the blow jobs and thus revered by the men-in-the-know on campus when she was in college.

On Mark and Teeny's wedding day, there were those men who mourned the passing of her days of free and generous oral loving. But I'm sure there were as many men who wiped the sweat from their brow and thanked their lucky stars for having been spared a lifetime of Teeny draining the depths of their souls, despite the other things she was so good at draining.

So, the fact that Teeny and Mark are breaking up doesn't exactly surprise me, now that I think of it; rather I'd say it took me off guard. Kind of like deep down you realize that sometime during your life you're going to break a bone, or have to get stitches, but when it happens you're just never ready for it. I had assumed that at some point Mark realized his wife was a narcissist but decided to suck it up and deal, thus becoming immune to even the mere notion of leaving Tina.

Shortly after they were married Mark became a corporate attorney, and was pulling in a highly sustainable upper-six-figure income. A few years later he joined her daddy's practice and started reeling in the really big bucks. I think "billable hours" was his middle name. From what I heard, Teeny was happy with the lifestyle this afforded her, and even took to traveling on holiday with her hairstylist, a chef, and two nannies. There was no expense too great for Teeny's insatiable wants.

"Mom," I say, snapping my thoughts back to the present. "What on earth happened with them? I just figured one day Mark would die in his sleep and that Teeny would cash in her earnings and hook up with a cabana boy at their retreat on Mustique."

"I don't know," she says. "I hear he gave her everything in the divorce settlement: the house, three cars, two vacation homes. She got the kids and the pets, too."

"What exactly did he get out of the deal?"

Jack steps into the kitchen, having overheard much of my conversation.

"His freedom," he says, picking up an apple from a bowl on the counter and taking an exaggerated bite.

My mother continues on for a while, speculating on the mercurial nature of marriages today, and wondering if she can get back the Limoges tea set she gave them as a wedding gift.

"I hate to tell you, but I suspect there's a statute of limitations on wedding-gift reclamation. I know the bride gets a full year to write thank-you notes, but I think the guests might get a thirty-day-back guarantee and after that it's lost to the Fates."

My mother moans about failed commitment and about whatever happened to "in sickness and in health as long as you both shall live," and I just really don't want to think about failed marital vows right now, so I bid my farewells and hang up the phone.

I look over at Jack, who is attacking his apple with a vindictive zeal. "You knew about Mark and Tina?" I ask him.

"Didn't I tell you?" he says to me with such fucking

insincerity I want to cram his words back down his throat with a serrated gardening shovel.

"Uh, I'm pretty sure I'd have remembered you telling me about the end of Mark and Tina as we know it." Particularly because theirs was a somewhat memorable wedding for us: Jack and I ended up enjoying a potentially compromising encounter in a supply closet at the country club where their reception was held. It was one of those needs that seemed so urgent at the time (we were finished in plenty of time to see Mark and Teeny cut the cake). Clearly *that* was a long time ago. I think if I found myself in a broom closet with Jack nowadays, I'd hand him a bucket and a mop and tell him to get to work.

"Oh, well." He shrugs.

"Oh well?" I am a bit taken aback by Jack's blasé attitude. "I cannot believe you knew about this and failed to mention it to me."

"Oh, come off it," he says.

I look at him with suspicion. "What else do you know that you're not telling me?"

Jack throws his apple core into the disposal and turns it on. Clearly he's avoiding conversation if he decides to go to all the trouble to actually use the thing, rather than leaving the food waste in the sink for me to deal with, like he normally does. "I met Mark last week for lunch in town," he finally admits over the grinding noise of the trash disposal. I'm sad to hear this, because there was a time in which I would have known about this luncheon date the instant it went on their schedules, and now I'm hearing about it only by postapocalyptic accident.

"And the catalyst for their breakup was . . . ?"

Jack gives me a detached shrug. "Nothing, really."

"What?" My tone of voice is elevating, verging on shrill. If I were on *American Idol* I think the judges would complain about my pitch. "You mean there wasn't another woman? Or another man? No one was having an affair?"

"Well, there wasn't an actual *catalyst*. Mark told me they'd been in therapy for years. He felt that he evolved and she didn't. She was so fixated on her own issues that she couldn't meet his needs."

I pause briefly, wondering what exactly were Mark's needs, after all these years. Did he want three women at once or something? Wife swapping? Did he have a thing for whips and spankings?

"Elaborate," I say.

"There's not much to say. He just said that Tina took and took and took and never gave. And one day he just got sick of her taking."

I'm silent, the hard drive in my head whirring and whirring and whirring away, trying to process not only this somewhat unexpected information, but also, worse still, my husband's obviously defensive take on it.

"So Mark was always the generous *giver* in their marriage, and Tina *took* constantly," I summed it up. Somehow, as a woman, I have a sneaking suspicion there's more to this story. Granted, Teeny was a veteran taker. But Mark knew that from day one, and, in fact, that's why he settled on her. In a perverse way he benefited from this relationship because he needed to be needed.

"Yeah," Jack says. "And he's screwed."

"He's screwed." I mull over this comment, swirling it about my head, a soup on my mental stove that may need more seasoning. I toss in a dash of salt. "But he's happy. Because he's free. The kids are her deal, he's getting laid with all the young chickie-poos, and he doesn't have to bother with the daily burden of marriage and family ever again."

"Well, he *is* very happy now," Jack reiterates. I cock an eyebrow at him, feeling the unspoken message being broadcast my way. "But I know he feels that's he's the one who was wronged, because Tina wouldn't meet his needs one bit."

I look Jack in the face. "What exactly *were* those needs that weren't being met?"

He looks just as directly back at me. "Well, for one thing, she failed him sexually."

Oh, ho, ho. Here we go. Hit Claire below the belt, why don't we? "What? She wouldn't do what he wanted?"

Jack shook his head. "She wouldn't do *it*. Period."

I'm starting to wonder if maybe Mark is Ward and that's why Teeny wouldn't do it. After all, we're talking about the blow-job queen here, not the Frigidaire queen. That skill (and the fact that she loved doing it) doesn't just dissipate without something precipitating it. I mean, from what I heard it was a hobby of the woman's.

"So, maybe there was a legitimate reason for her not doing *it*," I say, feeling solidarity with the sexless Tina. "Maybe Teeny woke up one day and realized that Mark was an incredibly controlling person, and she grew up enough to know that she didn't need to be controlled anymore. Maybe she tried to get Mark to stop being so controlling but he wouldn't listen to her. He thought he was doing her a favor by telling her how to dress and what to do and how to do it. But you know, Teeny was young when she got married. Maybe she really did grow up. And once she did, she realized that it was revolting to be married to a guy who was bossing her around like . . . like . . . like—"

"Like what, Claire?" Jack glares at me.

"Like he's her father or something," I say.

Jack laughs. "Oh, that's a real good one. Sure. She

didn't want to have sex with someone who treated her like her father. Yeah, right."

Well, I guess Jack can see the parallels from his self-ish perspective, but not from mine. I really don't have the energy to get into this argument right now, so I try to reroute the direction of the conversation.

"So, Mark gets a dope slap of reality in therapy." I am performing my mental calculations on this nuptial-demise equation. "Eventually he realizes that Teeny's taking him for a ride, and he suddenly wants her to pony up on her end of the bargain."

Jack's noisy silence is loud and clear to me, and his smug look betrays him.

"I know *exactly* what you're thinking," I say to him.

"What?" he asks, pretending that I don't know, but he knows that I know, which makes this all the more infuriating.

"You're wistfully jealous of Mark," I say. "In the big-screen adaptation of *The Breakup of Mark and Teeny*, you've cast Claire Doolittle in the starring role of the narcissistic Tina, and yourself as the magnanimous Mark who's been wronged and is now happily free of his burdensome bride."

Jack grunts. "Stop it, Claire."

But I can't. Because I know it's true. And it pisses me off. Now, I suppose this has some slight component of sisterly solidarity to it: I can only presume there is more to this than the cut-and-dried long-suffering-unloved-male sob story that Jack's been fed by Mark on the soupspoon of his laments. But the fact is, I *know* that Jack is seeing himself as the one who's gotten the raw end of the deal, too. Poor, poor, pitiful Jack, who doesn't have a nymphomaniac wife and instead has to suffer in silence, unlaid and unloved, week in and week out. Fuckless. No, make that feckless.

"No, you stop it." I bristle. "Own up to it."

"If you're going to force this out of me, yeah, I do see some parallels here." He bashes me over the head with the insult.

Now, even though I know in his self-absorbed mind he's seeing himself as the victim, to actually hear him enunciate these beliefs seems to amplify my rage. Besides which, I'm the forager here. I'm the one who has gone for long stretches without affection, without simple gentle kindnesses. I'm the one who has had to deal with Jack and all of his erratic, moody ways.

"Parallels? You dare to compare me to one of the most self-absorbed people we know?" I yell at him. "Me, who drove *myself* to the hospital when in labor with our fourth child because you were in the middle of an important meeting with a client? Me, who scrubs the toilets twice a week, scrapes bird shit off the floor daily, vacuums and dusts and mops and cooks and cleans and never asks for a goddamned thing? I don't have the butler, the chauffeur, the chef, the traveling hairdresser, the personal trainer, the personal ass-wiper doing anything for me, Jack. So don't you dare paint me in the same light as her. In fact, it would have been nice to have someone—like, say, a *husband*—fulfill the roles of some of those things every once in a while."

I'm rifling around my miscellaneous kitchen drawer in search of a Band-Aid, but can't find one. The blood has soaked through the paper towel I've been holding against it, so I toss it in the trash and rip off another sheet from the roll and press it against the cut. It doesn't escape me that Jack couldn't care less that I've been bleeding for the duration of this little spat. Good ol' caring Jack.

"Just forget it," Jack yells at me. "You don't understand."

"Oh, I understand more than you'll know. Believe me, I'm seeing things very clearly."

"Christ, this is why I never said anything to you about my luncheon with Mark to begin with," Jack says. "Because I knew somehow you'd thrust this back in my face."

Huh. Well, that's about the *only* thrusting he's gonna get from me; that's for damn sure.

"First of all, your assertion that I would *thrust* something negative at you doesn't really help you out in your self-defense argument, and only serves to engender hostility," I say. "And second of all, how on earth do you expect me to react when you have that sort of far-away dreamy look in your eyes, just like Gidget pining over Moon Doggie, that as much as *tells* me you're secretly yearning for your own longed-for freedom? Pondering where you can find *your* escape hatch?

"How do you think that makes me feel? I'll tell you: left to wonder if you're mapping out your own personal exit strategy." I stamp my foot on the ground for emphasis.

"You know what?" Jack rolls up his sleeves. Looks like this argument isn't going to wrap up anytime soon. "How about you stop making a habit of trying to figure out what's going on in my head? How about you leave my thoughts up to me, for once. Because you know something? You don't have a *clue* what I'm thinking. Not one goddamned clue. So don't presume to put words into my mouth or my head, because they're not yours to insert them into there, or anywhere. Do you understand, dammit?" He pounds his fist on the granite countertop so hard I think he might break his hand. God, I hate the male temper. It's so hostile.

All of a sudden I hear RePete repeating *dammit* in my voice, over and over again. It's hardly fair that he picks up my vulgarities when Jack's the one cursing right now.

"Maybe instead of spending all of your spare time

figuring out how my brain works, Claire, you can just put more of your own charming words into that damn parrot's mouth."

With that he strides purposefully and angrily from the kitchen and retreats to his office, where he will no doubt remain until I'm fast asleep.

I ponder this most recent confrontation as I go up to my bathroom for a little belated first aid. Not only is my hand still bleeding, but I'm pretty sure there's a sliver of crystal embedded there. Dammit, I hate using tweezers in a cut.

I rifle through the Drawer of Excess and find the needle-nose tweezers, the ones so lethal that they would definitely be confiscated in carry-on luggage before boarding an airplane. They're surgically sharp, and I try to fool myself into thinking I'm not going to hurt my hand as I dig into the cut in search of the shard of crystal. But it's like trying to tickle your own sensitive spots to elicit a reaction—it's impossible to fake yourself out.

Instead, with the pain from the tweezers piercing my flesh and the pain of Jack's words searing my heart, I begin to cry, which makes it hard to focus on the job at hand. I wipe the tears on my shoulder and dig, finally extracting the culprit, a chip of crystal no bigger than a flea. Funny how something so minute can cause such overblown discomfort.

I mull over Jack's words. *Parallels. Parallels. Parallels!* There are few, if any, comparisons between Jack's and my relationship and that of Teeny and Mark. I mean, if you want to talk in broad, sweeping generalizations, yeah, they were unhappy, and we're relatively unhappy. Of course, I don't dare speak that truth out loud to Jack. Instead, in between fights, I pretend things are hunky-dory, that we're just as happy as can be.

But just because things weren't right with Mark and

Teeny doesn't mean we're in the same boat. After all,
I'm thoroughly convinced that if Jack just resumed being the man he once was, I'd be perfectly happy with
him. Probably would *love* to have sex with him. I
know they say you can't change someone. And I have
to agree with that adage. But if someone changed
themselves, then cannot the corollary be true as well?
Can't they then change themselves back to whom
they once were? It's not that I don't love Jack Doolittle;
it's that I don't love who Jack has turned himself into.
And to extrapolate on that truth, by extension it's
therefore pretty damned hard to lust after him, either.

Does Jack have a point, telling me not to put words
into his head? On the one hand, I suppose so. It's not
exactly fair to presume what someone else is thinking,
right? But then again, come off it. I know and he
knows what he was thinking. He as much as said it.
And his look said it, too. I only took the liberty of filling in the blanks that were laid out before me. The
consonants were there; I just needed to fill in a few
vowels to complete the sentence.

And how fair is it of Jack to simply *deny* it? Should I
be insulted that he thinks I'm that stupid? It's like a kid
who swipes a lick of icing off a birthday cake. He's
standing there with residue on his finger. There's a telltale trail from a finger swoop in the icing. And yet he
denies culpability. All I did is put two and two together
and peg Jack as the icing thief, that's all.

But by Jack's indignantly denying it, he leaves me to
wonder if I'm next—if the next time my doorbell rings
it'll be someone serving *me* divorce papers. To me
that's copping out, just calling it quits without a fight.
You aren't willing to work on the problems, and instead just throw the blame at the partner and give
yourself carte blanche? Divide up the assets, apolo-

gize once or twice to the kids, maybe set aside some cash for therapy for them, and be done with it.

There is an irrefutable—and crucial—difference between the Doolittles and the Grays: Tina and Mark really did have inherent toxicity in their relationship. From the minute they bonded it was in a codependent, unhealthy way. Whereas with Jack and me, at least our relationship started out healthy.

With them, it was as if Teeny were a delicate orchid that required perpetual attention, and by lavishing it on her Mark forgot about himself. That's not how we are. We're more like a once-lush field that's been tilled over too much, without benefit of fresh, rich compost, with no rest time to regenerate. No farmer lovingly working the soil. Where once were flowers and healthy crops are now straggly weeds. But I take heart, because I know that flowers can still grow in an overgrown patch. It may take a little effort, but it's not an impossibility. If only I can get Jack to see that.

Chapter Thirteen

Sometimes I wonder if our clever brains try to tell us things that our hearts just don't want to hear. Maybe deep within the primal recesses of our gray matter, we know all, but we admit things only if our minds surreptitiously sneak them into our consciousness. This is the kind of deep thought that plagues my late-night brain as I try to drift off to sleep lately.

The thing is, my recent slumber is punctuated by stressful dreams, and I think my dreams are speaking to me.

Consider this one:

I'm washing the dishes, my mind whirring away, processing random thoughts, when I'm startled by the sound of the doorbell.

I'm dressed in a weird assortment of clothing: my trademark SAY NO TO CRACK nightshirt; a pair of black knee socks, rubbed through in the big toe; and graying white sweatpants with a gaping hole in the crotch, exposing the sadly dingy undies poorly hidden beneath. I've got a slick of bright red lipstick on, and my hair is partially rolled—make that tangled—in huge, fuzzy mesh curlers.

I'm also wearing an apron: a frilly yellow-and-lime-green chiffon apron with a three-dimensional daffodil springing forth from the pocket, in which I have tucked an embroidered handkerchief with a J—for June—on it.

The first thing I think when I hear the doorbell ringing is, *My God, I can't answer the door looking like this!* But then I realize if I don't answer it, who will?

So I skitter to the front foyer and start to dry my hands on my apron. The fabric's too pretty to mess up, though, so instead I wipe them on my shirt, a wet smear right across the fat guy's butt crack. I don't even bother to peer through the peephole. Instead I grab the brass handle (the Baldwin one that Jack insisted we put on the door, because we would be "far safer with a good, solid Baldwin lock") and swing it open to find Jack looking somber, almost funereal. Only, his name's not Jack. It's Ward. And he's standing before me in black and white. Whoa.

"Why, Ward," I say, primping my rollers and smiling a June Cleaver smile. "Whatever are you doing home in the middle of the afternoon?"

Jack/Ward, as seems to be the case when he's with me these days, doesn't look like he's in the mood for chitchat. Instead he knits his brow with displeasure. I notice he has an envelope in his left hand. A big white envelope with dramatic cursive scroll on it. The handwriting reminds me of the type of script expected of a schoolchild back in the fifties: sweeping filigreed letters, hardly decipherable without studying intently. Jack/Ward keeps nervously flicking the long edge of the envelope against the cleavage between his pointer and middle fingers. Flick, flick, flick.

He clears his throat—something he does only when

he's preparing to lecture me, an unfortunate habit of his—and steps into the foyer. For a moment I wonder why I haven't gotten the usual cursory peck on the cheek, the yes-we're-related-and-perhaps-long-ago-we-gave-a-good-care-about-each-other-but-right-now-you-know-what?-I-care-far-more-about-Baldwin-locks-and-how-the-stock-market-closed-yesterday-and-did-Cameron-cut-the-lawn-and-have-you-done-the-things-I-told-you-to-take-care-of-on-your-to-do-list-yet-than-greeting-you-with-something-resembling-an-act-of-true-affection kiss. It's almost funny that I even noticed the kiss didn't happen, it's such an antikiss to begin with. Who notices a bad thing when it's not there?

So, kissless, I ask Jack/Ward again, "Why aren't you at work?"

To which he replies with a hint of icy tundra in his voice, "We need to talk."

It's been my experience that the words "we need to talk" never preface good news. That phrase is always the precursor to information that somebody doesn't want to hear. And now is no exception.

"Is everything all right?" I look at him like someone might look at a hurtling locomotive when their car has just stalled on the tracks.

Jack/Ward breathes in deeply and exhales a sigh of immense proportions. His breath is warm on my face. But his words are cold on my heart. "As a matter of fact, I've been trying to find a way to tell you this, but—"

Of course we all know that "I've been trying to find a way to tell you this" ranks up there with "we need to talk" in the unwanted-phraseology department.

"It's just not working out," Jack/Ward says. He's not looking at me. Rather, his gaze glances over the top of my hair curlers, as if he's reading a thought bubble that's just popped up above my head. The thought bubble that should say something pithy and clever that I may or may not live to regret.

"I want a divorce," he blurts.

Huh?

I am not sure if I'm processing this information adequately. I mean, it's not like anyone's ever said this to me before. I. Want. A. Divorce. I want a *divorce*. *I* want a divorce.

My brain is trying to give birth to that thought bubble, trying to come up with just the right clever retort to let Jack know that . . . well, I don't know what I want to let Jack know. And so the thought just hangs over my head, wedged in my mental birth canal. Unseen. Unspoken. No words. No symbols. Not a "#" or "!!!!" or "*#&#**!!!!" Nothing. Claire Doolittle (played in this dream by June Cleaver), who once could slice into a chest cavity with the properly chosen word, is rendered speechless at the worst possible time.

Jack/Ward still isn't looking at me, but he's talking to me nevertheless. "Do you have any questions?"

Questions. I have many of those. Some that have lingered since childhood. Like, Why is the sky blue? I never bought into that whole reflecting-the-water thing, because why, then, is the Caribbean water almost green, it's so blue, but the sky is just plain blue? Why is water different colors everywhere, but for the most part, depending on cloud cover, barometric pressure, and time of day, a sky is a sky is a sky: blue?

I guess, too, I'd like to ask about the relevance of pi. I mean, why does that whole pi thing matter? It's a sequence of numbers. So what?

And maybe I've always wondered why some people have all the luck. Why do some women marry men who cherish them and treat them like queens, but other women marry men who dump them when the going gets rough, after having treated them more like worker bees up until that point anyhow?

The worker bee in me is rearing up and preparing to plant a stinger smack into the entire being that is Jack Doolittle—or is he Ward Cleaver? I practically hear the *buzz-buzz-buzz*ing as the stinger is readying its aim. But then he stings me first yet again.

"You see, I don't love you anymore. There's someone else. Someone I've fallen deeply in love with." His deadpan look makes me want to smack at least some sort of emotion onto his face.

There's a full-length mirror near the front door. Jack and I bought it at an antique auction back when we were dating. The mirror's always had a crack in it, splintering right down the middle, but we loved it for the frame's intricately carved mahogany woodworking, with mermaids climbing up the sides, Poseidon holding a trident spear, peering judgmentally from above. We cherished the idea of loving something so old, so treasured, flaws and all. So we never bothered to fix the crack.

I glance into the broken glass now and see myself poised for a meltdown next to the very composed Jack/Ward, who's still *tap-tap-tap*ping that envelope against his finger furrow. I gaze at myself, at my disastrous self, and hate that not only is Jack/Ward coming out as the victor in this whole charade, but also he even *looks* so much better. He's weathered the marital storms while I got drenched and battered by the squalls of discontent.

To look at us now, any reasonable-minded person would completely support Jack as he unseats me from my connubial throne. Jack in his Hickey Freeman suit, his freshly groomed hair, those three-hundred-dollar Italian loafers he buys twice a year. And me. Well, you've already heard how I'm dressed.

The Wicked Witch meets the proprietress of the local insane asylum.

Jack/Ward rifles in the envelope for a moment as I stand, dazed, before him, a supplicant at the altar of the betrayed. I can clearly see the dramatic lettering on the thing now. It reads: *Divorce Papers*. Stating the obvious. Jack/Ward always was a stickler for details.

He pulls out an inch-thick document and begins to elaborate on the contents.

"I've had my lawyer draw up these papers. I think you'll find the terms to be completely fair. I get the house and all of our assets. And I, of course, get full custody of the children. You will be able to visit with them one hour every other week. And don't worry: they'll be in good hands; my fiancée is looking forward to being their mom."

I have to stop my hand, which seems to have a mind of its own, from reaching up and slapping Jack/Ward across his smug face. Something in my mind is telling me that assault charges will only lessen my position if and when I can get this adjudicated fairly. I force out a constipated smile, and I can see in the mirror that my red lipstick has bled into the laugh lines surrounding my lips, mimicking the stippled marbling in the mirror.

"What exactly do *I* get?" This seems to be the only thing I can utter that makes sense.

Jack/Ward paints me with a smirk, then locks eyes with mine. His are seething with disdain. "You can keep your wardrobe."

I'm so glad that the kids are still at school, because I feel a Harpy wail coming on, and generally speaking I don't think it's a good idea for the children to witness their mother calling for the dead, or whatever it is that Harpies do.

The sound of despair seems to work its way up from

somewhere between my gut and my now-broken heart. It's a reverse avalanche, cascading its way upward through my windpipe, gaining momentum, and collecting bad language and every mean thought I've ever entertained about Jack/Ward, maybe even mean thoughts I've felt about other people as well. By the time it erupts through my red-tinged lips the sound very much mirrors my lip color, and even Jack/Ward covers his ears from the aural assault. Covers his ears, maybe, but barely flinches nonetheless. His face is a wall of glacial indifference, and I feel powerless against the sheer force of his emotional detachment.

"Jesus H. Christ, haven't you got some sort of soul left in that hollowed-out body of yours?" I scream at him. "You take everything that you can from me, then stand there haughtily acting as if you've done me some huge fucking favor?"

"I've told you a thousand times, I'm tired of your attitude," he replies. "I've been asking you to change for years, Claire. I've tried to mold you as I wanted you, but you refused to be molded. I had no choice but to do this."

It is true. I've felt in some ways as if Jack's been standing above me with an X of plywood and a bunch of strings attached to various parts of my body. Two to make my arms move one way, two to move my legs, one to make my mouth shift up and down. One attached to my rear end, probably to give him better access. The only string he wasn't able to successfully attach was the one to my mind. And that's what's led to this scene.

As I stand there helplessly trying to figure out how I went from washing dishes to picking up the pieces of my life in a matter of a few short minutes, I have nothing left to do but to tell it to Jack/Ward as I see it.

"The thing about you is this," I say with the intensity of someone who has just been informed that they are about to lose their citizenship and will be left without a home and country, and there's nothing they can do about it. "You diminish me."

Jack/Ward stares at me, thoroughly clueless about what I'm saying.

"That makes absolutely no sense."

I grit my teeth against the frustration of speaking to a potted palm instead of a once-loving, caring spouse, and continue. "Sure it does. It makes a world of sense. I'm thinking back to that sweet movie. What was it called? Oh, yeah. *Jerry Maguire*. And in the pivotal scene in that movie, the actress—what was her name . . . you know, she used to be normal-sized but now she's scary thin?"

"You mean Renée Zellweger?" he asks, now swirling further into his vortex of befuddlement.

"Yeah. That's her. Renée Zellweger. Someone really ought to feed that girl a meal," I say. "Anyhow. So Jerry Maguire realizes what an ass he's been, and he shows up at her doorstep or whatever, and he says to her— maybe he even says it in sign language, I don't know, I can't remember—'You complete me.' Sighs all around from the audience; we're all swooning at the man's capacity for romance. And she melts when he says this, because she realizes he finally *gets* it."

"Claire, can you cut to the chase, here?" Jack/Ward glances at his watch as he strums his fingers impatiently against the envelope that contains the death knell for our marital partnership.

"That's just it, Ward. See, for Jerry Maguire, Renée Zellweger *completed* him. But for me . . . well, you *diminish* me. In your gravitational pull, Ward, I've become smaller, more insignificant. I'm one of those cosmic blips on the radar screen of your life. A blip that has now become more bothersome than you want to deal with, so you're deblipping me."

Jack/Ward begins to laugh, this deep, dark, sinister laugh, and as he opens his mouth with the force of it I almost expect to peer down his throat into the bowels of hell; it's that nasty a laugh. I'm now so incredibly riddled with rage that I begin to scream at the top of my lungs.

"You'll never get away with this, you'll never get away with this, you'll never get away with this," I wail, but like in one of those bad nightmares where you're being attacked and you try to scream but your voice is silent, I am inaudible, or at least I think so. Until I feel Jack shaking me, shaking me.

"You okay?"

I open my eyes to see Jack in front of me in his pajamas. I reach a sweaty palm up and down to feel what I'm wearing, and sure enough, I've got that SAY NO TO CRACK shirt on, but no rollers, no red lipstick, and certainly no chiffon apron.

Oh, thank God, it was only a bad dream. My ongoing anxieties about my marriage are now manifesting themselves into nightmares about infidelity and usurping stepmoms.

"Is everything all right?" Jack asks me.

I eye him with more than a whiff of suspicion. "What's her name?"

Jack looks at me as if he thinks I'm still asleep. "Whose name?"

"You know who I'm talking about," I accuse him.

"I haven't a clue. You were shouting out in your sleep, and I woke you so you'd stop."

"You're sure there's no fiancée?"

"Go back to sleep, Claire," Jack says as he turns the

light off again and flops back onto his pillow, pulling the covers up to his shoulders.

After he rolls over and returns to his sleep, I lie awake staring at the shadows being cast on the walls by the occasional late-night car driving past our house. My eyes follow the trails of slatted light as they course through our bedroom, lighting then darkening even the most hidden of recesses.

Good God. Is my brain trying to tell me it's time to fight? Or time to flee?

Chapter Fourteen

Ever since I woke up from that damned dream, I've had the unsettling feeling that I should be angry at Jack—not for the reasons I was already mad at him, but for other ones. What may be even more disquieting about this notion is how frequently it seems to occur. After all, probably a sure sign that you're in need of a relationship fix is if you have to ask yourself each morning if you're angry with your spouse.

It makes me want to cry. Add to it that that one early morning resentment just seems to get buried beneath the next one, until what we have is a slag heap of a marriage masquerading as business as usual.

I remember when I used to wake up practically beaming, so filled with the optimism that comes when you know that someone treasures you, really thinks the world of you. When mornings would be sunshine and smiles, not bitter thoughts and recriminations.

Once, when Jack and I were engaged, I woke up to him bringing me breakfast in bed, complete with the Sunday *New York Times*. And on my breakfast tray, in between the coffee (served in china) and the butter dish, was a silver box tied with an organza ribbon. I excitedly opened the box, and in it I found a piece of paper, on which Jack had written this: *I love you more than you'll ever know.*

That's it. No histrionic declarations, no diamonds or semiprecious gemstones, no keys to a fancy sports car. But you know what? It was one of the nicest gifts I ever received.

I think about that note. *I love you more than you'll ever know*, he said. Does he still? I wonder. I really wonder.

Tonight Bubba's got a Cub Scout meeting, and Cam's going to basketball practice. The girls are studying at a neighbor's house. I'm meeting my sister for drinks in Old Town, taking advantage of the rare occasion when Jack is off with Bubba and I'm commitment-free.

I enter the Hard Times Café and realize that if one could have a soul mate that's a restaurant (as opposed to another human being), this place must be it for me. Each time I come here I feel a little more like I'm home. It's a hardscrabble Depression-themed bar (which fittingly matches my depressing mood) best known for its chili and wailing country and blues music. I tuck into a booth and wait for Syd to show up.

I hear Buddy Guy crooning "You Damn Right I Got the Blues," and I can't help but relate to his lamentations.

"You damn right, I've got the blues, from my head down to my shoes," he sings.

The waitress asks me if I want a drink while I wait, and I tell her damn straight and order a Lone Star. The name seems appropriate.

Syd shows up a few minutes later, the chill in the air adding a rosy flush to her cheeks. Or maybe that's from all the sex she's been having lately. Lucky girl.

I stand and give her a hug.

"You look like life's agreeing with you," I say.

"Things are great, actually. But let's not talk about me. I want to find out what on Earth is happening with you! You send me these cryptic e-mails, then leave me dangling. Is everything okay with you and Jack?"

The waitress brings my drink and I suck down a huge gulp. Nothing like a cold beer and the blues to help me put it all in perspective.

"I don't want to bore you. It's just marital stuff, I guess."

"Marital stuff? Come off it, Claire. That's a bunch of nonsense. What's going on with you two?"

My sister always did have a professional bullshit detector. Like that time back in high school when I told her I was going to a friend's house one night when I was actually going on a date with this guy whom she was nursing a serious preteen crush on. She didn't speak to me for a week when she heard that I was seen driving down the main drag of town in the front seat of Ricky Dagostino's souped-up Gran Torino.

The waitress hands us menus, but they really aren't necessary because we always order the same thing here: Texas chili topped with cheddar cheese and sour cream, onion rings on the side for me, fries for Syd. Been ordering it that way for almost fifteen years.

We hand the waitress the menus, and Sydney orders a beer and waits for me to continue.

I go into the whole boring explanation of things with Jack and me: how the spark has been extinguished, how it's all just so darned dismal.

"Geez, that sucks, sis. Especially because this guy Philip who I've been going out with . . . well, I mean, it makes me think that a long-term relationship with a man can be a good thing. I mean, he's so, well, different like that—"

"Yeah, say no more. I can tell by the sparkle in your eyes."

"And I can tell by the lack of one in your eyes. It worries me. It's just not like you. You're usually the up-beat, happy-go-lucky one. I don't know, Claire. Maybe you ought to have an affair," Sydney offers.

I look at her, aghast. "Sydney Mooney! I would never!"

"I'm just joking; you know that. But not *ever*?" She winks at me.

"Sydney, I married Jack for better or for worse," I say. "I don't remember the vows saying anything about 'if the guy turns out to be a real jerk sometimes, well, then, just sleep with someone else.' "

She shrugs. "You got a point there."

"Plus, Jack knows I'm as faithful as a dog," I say. "Woof."

The waitress is back with our food already. She puts two beers in front of us—I don't even remember asking for a second one, but she must be omniscient.

"So, what do you propose you do about this, then?" Sydney asks, waggling a french fry at me as if trying to point me in the right direction.

"That's just it. I don't know what to do. I mean, any-time I gently make suggestions for him to lighten up, he bristles at me."

Sydney laughs. "Like a porcupine?"

I pick up one of her fries and toss it at her. "Ha, ha. Funny. Even more prickly. Like someone who's acting like a real prick."

We both laugh at that while Gene Autry croons some old-timey cowboy song from the jukebox.

"Seriously, Claire. I just hate to think of you and Jack in this way. I mean, you guys were so in love!"

Were so in love. Is that verb doomed to be relegated to the past perfect (or is it imperfect?) tense when it refers to me and Jack?

Past perfect. "It was a really perfect past," I say out loud to no one in particular.

My mind wanders off to an earlier time in our relationship. I'd been flying for several days without a break and arrived home late one night, expecting Jack to be out of town. I put the key into my door and opened it, only to discover Jack in the kitchen fixing dinner. He didn't see me, so I just watched him for a few minutes. He had Jeffrey Osborne on the stereo and was dancing with a wooden spoon in his hand, his arms raised, just completely lost in the moment. Happy, relaxed, at peace.

"Surprise!" I shouted above the music.

Jack jumped. "Oh, Claire! I wasn't expecting you for at least another hour. God, you scared me half to death!"

"I didn't expect to see you at all, so we're even!"

"My trip got canceled," he said as he came over to relieve me of my suitcase and give me a kiss.

"Their loss is my gain. Lucky me!"

We walked over to the kitchen, where Jack had some Cajun dish simmering on the stove.

"You shouldn't have done all this for me!" I said, but I was thrilled that he did.

"Sweetie, you can always count on me being there for you if I can," Jack said, kissing me on the forehead like a protective mother would her beloved child.

"Promise?" I teased.

"Promise. Forever and ever."

My mind wanders back to the present. I can always count on him being there for me? Fat likelihood of that now. Huh. If I ever came home to my husband affectionately fixing dinner for me—and dancing without a care in the world—I think I'd keel over. That's something that would never happen. Not ever.

chapter Fifteen

"I haven't seen your travel itinerary for the weekend yet." I'm just back from dinner with Sydney and decide to quasi-toss out an olive branch and attempt to conduct a conversation with Jack. With but a half a day until he leaves, we're at least finally on speaking terms, of sorts.

"Just call my secretary and she'll e-mail a copy to you."

I really detest that I seem to be so insignificant in this man's life that he can't even be bothered to replicate a copy of his travel schedule for me, his next of kin.

"Maybe it would be a novel idea if you actually just cc'ed me on these things in the first place."

"What's the big deal? Call Judy and she'll be glad to get it to you."

Of course Judy will be glad to handle what Jack can't be troubled to do for me. Is it just me, or does every wife become a nuisance appendage with limited assignments (i.e., the obligatory Sunday-night fuck) after a certain period of time? Is it true that I have become his glorified tonsil or gall bladder—no, wait, how about a spare kidney, whose sole purpose is to filter the toxins from his life? If that's the case, then I must not be doing my job.

Jack is folding clothes into his suitcase, packing for the weekend. I try to glean from his packing job what the true intent of this trip is. I note he's slipped his swim trunks into the luggage.

"So, uh, what do you have planned for the weekend?" I feign nonchalance.

"Hmmm? Oh, nothing, really. Just lots of meetings."

"Then why are you packing your bathing suit?"

Jack gives me one of those looks you give to a driver who cuts you off in traffic. "Well, Claire, I *am* going to *Miami*. As in, *beach*. Just in case I get a chance to get out there and enjoy it for a few minutes."

I imagine Jack with Julia Julliard, frolicking seaside, her thong wedged in between her firm little youthful and dimple-free buttocks as they bat a volleyball back and forth to each other. Her upturned breasts, undaunted by the ravages of time, nursing, and gravity, jiggle, virtually unrestrained by the minuscule patches of macramé she calls a halter bikini top. At least she doesn't have implants, I think. Er, I don't remember thinking she had them.

I picture her and Jack salsa dancing, Julia shaking her little architectural booty to the pulsating sounds of Cubanismo. Well, if they plan to shake it to the salsa beat, then I plan to shake them right out of whatever palm tree I find them lurking in.

"You don't have anything fun planned for the entire weekend?"

"Maybe a dinner or two, but really, this is *not* a fun getaway."

"Well, you know what they say: All work and no play makes Jack a dull boy."

Jack doesn't respond.

"Mommy!" Matthew comes running into my arms. The bill of his baseball cap jams into my solar plexus.

"Oof! Honey! Careful. You hurt Mommy with that hat of yours!" I look at my watch and wonder why Jack didn't bother to put the children to bed when they got back. Figures. Leave it to Claire to do the dirty work.

"Mommy! Lindsay says my hat is yucky and it smells like dog poo."

"Lindsay is just teasing you." I do, however, notice a foul odor wafting my way.

"What is that stench?" I sniff his head and realize that his hat does indeed smell like dog poo.

"My hat dropped in the potty." Only now do I notice that his hat is also wet and reeks of the smell of dirty diapers or something.

"Matthew! You can't keep that hat on. We have to wash that out. It's not clean."

Matthew's face turns ashen. "Moooooooooooooooo-oooommmmmmmmmmmmmmmmmmmmmmmmmmm-mmmmmmmmyyyyyyyyyyyyyyyyyy!!!!!!!!!!! You can't wash my hat!!!!!!!!!"

Oh, brother. I had this problem when Cameron threw Matthew's stuffed emu into the toilet one time, and that was in a relatively clean bowl, not an unflushed one.

My husband continues to pack, oblivious to the trauma unfolding before me.

"Jack, I could use your assistance here," I growl.

"What?"

"Can you please persuade your son that his bacterially compromised hat needs to be sanitized in the wash?"

"Bubba, listen to your mother," he says, sounding like a school principal.

"I don't wannnnaaaaaaa," Matthew cries.

"Matthew Doolittle, give your mother that hat this

very minute or I will snatch it from your head and you won't get it back again. Ever."

"Waaaaaaaaaaaaaaaaaaaaaaaaaa!" Bubba is inconsolable. Jack hasn't helped matters here. I have to think on my feet.

"I know! How about if you help me put it in the washer so you can see that it will be okay? You can help me turn the water on and put the soap in and—"

"But my hat will drown!"

"Sweetie, your hat knows how to swim. It'll be fine."

"It does? It can swim?"

"Sure," I assure him. "Trust me. It will be just like new."

Matthew reluctantly hands me his treasured cap and wipes his tears from his eyes as we head toward the laundry room.

Well. One life crisis dodged. Another to be broached in T minus twelve hours.

The phone rings. I reach the two feet to get it, and Jack picks up as I do. I hear a woman's voice on the other line. A soft, gentle, coaxing woman's voice. An I'm-ready-to-fuck-you-in-Miami tone of voice. I don't dare hang up, and instead cover the mouthpiece with a nearby dishtowel.

"Jules!" Jack says in a bon-vivant sort of way. Jules. Now they're on intimate-nickname terms? Jules. I'll show her Jules. Better yet, I'll show *him*, right where it counts: in his family jewels.

"To what do I owe this pleasure?" he asks her, and he means it. Christ, I can't imagine the last time Jack's voice registered happiness upon realizing *I* was on the other end of the line. Probably if I called to say I was able to pick up his dry cleaning on time or something like that I might get a lukewarm response. Better yet, if I called to say I wanted to give him a blow job. That would definitely bring forth a choir of angels from his mouth. But certainly the mere existence of my trilling voice would not elicit a moment of joy in him.

"Hi, Jacks," Julia pants to my husband. Well, maybe it's not exactly a pant, but my imagination is getting the best of me. Wait a minute. Just a cotton-picking Ward Cleaver minute. She called him *Jacks*? Okay, as I extract my pointer finger from down my throat, I mull that cute little name over in my head. Jacks. As in Jacks and Jules? Jesus, this thing must be more serious than I'd thought. My heart sinks.

"Are you getting ready for the big weekend?" he asks her like he's Santa asking a child what she wants for Christmas. *The big weekend that my wife's not going on*, he should say. *Yeah, baby, I've got a jumbo-size carton of condoms packed; are you happy now?*

"Well, actually, that's why I'm calling you," Julia says, her soft, coaxing voice a panacea to my haranguing, no doubt. "I was trying to pack for the trip, but since I haven't been to one of these things, I wasn't sure exactly what to bring along. I mean, do I pack professional suits, or should it be resort casual? And for dinner is it dressy casual or cocktail wear?"

Since when does the hired help call a boss to be a fashion consultant? I wonder.

Oh, maybe when the hired help is *doing* the boss. I shudder at the thought, and listen intently to Jack's reply.

"You should definitely pack the gray suit you wore to the meeting with the Cambridge group last week," Jack says. "That was very flattering yet still quite professional."

Okay, let's back up here for a minute. The last time I consulted with Jack about what to wear to something, he got furious with me for asking. He insisted that whatever he suggested, I would then contradict it anyhow, so he refused to participate. He said he didn't care what I wore. Yet right now, as I eavesdrop on this personal conversation, I am realizing that Jack does have a fashion sense, only not where bedraggled housewives are concerned. *Flattering yet still quite professional?* I get the feeling he's been watching the Home Shopping Network when I'm asleep.

I fight the urge to scream like a fishwife into the telephone line, to warn Julia Julliard that I'm fully prepared to jack her up this side of Sunday if she doesn't get her designs—architectural or otherwise—off my dirty rotten husband. Oh, God, if I did that, though, I couldn't glean more information, nail down that incontrovertible evidence of his infidelity. So I bite my tongue and listen some more.

"You should definitely plan on wearing something elegant for dinner," Jack offers up. "We have reservations at a swank restaurant where you'll want to look your best."

My hands are a little bit numb. I realize it's because I'm clutching the telephone in a death grip. I relax my fingers slightly when I realize my knuckles have turned white. It's really quite remarkable that I have been able to maintain my composure while I listen to my husband verbally masturbate his professional underling with fashion advice. His sexy, blond, perky underling. The one with the heart-shaped fucking lips.

"I can hardly wait to get to Miami, Jacks." She strokes him with her words. "Miami's such a *hot* town." She says *hot* as if she's talking about her body (or his), and not about a major metropolitan city with a humidity problem.

"I've been reading *People* magazine, and all the most beautiful celebrities flock to Miami," Julia goes on. Oh, this will be a real reason for Jack to go there. He's about as fascinated with celebrities as I am with carbuncles. Of course, I don't exactly know what a carbuncle is, but I'm thinking it's an abscess of some kind. Sort of like Julia Julliard. She most definitely has become a human carbuncle. At least for me, anyway.

"Oh, really?" Jack says, sounding interested. "Like who?"

Julia begins to rant off a list of celebrities of dubious distinction who frequent the many watering holes and VIP lounges of Miami. Right about now, if that were Claire regaling Jack with such vital information, Jack would hit the off button in the hopes that Claire would shut up. Instead he clings to Julia's every word.

"Enrique Iglesias?"

"Oh, really?"

"Ben Affleck?"

"He's a great actor. And all those Jens."

"Paris?"

"Is she back with that Greek tycoon?"

"Oh, that's too bad they broke up. But you never know. Maybe they'll reunite someday."

Before I know it, Julia has named at least fifteen famous actors and singers whom she hopes to spot on the beaches of Miami this weekend. One wonders when all of this important architectural work is going to get done if she's planning to do so much jock sniffing.

Jack usually gets annoyed with people who have a fixation on fame and fortune. He sees it as trivial, a real waste of brainpower. But with Julia he seems to have forgotten that policy. All systems are go. Lock and load, mud marine.

From a purely anthropological viewpoint, it's fascinating to see this dark/light side of Jack. Jack Doolittle in chiaroscuro. I mean, he hasn't been able to be jovial and light about trivial nonsense in so long that I just would never expect it from him.

But from an on-the-verge-of-jilted-wife standpoint, this is all quite disturbing.

"So, is your wife staying home with the kids this weekend, then?" Suzy Innocent asks. Like she cares. Well, I'm sure she does, to the extent that she wants to be sure I don't show up surreptitiously and put an end to her fun and frivolity.

"Who, Claire?"

Who, Claire? Me, the wife? The mother of your children. The one who scrapes the bird shit off the floor with regularity.

"Is she staying home with the kids or is she coming along?" she asks him again, for clarification.

"Oh, Claire really hates to travel," Jack lies. "She's happy to stay home with the kids. She understands that this is all about work for me."

My blood pressure instantly skyrockets, and I think I need an infusion of some sort of ACE inhibitor before I suffer a coronary right here on my living room floor. I wonder how long it would take before anyone noticed. My best bet is at least seven to ten splotches of bird poo would have to accrue on the hardwood before anyone would even notice me missing. In fact, people would probably just step over me, like they do the myriad other crap piled up on the floors around here.

Amazing, the amount of denial in that statement he just made. *Claire*—former flight attendant and professional traveler—*really hates to travel*, he says. *Claire's happy to stay home; she understands that this is all about work for me.*

Yeah, right. It's about working it, all right. Or getting a workout, of sorts. Working some kind of angle on this willingly adulterous participant who obviously reveres the man.

If I didn't have an outright game plan, why, I'd . . . I'd . . . I'd *make* one, that's what I'd do. But I'm going to keep my cool, because I've got it all under control, and Claire Doolittle is going to snare this Spanish fly in her sticky web. And the black widow in me is going to swallow that bastard whole the minute I can prove anything is going on.

For a minute there I think I am beginning to hyperventilate into the phone, what with my heart rate high enough to rupture a sphygmomanometer. I take a deep breath to calm myself and listen on.

"I am so excited to be working with you on the group conference, Jacks," Jules the Wonder Dog says. "I will learn so much from you, I just know it. I've admired your work from afar for so long."

Sweet Jesus in heaven. I didn't know one could admire the man's work from *any* position. I just thought he was an architect. You know, decent enough, but not particularly outstanding in his field. Then again, I guess Jack was considered a real up-and-comer back when we were young and in love. It's been a long time since I even paid attention to Jack's career. Well, it's not as if he actually shares it with me. I mean, Jack does his thing and I do mine. We don't exactly compare notes regularly. Who's got time for it, with the lives we lead? So, why do I feel so guilty just thinking that thought? I wonder.

My mind is snapped back to the immediacy of Julia's and Jack's scheming by this line, uttered with gusto by my spouse:

"Oh, and don't forget to pack your bikini!"

"You too! I can't wait to see that cute bum of yours in a swimsuit!" She giggles schoolgirl-like into the phone.

I damn near drop the phone. Or birth a cow.

Don't you worry, honey. Jack will be packing a suit. *Jacks* will be packing a *law*suit soon. Going to Miami to *work*, he said?

If I were a really malicious woman I'd do something cruel, like go to the joke shop and buy itching powder and coat the lining of Jack's swim trunks with the stuff. After all, he'd have a hell of a time getting it on with Julia with his crotch on fire. Maybe I should instead douse the crotch of his suit with some sort of scent that would attract sharks. That would teach him: one swift chomp in the groin from a carnivorous *hot* Miami water-loving shark.

"Well, I'd better get back to packing and get caught up on my beauty sleep." Julia sighs.

I haven't had beauty sleep in about fifteen years. In fact, I was under the impression that it was one of those urban legends, that there's no such thing as beauty sleep anyhow. Like Santa Claus, or crocodiles in the sewers in Manhattan. But, judging by the looks of Julia Julliard, maybe there really is such a thing. The bitch. Jack dope-slaps me back to his conversation.

"You couldn't get any more gorgeous, Julia," he says. "You're as beautiful as they come, on the inside and out."

I'm not much of a churchgoer, but being born Catholic, it's hard to shake some of those prayers that were figuratively beaten into my memory as a child, and right now all I can think of, on Jack's behalf, is this:

Holy Mary, Mother of God, pray for us sinners now, and at the hour of our death. Amen.

Because I think that is the prayer that my husband needs to get him through this night and prevent me from throttling the last gasp of breath from his dying body. For his sake, he'd better hope he's got Holy Mary, Mother of God in his corner.

Wednesday morning is finally here. It couldn't have come soon enough, if you ask me. Jack's flight leaves in a couple of hours, and he's gathering his last-minute things before saying good-bye to the children.

"Kids!" he hollers.

"One sec!" yells Lindsay. She is the queen of post-

ponement. If she ever did something at the initial bid-
ding, I'd probably keel over from shock.

"Coming!" shouts Cameron. He's no doubt IMing
some hot little thirteen-year-old girl and can't drag
himself away.

The other three hustle down to the kitchen, lining
up to kiss their father good-bye.

"Now, children, you be good."

"Okay, Daddy," Bubba says, batting those innocent
brown eyes of his.

"And I'll call you on my birthday."

"Your birthday?"

"Yes, Daddy will be in Miami for his birthday," I tell
them with malice aforethought, knowing that will stir
the pot and cause him to have to leave amidst the cacophony of tears and recriminations.

"Daddy, you can't be away for your *birthday*!" Charlotte stares, unblinking, at the man, so deeply offended by this news that tears are welling in her eyes.

"Well, honey, sometimes daddies have to do things
that they'd rather not do."

That lying dog. I want to kick him in the shins for
pretending that he doesn't want to be off to Miami
with the homebuilding home wrecker for his birthday.

"But, Daddy, it's your *birthday*." This time Chrissy
pipes in.

"What about birthdays?" Lindsay enters the room.

"Oh, come off it, you guys. Big deal. So Dad's not
gonna be here for his birthday. It's no biggie."
Cameron adds his two cents' worth, and I'm struck by
how blasé he's become in his dotage.

"Well, you could have a little bit of remorse, son,"
Ward intones.

"Well, Dad, *you're* the one who made plans to be
away despite it being your birthday, not me." Aha. He,

too, is upset that Dad won't be back. He was just putting on a brave front.

I look at Jack, who looks like his temperature's heating up, and not in a good way.

"All right, kids, everyone, give Daddy a hug and a kiss and tell him you'll call him on his birthday, okay?" While I do want Jack to feel guilty for leaving everyone, I don't particularly want to deal with one of those familial confrontations right now.

The younger kids begin to cry; then Tripod joins in, his piercing yowl making my ears pin back just like a dog that's heard one of those high-pitched whistles. RePete chooses now to join in the chaos, his shrill jungle chatter inducing a headache that only a margarita will dispel, even if it isn't quite five o'clock somewhere.

Out of nowhere, Dolly Llama jumps down from the kitchen counter in front of Tripod, who takes off like a shot after the poor feline. RePete, who has been perched atop his open cage, starts flapping his wings furiously, and gives himself enough loft with the power of the flap to simply lift off the perch, but then plummet, leaden, to the ground. Tripod hears the thud and skids back into the kitchen, but we know the routine and have encircled the bird in a protective shield from the clutches of our maybe–bird dog's jaws just in time.

"Well, so sorry to be leaving everyone right now, but *I* have a plane to catch."

And with that, Jack slips out the breakfast room door and into his waiting car in the garage. No kiss for me, no, *Have a great weekend yourself, Claire*, no nothing.

Well, that's just fine, Jack Doolittle. Just fine. I'll show you, you smug son of a bitch. I'll just show you and your little slice of architectural pie.

"Mommy?"

"Yeah, sweetie?" I'm in Matthew's room, tucking him

in for the night. Normally when Jack goes out of town, all the kids join me in my bedroom, but as I'm leaving tomorrow myself, I didn't want to get their hopes up, only to dash them tomorrow when I blow out of town, vacating my own warm bed.

"What do you think Daddy's doing right now?"

Oh, I can only imagine what Jack is up to. "Well, maybe Daddy's already gone to bed. He might be tired after traveling, you know?"

"I hope he's not having too much fun without us there."

I smile at how perceptive the child is. "I know what you mean, Bubba. I know what you mean."

Chapter Sixteen

While life with Jack has hardly been a picnic lately, it hasn't been bad throughout our marriage. Of course, our earlier wedded bliss was tainted with the immediate aftermath of his brother's untimely death, but between the moments of sorrow were tender moments of loving kindness.

I remember a trip we took about a year before Cameron came along. Jack had been a little bit uptight—of course, he'd been like that pretty much since Colin's death—but he really seemed to unwind on this trip. We were wandering the beaches of Acapulco, with all of the beggar children trying to sell us Chiclets and jewelry and leather tchotchkes and such.

"You know, I owe you an apology for sometimes getting wrapped up in my own things." He surprised me with this statement.

"What do you mean?" I knew damned well what he meant, but just like when you've sneaked a peek at some private diary you weren't supposed to have read, I felt the need to pretend I was clueless.

"Well, I just haven't been completely myself, that's all."

We strolled along in silence for a few minutes. Those sad, straggly little kids kept tugging on Jack's hand and bickering at him in Spanish.

"But I look at the tragedy of the poverty here, and realize that my problems are insignificant compared to other people's problems," he said. "Look at these poor beggar children. They don't have time to wallow in misery. They have to work from dawn till dusk to make enough money to just get by. How hard a life that must be."

At that moment I felt that perhaps Jack had truly experienced an epiphany—that he saw something for what it truly was. I must say, it was quite a relief knowing that maybe we'd soon be able to put his silent mourning behind him. I grabbed Jack's hand and squeezed tightly; then we stopped and kissed. For a little while, Jack had returned home to me.

It wasn't until after the kids were a little bit older that Jack became so very Ward-like. It was also when he started doing all sorts of peculiar things. At first I just shrugged them off as idiosyncratic nuances, little hard-to-love quirks that came with the territory. The behavior of someone who maybe just needed to have control over his environment, which, I suppose— considering the early demise of both his father and then his brother—was understandable.

I remember the first really strange thing he did: he decided to plant plastic flowers in our yard. We were living in a cute little rambler in Alexandria. All of our neighbors were very proud of their yards, and toiled endlessly to edge and weed and prune and all of those things one must do to a yard if you're so inclined.

Well, I sure as hell wasn't inclined. I can't even bother to keep alive a little desktop cactus, which requires a tablespoon of water twice annually, so I certainly had no interest in spending my very limited free time trying to maintain a lawn and flower beds. I was too busy watering the kids. Hell, as far as I was concerned, letting the land return to its natural state was the perfect ticket. But Jack wanted things to look nice. And so, because I just couldn't deal with planting bulbs and all sorts of seasonal flowers, he decided to plant plastic ones.

Plastic flowers sticking out of the ground in the summertime actually aren't so bad—from a distance, at least. Really, if you're just driving down the road, you notice only that the flowers look unnaturally colorful, or oddly flawless. But let me tell you, plastic flowers poking out of two inches of snow in the dead of February look downright ridiculous. I tried to explain to Jack that this faux-garden pursuit of his was really quite insane, almost laughable. But he would hear nothing of it. He'd just shrug and tell me that unless I planned to do something better, then I should be happy that at least it looked that good. It was a fight I chose not to pick.

For a while he had another strange habit of wearing shorts in the winter and sweaters in the summer. Again: Quirky, yes. Committable? Not so much. I mean, if you want to freeze your ass off in the dead of winter, then by all means, be my guest. And if schvitzing through the summer in Washington, DC—which, I might add, was built atop a swamp—then that's really your own business. Whatever. So I let him dress in his own little peculiar way, if that helped him feel in control.

But eventually his control issues spread. And it wasn't controlling the appearance of the exterior of our home anymore; it was controlling the residents therein. Particularly me. When I realized that Jack was becoming so intent on telling me what to do and when to do it, I reflexively wanted to slug him. And so, after enough time of him chipping away at my psyche, insisting that my parenting skills weren't necessarily up to his high standards, or that my cleaning prowess was lacking—it was, but I didn't see him pitching in to help out—I started to take offense.

Jack (standing idly by): "If you'd just fold the clothes as soon as they were done in the dryer, like I asked you to, we wouldn't have such a problem with wrinkles."

Claire (nursing a baby while reading a book to three other children): "In case you hadn't noticed, I've got more important things to do with my time than wait for the dryer to turn off. Feel free to fold them yourself."

Or how about—

Jack (standing idly by): "It really is unsightly having dirty dishes stacking up so high in the kitchen."

Claire (changing a diaper on one child while pushing the baby swing with her spare foot for another): "In case you hadn't noticed, you did not marry a bald guy with a bulging chest wearing a white T-shirt and pants, sporting a hoop earring, okay? I made no pretense of being Mr. Clean then, nor do I make such a contention now. If the mess is bothering you, well, then, you know where to find the rubber gloves."

Truth of the matter was, he couldn't have found a pair of rubber gloves even if it were something he needed to service his libido—which would be pretty much the only circumstance in which I'd expect him to at least search high and low for them.

Okay, so our reactions to each other were probably not so healthy. After a while, Jack realized that I had no interest in dealing with his controlling ways, and so he redirected his efforts to our children, one by one.

Why, you might ask, did I let this go on so long unchecked? Why did I not seek counseling for him?

Why did I not nip it in the bud? Well, the easiest answer to that is that I was just so caught up in the fog of motherhood that it just wasn't possible. Plus, I have to say, I hardly know a person less inclined toward confrontation with a man than me.

Let me clarify that. I'll be happy to jump down some man's throat if I feel that he has betrayed me, or stolen my parking space, or cut me off improperly on the Beltway. In fact, I've been known to flip the finger on occasion for such transgressions. Well, not so much nowadays, because you get shot for that. But way back when, sure. One thing I just could not bring myself to do was to *really* cross the man who willingly took it upon himself to marry me.

I know, I know: that sounds downright crazy. But you have to remember, I took up with Jack on the heels of a jarringly abrupt end to the most permanent and trustworthy relationship I'd ever known. I mean, I had complete faith in Todd, and look what he did: he just pulled the rug right out from under my feet. And I didn't even do anything wrong! So after that, I think I was subliminally reluctant ever to give reason to any man to give me the shaft, particularly this man with whom I'd once been so blindingly, passionately in love.

Okay, so then, you ask, why would I just sass back at Jack—and occasionally tell him to fuck off, I admit—when he was so busy criticizing me? I don't know. I guess that's part of my bad habit of impulsivity. But extemporaneously spewing vulgarities is different from picking apart someone's personality with the intent of radically altering freakish behavior. And that is what I would have been doing had I confronted Jack with all of my gripes about his strange attitudinal decline.

Too, you might wonder, if I was intent on not putting more nails into the coffin of our marriage, then why have I allowed myself to become so sexually funereal with my husband? After all, there is probably no better way to drive a man into another woman's arms than by rejecting his sexual overtures.

And you're right. You're so bloody damned right. I can't explain it to you. I guess it is some bizarre instinctual survival tool: you reject intimacy with the one who has covered your mouth with the chloroform-drenched cloth, just in case his intent is to suffocate you.

I'll never forget our first really bad Ward Cleaver dinner. Cameron was maybe ten years old; that makes the girls eight, Lindsay six, and Matthew just turned one. The kids were, as always, bickering at the dinner table.

"You are *not* the boss of me," Chrissy was screaming at Cameron.

"Well, if you weren't such a stupid-head," Cameron snarled back at her.

"You're a bigger stupid-head," Charlotte defended her sister. "You big, fat stupid-head!"

"Kids! Stop it now," I warned.

"Stupid-head! Stupid-head! Cameron is a stupid-head!" Lindsay couldn't help but join in the fun.

Cameron propped himself up on his knees on the chair, reached across the dinner table, leaned over the meat-loaf platter, and whacked Chrissy right on the head with the back of his hand. Chrissy howled in a deafening tone.

All of a sudden the noise was broken by this slamming sound at the head of the table: Jack had taken the huge wooden salt and pepper grinders that we got as a wedding gift from my aunt Mona and uncle Tippy and began pounding them into the wooden table.

"STOP IT!" It sounded like the voice of the Almighty himself. "Stop it, *NOW!"*

A hush descended upon the table, much as it would at some swank soiree if a really drunken man had loudly insulted the host's wife as being a two-bit slut. Kind of like when that Washington Redskin John Riggins, notorious for his disgraceful behavior while intoxicated, advised Supreme Court Justice Sandra Day O'Connor at an exclusive Washington dinner to "loosen up, Sandy, baby!"

Now, mind you, oftentimes what is said needs to be said, on some level. But *when* you say something is as important as *how* you say it. And so, as our young brood sat tableside, stupefied at the voice of impending doom emanating from the head of the table, I knew we were mere seconds away from an enormous meltdown of near-biblical proportions.

"Daddy doesn't love me!" Lindsay wailed first, tears streaming down her face, her mashed potatoes combining with her saliva and choking out of her mouth in a lava of pasty starch.

"Wahhhhhhhhhhhhhhhhhhhhhh," Chrissy bellowed, knowing she was the initial source of her father's ire.

"I didn't do anything!" Cameron defended himself, despite all evidence to the contrary.

Charlotte, my internalizer, sat silently repressing her impending tears, which broke my heart more than the rest of the lamentations combined. I stood to comfort her and Jack chastised me, as if I had been part of the problem.

"Get away from her right now!" he hollered at me.

Matthew started to scream, that shriek all one-year-olds have mastered even before they learn to walk or talk. I was speechless. How *dare* he tell me how to respond to my child's needs?

"Well, who the hell are you? Nikita fucking Khrushchev? I've got news for you, Jack. This isn't the goddamned United Nations. We don't pound the table with our shoe *or* the salt and pepper shakers to express our displeasure around here. There are more civilized ways to handle it. And roaring like some god-damned lion on the savanna who's waiting for his li-onesses to bring back his freshly slaughtered zebra *isn't* the way we do it."

Jack glared at me in a way theretofore unknown to me. He spoke through exaggeratedly gritted teeth. "You are my wife, and you are supposed to be support-ive of me in this endeavor as parents of these children. You *will not* contradict me as master of this house."

I laughed. I actually laughed. *Master of this house?* To paraphrase old Ward Cleaver, was he out of his cotton-picking mind?

"Well, let me tell you, sonny boy. First of all, my re-sponsibilities and my loyalties are to *everyone* in this house. Yes, you and I are partners as parents, but that doesn't mean I just silently accede to your actions whether I agree with them or not. And, in point of fact, I absolutely do *not* agree with what you just did. You don't take a bad situation and make it worse by throw-ing a grown-up temper tantrum into the pediatric one occurring already."

At that, Jack stood up, grabbed his dinner plate, and stomped away, his feet pounding the heartbeat of a bad conscience, like in some Edgar Allan Poe story. *Thump-thump. Thump-thump. Thump-thump.* Storming off in much the same way that the children are *not* al-lowed to do. Do as I say, not as I do.

It was the first time that I realized that I was starting to detest the man that Jack was becoming. I hadn't an-alyzed exactly when he went from being the Jack I fell in love with to the Jack who was now turning into the itinerant tyrant of our home. But it didn't matter. The mere fact that he had turned into this middle-aged man who was capable of throwing a vitriolic temper tantrum, who would hold us all hostage to his mood, really stuck in my craw.

Chapter Seventeen

I wake early, excited that today is the day I get to leave on my first-ever, self-indulgent vacation/spy mission. Last night, before drifting comfortably off to sleep, I cleverly inserted little snack treats into each of the kids' backpacks, knowing that this way even if they leave their lunch boxes at home, they'll have enough food to sustain them until day's end. Today I am not adding a run to the school with lunch boxes to my list of lunch-hour chores.

I shower in peace, kind of enjoying the solitude and the lack of friction in the bathroom this morning. Oh, if only I didn't have to go to work today, I'd relish one of those fine General Mills moments with my powdered faux cappuccino in a can. Well, not really. That stuff disgusts me—those dreadful Irish cream coffee drinks and such. But it sure would be nice to sit and soak in the silence for a while longer. Alas, I must awaken the kids and pack them all off to school with their complete breakfasts.

Once all kids are roused I head downstairs, but am

hit with a strange nutty aroma. At this early hour my nose can't quite place it, but it's kind of pungent. I turn the corner and flick on the light to see a very guilty Tripod, his sneaky little tail practically wedged between his hind leg and his stump, ears pinned back in the universal canine sign of "I did it, but please don't hit me!" Strewn about him lies the evidence of his obvious nighttime foray into the kids' neatly packed backpacks: wrappers of Skippy peanut butter sticks, foil packaging from Nature Valley honey-oat granola bars, and puddles of Minute Maid fruit punch, the dog's teeth having punctured but not completely destroyed the foil pouches once containing the drink.

I should've known better. Tripod absolutely adores peanut butter; it's so like him to sniff it out and snatch it right from the open knapsacks on the floor.

"Tripod!" This is no way to start the day, especially when I'm the only adult around to deal with this mess on top of the usual morning routine.

The dog slinks toward me, acting as if I am about to beat him. And while I have yet to employ that tactic, I must admit I'm sorely tempted right now. But who could hit a three-legged dog? I open the door and toss him outside and set to work wiping up the smeared peanut butter remnants and juice drippings.

"What the hell was that dog thinking?" I yell to no one in particular.

"Mommy, language." Lindsay comes up behind me. She is my perpetual conscience, and keeps me from randomly spewing vulgarities about seventy percent of the time. The other thirty percent I cannot be held accountable for.

"Honey, can you get the cereal and the milk out for everyone while I clean this up?"

"Sure, Mom."

Cameron comes down, fresh from his shower—a

new teen thing he does in the morning—and sits down, demanding his breakfast.

"Excuse me?" It always amazes me, his sense of entitlement, even now that he's old enough to make breakfast for himself. "In case you hadn't noticed, I'm dealing with a disaster à la Tripod, so I'll greatly appreciate your starting to fix everyone's lunch."

He grumbles a bit to himself, but reluctantly complies. Somehow over the next forty-five minutes I manage to wrangle the kids, the dog, everything under my roof with a pulse, and get everyone off to school and on the right bus.

I've got exactly forty-five minutes before I have to leave for work. Just enough time to jot off an e-mail to Todd.

Hola, Todd!

Just practicing my Spanish, as I leave this evening for Miami! Can you believe it? Twelve hours from now I'll be in the tropical warmth of the Four Seasons hotel, maybe dining on some puerco with frijoles and plantains and sipping that much-longed-for mojito. Oh, or maybe I'll go to that hip restaurant I read about in People magazine where everyone dines in bed rather than at a table. But it does sound a little bit uncomfortable. Plus, how weird would that be, eating alone in bed in public?

But I really wanted to get off a quick note to you to thank you for your wonderful pep talk the other day. I didn't know how much I've missed your philosophical musings over the years. I guess you made up for it with that fifteen-thousand-word dissertation you wrote to me ☺.

BTW—"spoilage in the refrigerator of love"? My, my, my, aren't you poetic? Ha, ha. I do, however, appreciate your male insight into the potentially puerile workings of Jack's mind. I know there is this bizarre uncontrollable testosterone thrust by which you men seem to be invisibly steered. Some sexual rocket booster or something.

I just don't understand, even after all of these years, how clearheaded logical thinking can't, however, prevail over irrational hormonal urges. But that, I suppose, is one for the history books, as I am not the first, nor will I be the last woman to shake her head in dismay at men and their below-the-belt priorities.

Besides which, I'm sure he'd readily launch that hormone-excuse grenade right back at me. After all, what woman can't comfortably rest on her estrogen-laden laurels as an excuse for bitchy behavior?

I have taken your advice to heart, though, Todd. I am becoming a veritable Nancy Drew. I am off in search of the truth as far as my husband's potential infidelity is concerned, and in between a scheduled massage and several hours per day poolside, I plan to surreptitiously follow that husband of mine all over the city until I can know with confidence what is up— or not—with him.

Alas, I couldn't bring myself to sniff him down after I'd read some of your suggestions. Though I will say, I ran into one of his partner's wives after that party, and she too picked up on the vibes between Jack and Julia, so I certainly wasn't crazy imagining it. Of course, this woman was reveling in my misfortune, which made me want to beat her senseless with the spiked heel of her shoe.

But the idea of him smelling like that Julia girl—in that way—oh, Todd, that just damned near destroyed me to think of that as a possibility. Please tell me that a man with a conscience has a far harder time than you seem to describe in committing such an act of betrayal. I mean, a kiss is one thing—that's bad enough—but the other act? Blech. I'll castrate him if I find out he's been doing that. I've already got a dog amputee at home; what's one more male with some dismemberment?

Well, your description of my once-revered kiss certainly did drag me out of the swamp of despair into which I'd been wallowing, though. Was I really that great? Wow! What happened? I wonder. I went from a lush, sensual woman to, well, what? A lush? Ha, ha. Just kidding. Have no fear; I'm not a lush. Not yet, anyhow.

I must say, it certainly is reassuring that you now miss me. It's a shame you dumped me the way you did, but at least you see the error of your ways finally! And to think, you ditched me for someone named Vanna Black! That should have been a red flag, Todd. Vanna Black? Well, enough beating you over the head about that. But I do want to tell you my own bit of advice about old Vanna girl.

You recognize that the fate of your fatherhood is now in the (prayer-clasped) hands of your ex. But do not forget that while she's working the strings now, the fate of your relationship with her was once in your hands and you blew it, and so you must make it abundantly clear to her that you really mean it this time. And you are going to have to woo your son, make him fall for you. Make him—no, better yet, let him—see what he's been missing out on. And by so doing, you will realize, too, what you've been missing out on.

Old Vanna isn't going to like it. Not one bit. But she's also going to want to do what is best for him, even if that means letting you into her son's—your son's—life. So persevere, I say, for the sake of that boy of yours.

You have given me much food for thought, with your man's perspective, Todd. About working at marriage, striving for intimacy, even how onerous it is for a man to have to provide for a family. I just hadn't looked at things through those eyes before.

So I've decided that this weekend is the beginning of the rest of my life, Todd. I am officially going to add some color back into my world. To appreciate my children more.

To value my life more. And—provided that my husband isn't making a cuckold of me (well, I guess really only a man can be cuckolded, but you know what I mean)—to truly appreciate the man I married. And I have you and your learned advice to thank for this. Who'd have known that a man I've spent so many years holding in contempt could actually be so erudite? In honor of that, Todd, I'm going to carpe my diem, dammit. Just as you're carpe'ing yours.

Isn't it exciting? After feeling as if I've been going through the motions of my life for so very long, I'm ready to get out there and join the living again. And who knows? Maybe I'll find myself in an elevator in Miami. . . . Oh, I guess that's not possible, as I'm married. Well, you know what I mean. How about maybe I'll find myself throwing caution to the wind for the first time in a very long while. I'll let you know what happens. In the meantime, get to work, my friend!

C

I have one foot out the door when I notice Cameron's lunch bag—he's far too cool to use a lunch box—lying on the dining room table. Damn. Thought I got away without that duty today. But as the snacks are gone . . . I throw it into my car and rush, now with the added diversion to the middle school to drop off his meal.

I arrive at work ten minutes late, but am surprised by Kat sitting at my desk, sexy kitten heels kicked up, about the last thing I expected to see. Kat looks disgustingly sexually sated, her glossy ebony hair slightly tousled, her verdigris eyes harboring all the secrets of her recent pleasure.

"Claire!" She stands, giving me her little European dual-cheek kiss.

"What are you doing in my humble office, girl?"

"I just dropped Robert off, so I thought I'd poke my head in to see if you'd gotten here yet."

I close the door.

"Whoa—this is getting serious. You've spent all of your waking—and sleeping, God forbid—hours together, and now you're driving him to work?"

"Since he lives right here in Old Town, Robert usually just walks to work, but it was cold today, and I was driving right by the office anyhow. . . ."

"Yeah, sure," I say, knowing damned well that even if Kat had been driving to Baltimore she'd conveniently divert herself fifty miles out of her way to accommodate her guy.

"So, I guess this really is getting serious?"

"Sometimes things get serious quickly, right? I mean, look at you and Jack."

"Yeah, right," I grumble.

"What do you mean by that?"

"Only that I think my husband is off in Miami having a little tête-à-tête with some young floozy from his office," I moan.

"Oh, come off it. Jack would never do something like that."

"I'm glad that you're so certain of that, because I'm not. In fact, I am planning to find out for myself."

"What? Did you hire a private investigator?"

"Nope. I'm off for the weekend to stalk him."

"Please tell me you're joking."

"Not exactly. I'm going to Miami, where Jack just so happens to be, and while I enjoy some time to myself I'm just going to see what I can find out."

"You are insane, Claire. What do you think you're going to find out?"

"Well, for one, I can see if the two of them are hanging out together. Or holding hands and behaving affectionately. Or, well, worse."

"Oh, honey." Kat hugs me. "You can't actually *believe* that Jack is cheating on you!"

"I don't know, Kat. I just don't know." I pace my tiny office, running my hands through my hair with a sense of exasperation.

"Well, I for one trust Jack completely. And I think you should just go to Miami and relax for once."

"What do you mean, relax for once?"

"It's not like you ever get a chance to just take it easy, right?"

"Duh. Of course not. When would I?"

"My point exactly. So just go down there and take advantage of being away and stop worrying about Jack."

"And if he's having an affair?"

"Claire Doolittle. If your husband is having an affair, well, then, I'll—"

"You'll what?"

"I'll . . . I'll marry Robert!"

"Ha! That is the best one I've heard in ages, Kat! You? Marry again? Plus, doesn't Robert have a say in that?"

"Well, Claire, sometimes you just know when something feels right. And it just so happens that Robert has already asked me."

My ears must be deceiving me. "He asked you what?"

"He asked me to marry him."

"Wait, wait, wait, wait, wait! Robert—my boss—asked you—my best friend—to marry him?"

Why is it that the best friend is always the last to know?

Kat smiles a Mona Lisa smile. "Like I said, sometimes when you know, you know."

"Do you mean that you'll agree to marry Robert only if you find out that my husband is having an affair? Or are you planning to accept his proposal regardless? And isn't this all a little rash? I mean, you've only been dating for a few days!"

"Days, shmays, Claire. It's love. Time is insignificant where love is concerned."

I roll my eyes at her. "Yeah, right."

"Why, just imagine the possibilities!" Kat winks at me. "Isn't it romantic? Love at first sight and all?"

"I think it's just that you haven't been laid in a while and you're equating sexual gratification with domestic permanence or something. Kat, dear, you of all people should know about making such mistakes."

Kat glares at me now. She does not like to be reminded of her lapses in judgment, particularly those that have led to erroneous and doomed marital unions.

"Okay, so fine, whatever. You think you should marry Robert, that's your business, Kat." I tell her that, but the truth is, I don't get it. I really don't get it. Kat is happy. She's got her independence. She's got her life, for Christ's sake. What in the world has changed her mind?

Kat remains silent.

"I'm sorry. But I just have to ask you: why in a million years would you throw away what you have for an impulsive act of passion?"

Kat sort of glares at me. "Do you not get it?"

"Get what? All I know is that you were very unhappily married to three men who suffocated you. You struggled mightily to rebound from those bad relationships and to make something of yourself. Now you are in a situation where you're single, free, and happy. And you're talking about just impetuously throwing all that away?"

"There's where you're wrong, my friend. Well, maybe not wrong, but where you've been subjecting my life to your own murky interpretation. Yes, I have been free. At least, I haven't been under the thumb of my ex-husbands, if that's what you mean. And I've loved every minute of that part of it, of being rid of them. But you know what? I'm lonely. Christ, I'm lonely. I look at you with your house full of love and activity and always something crazy happening, and yeah, you tell me you're feeling like you're coming down with a bad case of marital malaise. But I tell you, Claire. You ought to think long and hard about that."

Kat picks at an invisible hangnail, and I think I see a glimmer of moisture in her eyes.

"Try being alone and middle-aged. It's not all it's cracked up to be. Try spending a few solitary nights without the company of anyone, just you and a glass of wine or two. The most exciting event of the week being when *The Bachelor*, or some equally maudlin program, comes on TV. So you can watch some other poor desperate woman publicly launch herself at an unsuitable man, simply because she'd rather settle for some loser she finds on a reality program than spend another empty night feeling that she lost in a cosmic game of musical chairs—the music stopped and everyone else had a partner but her.

"You know how pathetic it is? I'll tell you: do you know that every night when I go to bed, I cover myself from head to toe, tucking the blankets in beneath me to ward off the loneliness?" She laughs, but it serves only to mock her. Or me.

"Like hiding my extremities from the dark night air will protect me or something. In fact, it has taken substantial restraint not to have my daughter snuggle up in my bed on the nights that I have her with me. Tallulah, my only other talisman against my unwanted solitude. But I don't want to make my daughter any more neurotic than she's already doomed as my child to be. But for the past several weeks, not only have I enjoyed the luxury of having company while I sleep—peacefully, I might add— but I've slept naked. Naked and uncovered. Gloriously free of blankets and sheets and any protection from my lonely nights. So here's the truth of it, Claire. I'm thirty-nine years old and I've found a man who has ignited a fire—no, more like he launched a goddamned rocket—

deep within me. I've been earthbound for so long, pretending I was happy just being Kat. But it wasn't until Robert came along that I realized how much I've been missing out on. And now I'm floating around the stratosphere, orbiting all of those earthbound fools, whom I pity because they don't know how great they could have it. I've been happier these past couple of weeks than I have been the past fifteen years combined. Do you understand what I'm saying to you?"

I can hardly look at her. I feel foolish for being so judgmental, and like I must be a really shitty friend for having no clue that Kat felt so low for so long. I mean, really. Have I been wandering around with my vision *that* shrouded by my own experience? Am I so entrenched in my own woes that I lost sight of the fact that others are busily drowning in their own troubles? Have I been peering through my own sort of camera obscura, with my view being inverted and I didn't even know it?

"Kat," I start to say. But I can't find the right words.

"I'm sorry about that outburst—" she begins.

"No. *I'm* sorry. I'm sorry that I never noticed—"

"Nobody notices. I think that's the thing. You're upset because things aren't as you'd like them to be with Jack. But Jack doesn't notice, because he's probably wrapped up in whatever his troubles are. We all go along in life just embroiled in our own lives. Every once in a while our eyes are open to someone else's world, to really, truly see into their world. But usually we all just sort of plug along, sometimes to a fault. And that's when marriages start to unravel. When husbands and wives stop being able to see the world through the eyes of their partner. I speak from experience, Claire. You know that. The thing is, you and Jack are great together. Jack's such a wonderful man. And you're a remarkable woman. You can't let yourselves be dragged down by unspoken words, by bitterness and resentment that build to vendettas. I've always looked at you and Jack as the ones to emulate. At the very least, for my own selfish sake, you must not let go of what you two have."

She squeezes my cheek like an Italian uncle, then laughs, this time without a hint of irony.

"Wow!" I exhale. "Who'd have ever thought that all of those intense emotions were boiling beneath the surface of Sky's Slut little friend?"

"Indeed. Now, Claire. You are going to go to Miami and just relax. You're not even going to worry about Jack or this little Twinkie who'll be there, okay? I think the best thing for Claire and Jack is for Claire to get a little break, take a breather from the demands of your life. So, pack your suntan lotion, throw in a couple of steamy romance novels, and enjoy yourself! It'll do you a world of good."

She gives me a little hug.

"I suppose you're right."

"Now, then, I'd better get out of here and let you do some work or Robert will change his mind about me!"

I look at my friend with renewed respect. "You know, Kat, twenty minutes ago I would never have dreamed of endorsing a marriage based on great sex and a short period of perceived compatibility. But now I say, go for it, mazel tov, *salut*, *bonne chance*, may the Force be with you, and all that stuff. And I apologize for presuming to know what's best for you."

"Sweetie, that's what best friends are for!"

Robert turns the corner and pokes his head in. The man looks like he's gleefully getting away with murder. He knows he's out of his league with Kat. Clearly he cherishes her, though, and that's a first for her, considering the previous three lunkheads she suffered through. Maybe this will be good for Kat after all.

"Yoo-hoo! Robert!" Kat extends her hand, which he tucks comfortably into his own. They share a secret smile, and suddenly I'm a little bit envious that Kat's got what I had, and I want it again, too. I want to feel that same sense of shared intimacy, like the two of us are in on a private secret that no one else can know. Now I know that I must work to reclaim that with Jack. But first I need to know for certain that Jack isn't sharing secrets with a certain trollop from his office. . . .

Chapter Eighteen

Right now you must be wondering if I am a little bit off my rocker. If the real loser in this relationship might actually be Jack. After all, anyone else who sat through an emotionally jarring conversation like I had with Kat would probably be sold on her suggestions. Like sitting through a particularly passionate sermon in which the converted line up to have the preacher touch their heads and baptize them or something.

You might think that I'm courting trouble by not just trusting Jack, believing that he's in Miami exclusively for business.

Truth is, sometimes I do act irrationally. I can't help myself. I just have the propensity sometimes to follow my gut, or to act based purely on an emotional level. It makes no sense; truly it doesn't. And can occasionally get me into hot water.

I'm thinking back to a situation a couple of years ago. Jack had undergone some unexpected surgery. Now, normally I would have been a supportive wife, fluffed his cushions, served him orange juice in bed, all that stuff. But I was actually a bit peeved with the man, because the reason he was lying in bed incapacitated was that he played lacrosse.

You see, Jack was some sort of star lacrosse player when he was in college. I don't really get that whole lacrosse thing—a bunch of people running up and down a field with sticks with little nets in them, glorified little hobo sticks. Then they lob a rock-hard ball around and hope to God that no one gets a concussion or worse. Not my thing, really.

Jack kept insisting that he wanted to play lacrosse in some weekend league, even when we had five kids and the last thing we could afford to deal with in our lives was having one of the two of us out of commission. Especially as a result of a voluntary injury. I say *voluntary* because, to me, any injury that happens as a result of something we didn't have to do is basically an injury that you asked for.

Thus, playing lacrosse as a middle-aged man, in my estimation, constitutes volunteering for an injury. Sure enough, Jack ended up with a broken femur, and had pins put in his leg, and thus was unable to get up off the bed, not to mention unable to drive, walk unassisted, or anything. And, of course, that left me to deal with five kids, a three-legged dog, the bird, the cat, and the infirm husband.

Well, the little part of me that can be so unmerciful chose to pop up at that time. I brooked no foolishness, and I let him know I was displeased. Call me Nurse Ratched.

The timing was really bad for Jack, I'll freely admit. You see, as Jack lay there in bed, miserable and stoned on Vicodin and really just looking for a modicum of sympathy from his beloved, he sent me to the basement to look for something in some filing cabinet that hadn't been touched in years. Grudgingly I entered our dingy basement. I hate to go down to the cellar. Coated in dust and cobwebs, with light sockets that refuse to yield electricity when the switch is placed on, the dank, dingy room is hostile territory that just makes my eyes swell from mold allergies and brings on asthma attacks.

I flicked on the switch, and only one of the three available naked bulbs decided to illuminate the mess before me. I should have brought a flashlight. And a broom. As I worked my way through the dimness, wiping a cobweb from my face, I found the filing cabinet in question. I opened the drawer and began to sort through the files in search of Jack's elusive document. I got to the letter L, and my roving fingers happened upon a file named "Letters." Curious, I opened the file, and out fell one solitary missive.

It appeared to be from an old girlfriend of Jack's, something she'd written to him during the time that he and I were dating (*November 1988* was scrolled across the top in hyperbolic second-grade teacher's ass-kissing cursive, next to the words, "My Dearest Jack"). There were some bad attempts at references to his and her sexual prowess (she was clearly not a writer), and there was even a faded lipstick mark. How clichéd. Then she declared her undying love for him or something, begged his forgiveness, and asked if they could renew their engagement.

Engagement? *Engagement?* That was the first I'd heard of Jack ever being engaged to anyone other than me. Yet she wrote this while he and I were together, and he never made mention of it. But he saved it? For almost twenty years?

I stormed upstairs, eyebrows furrowed, mood decidedly altered for the worse, fury erupting from me like chunks of molten rock from Krakatoa.

I have to admit, there's a pretty decent chance that

somewhere in a box in that very same dismal basement I have love letters written to me by Todd, or maybe even from Jordan Fenstermacher, my old high school boyfriend. After all, who'd ever throw away anything that is written proof that someone out there thinks you're the best thing happening? You'd be a fool to do so.

So, you may think that I was being uncharitable in skewering my husband for saving a letter from so long ago.

But the thing is, he didn't just *save* the letter, stuffed in the bottom of some grimy old box; he made a goddamned *file folder* for it. Where he could instantly retrieve it one day if the need arose. So while he chose, lo those many years ago, to tuck this letter away for safekeeping, unbeknownst to him it was going to come back to haunt him. Timing, after all, is everything.

I slammed the basement door open and glared at him, my eyebrows furrowed.

"Honey? Can you get me some more water?" he asked, beckoning his nursemaid.

"Get it yourself," I huffed, leaving the room.

For an hour or so I festered with resentment. How could he have held a torch for this woman without my knowing it? How could he be so cavalier?

Finally, at dinner, he asked me, "Is there something wrong? I get the sense that you're angry with me about something, but I can't imagine what."

My eyes burned with tears. I felt so *betrayed*. But as I thought about the whole episode, I was beginning to see how laughable it was. But I couldn't let Jack know this.

"Does the name Nicole mean anything to you?" I asked him.

He looked blank. "Noooooooooooo. Should it?"

I stood up and went over to that kitchen drawer that

holds all of the odds and ends that have no other place in the world. It's still sort of my private drawer, because no one else ever thinks to look in there anyhow. I rifled through it, unearthing the offending letter I'd tucked away earlier that afternoon.

"How about this?"

Jack squinted to get a better look. I carried it over to him, holding it by the very edge with my fingertips, as if I were avoiding contracting germs from the thing.

The kids all stared wide-eyed, not knowing what to expect.

Jack looked at me. "Oh, *that* Nicole."

I stood there, arms crossed, waiting for his explanation. But there wasn't one.

"Don't you have anything to say about the letter?"

"Yeah. Where'd you find this?"

"When I was searching for your thing in the basement. I found it under L—the only item in the folder, I might add."

"I guess my organizational skills only extended to a short period of filing letters way back then." He laughed.

I didn't.

"You were *engaged* to someone else before me? You never said anything to me about this!"

Cameron hooted. "Ooooooh, Daddy was engaged!"

Jack looked confused. "I wasn't engaged to her."

"Yes, you were. It says it right here." I showed him the proof.

"Claire, just because this woman says in a letter that we were engaged doesn't mean we actually *were*."

The kids all looked at me, waiting for my reaction. I squinted my eyes at Jack, rife with suspicion.

"Nicole always exaggerated everything about her relationship with me. That's why I broke up with her. We weren't engaged. Maybe I had a date to take her to some 'engagement.' That's the only time I ever used that word with the woman, I swear it."

"But you saved this letter? That must mean something."

"First of all, I probably tucked it away just because the woman was a bit of a stalker, and I figured I might need proof down the road that she had read too much into our relationship. But second of all, what's wrong with saving an old letter from someone from your past? I'm sure you've done so, too."

Damn. He had me there. Not only had I leaped to conclusions without giving him the benefit of the doubt, I was hung by my very own noose.

"So this is why you stormed around here pouting like a petulant child all afternoon?"

"Well, yeah, sort of."

"Sometimes you amaze me with the way you overreact to situations. Come here." He extended his arms to me, his leg sticking out on the chair I'd placed next to the dinner table so that he could keep it elevated.

I tiptoed toward him, feeling a bit of a fool. "I'm sorry, honey."

"Oh, silly girl. You really shouldn't let your imagination get so out of control next time, okay?"

"Yeah, Mommy's 'magination is a bad girl." Lindsay laughed.

It is true: I have partaken in my share of irrational conclusion jumping in my day. Nevertheless, I can't help but think I must follow through on this mission to know for certain that things have not gotten beyond my grasp.

It's not that I don't *trust* Jack. But one of those brutal ironies of life is that you can't change people, and yet people are always changing on you. You can't count on them remaining the person you thought they were—my God, just look at Kat! So how do I know that Jack hasn't become someone completely out of character, some philandering wife-abandoning cad or something? Crazier things have happened in the world.

I think about Todd's e-mail in which he asked if I missed him. Ha. Missing Todd hasn't come up in my mind in many years. What's to miss? That was something that happened in another life, in some ways. And while I enjoyed the security and stability of what Todd and I had back then, I'm afraid that his destructive finale to our romance kind of took care of my ever actually missing him.

Although I don't think you necessarily ever really "unlove" someone. I think that an emotion as intense as love shape-shifts into some other passion that encompasses love but then can be tainted by hatred, anger, or bitterness. And certainly that is the form that my love for Todd transformed into: a sort of desperate anger that softened over time into a vague feeling of *something* for the man.

And so I wonder, is this the direction that Jack's and my love has taken? Are we beyond the love phase? To tell the truth, I'm having a hard time even recalling that phase of passionate *amore* with him. Jack and I are so out of touch anymore, I don't even like to revisit the past, as it's such a festering emotional lesion. That sounds ominous, doesn't it? Comparing our love to an open sore?

I finish work and pick up pizza for the kids on the way home. When I arrive home, Candy and Dick are waiting in the driveway.

"I'm so sorry to make you wait outside!" Damn, I forgot to leave the key under the mat.

"No worries. Dick took a little snooze and I read a

few chapters of my book. We were happy as clams!" Candy is a historical-romance-novel junkie, and is never without an old-fashioned bodice ripper featuring some raven-haired maiden with heaving bosoms.

The kids begin to trickle in amidst squeals of, "Grandma!" and, "Daddy Dick!" (I'm not kidding you about that), and I slip off to pack my suitcase and leave Candy to feed the children. Rummaging through my drawers, I pull out last year's bathing suit, hoping to God it still fits with some semblance of acceptability.

I toss in some exercise clothes (which will probably only be used to wrap a souvenir or two from the trip), some cute shorts, a few nice dresses, and my sexiest little mules—though I'm afraid my added weight tends to make me look like an ice-cream cone teetering on them, poised on delicate little tips and widening upward from there. Oh, well, tough. I am what I am, and I can't be in Miami without some sexy shoes. At the last minute I toss in the only provocative bra and panties I own. I don't even know why, unless I subliminally hope to pick up a cabana boy this weekend.

For a fleeting moment I ponder throwing in the old baby-prevention hazmat kit, but figure the chances of my needing that are next to nil. I certainly won't even be associating with Jack this weekend; he's made that abundantly clear. So why else would I need it, then?

In half an hour I am packed and briefing Candy on the weekend's events.

"So, Chrissy and Charlotte have ballet on Saturday morning at ten o'clock," I begin. "Cameron has a soccer game at one. Lindsay has a scrimmage at noon. Bubba has T-ball at nine—"

"How do we get the girls to ballet if Bubba's still at his ball game?"

"I'm afraid you'll just have to leave Bubba with the coach and tell him you'll be back shortly. Luckily, ballet is only about ten minutes away."

"I don't know about these crazy schedules for kids nowadays." Candy shrugs her shoulders. "Used to be you'd throw them outside to play in the morning and they'd come home in time for dinner."

I laugh. "And you walked uphill barefoot, both directions, in the driving snow, to get to school each day, right?"

Candy taps me lovingly on the head with the wooden spoon she pulls out of the drawer to mix lemonade.

"I hate to mention this, but that's only part of the schedule. Bubba has a birthday party to attend at four thirty. Cameron was invited to sleep over at his friend Brian's house, so he needs to get there by five. Here are directions for everything, emergency numbers, numbers for the vet, the pediatrician—"

"Don't you worry about a thing, honey. Just go and have a wonderful time with Jack."

I blanch. "Oh, about Jack. I'm going to surprise him, Candy, so if you can be sure not to mention that I'm heading down there if he calls—"

"That's so romantic of you. Of course I won't breathe a word." She winks at me, and I feel a bit guilty.

"Okay, children—everyone give me hugs and kisses!" I am struggling with the idea of truly driving off and getting on that plane. I don't know how I can leave these kids behind!

"Mommy, do you have to go?" I look down at Lindsay and see tears filling her little doe eyes.

"Oh, baby doll, it's just for a few days, and Grandma and Daddy Dick will take such good care of you guys, you'll hardly miss me!"

She wraps her arms around my thighs, and I look at the clock, realizing that if I don't leave immediately, I'll miss my flight. Sensing this, Candy corrals the children to let me make a break for it.

"Who wants to go get some ice cream?" Candy asks, and the kids fall into place in front of her. Well, Cameron kind of strolls over in her direction, not wanting to appear enthusiastic, which would be so uncool.

"Good-bye! I love you all!" I blow kisses as I quickly shut the door, not wanting to hear the guilt-inducing sound of crying that I know is imminent.

I board my flight, settling into steerage class with the rest of the unsettled masses. I swear, as much as flying can tax one's human dignity, it's almost preferable to the lack of solitude that is the hallmark of my existence. I say *almost preferable*, but not really. Truth of the matter is, I'm crazy about my family. I have grown to adore my captors, even though I am thoroughly enslaved by them and their level of expectation is unreasonable and unattainable.

I toast to that as I practically guzzle the overpriced beer I just purchased from the flight attendant. I laugh, thinking how glad I am not to still be one of those dreaded sky sluts anymore. Kat and I sure had a wild time of it when we were younger, but that is definitely a job best suited to someone other than me. I always feel sort of sorry when I see a flight attendant who looks ready for retirement and perhaps should have turned in her wings a decade ago.

By the time we land in Miami, I've got a bit of a buzz on, but manage to collect my luggage and hop a cab to the hotel without incident. I arrive at the Four Seasons to a cadre of pampering staff.

My room has a large and inviting bed, a spectacular

view overlooking the sumptuous swimming pool, and a complimentary bottle of champagne and chocolate-covered strawberries. How odd; why would I get any sort of special treatment? I notice a note set next to the tray, and open it.

Welcome to Miami. From a Secret Admirer.

Well, now, that's strange. Jack doesn't even know I'm here. This must be a clever little joke that Kat's playing on me, I think. *Oh, well, bottoms up and all that rot.* I crack open the champagne, taking my glass out to the deck to enjoy the night air. It's strange to be alone in a hotel without any responsibilities. Strange and a little bit lonely. I decide it's time to go out for dinner, before I get too tired from all of this champagne and just go to sleep without taking advantage of my newfound freedom.

I find a hip little Cuban restaurant a few blocks away on the strip, and sit down at a table for two. The sounds of Latin music and traffic mingle in the tropical night air, and I feel downright revitalized amongst all of this activity and pulsating energy.

My waiter, a sexy Cuban named Enrico with an irresistible suntan, a mesmerizing accent, and biceps that could have done some healthy double time wrapped around yours truly in another life, takes my drink order.

"I've been fantasizing about a mojito." I wink at him. Yeah, I'm starting to remember what it was like to be flirtatious and sexy.

"Make that two. And what about that *puerco* with *frijoles* and plantains?" I hear a voice behind me, and a set of hands covers my eyes. "Guess who, Claire Bear?"

Oh. My. God. It can't be. The only other person who ever called me Claire Bear besides my mother was Todd.

He leans forward, whispering into my ear, "Long time no see."

As he removes his hands from my eyes, revealing none other than Todd, minus a bit of hair and with an added middle-age paunch, I'm rendered speechless.

"Surprise!" He grabs me in a fat hug and then helps himself to the seat across from me.

"What the bloody hell are you doing here?"

"Claire, that's not exactly the reception I was expecting! No, 'Hello, Todd, good to see you'?"

The waiter delivers our drinks, from which I take an immediate and lengthy slug.

"Todd, I'm stunned to see you here. How did you know where to find me?"

"Well, you mentioned in your e-mail that you were staying at the Four Seasons. I just sort of read between the lines, thinking you might enjoy a little, uh, moral support. You may have noticed that I travel quite a bit for business. So I just decided to take advantage of my frequent-flier points and divert myself to Miami. I arrived a few hours ago, checked in at my hotel, then came down to your hotel to wait in the lobby until I saw you. I'd wanted to go straight up to your room, but they wouldn't give me your room number."

"Thank goodness." I breathe a sigh of relief. I can't imagine if I had shown up in my room to a naked ex-boyfriend lying in wait. I blanch at the thought. I swill from my very potent drink, knowing that I've had more to drink in the past six hours than I probably have had in the past six years. "I have to ask you. Why exactly are you here?"

"I just felt such a connection to you in the e-mails we've exchanged, I thought this was the perfect opportunity to really get to know each other again."

"Todd, I'm *married*. I can't be meeting up with old

boyfriends in posh resorts. What would my husband say?"

"Do you mean your husband who is right now very likely enjoying the company of a nubile and much younger coworker?"

Ouch. That hit below the belt. He has a point there. Sort of.

"Okay. Supposing that is true. Do two wrongs make a right? Plus, *you're* married!"

"I didn't intend for us to just hop into bed right away. Although in truth I wouldn't object to it. I just wanted to sit down with you and talk, one on one, face-to-face. All completely innocent. Really."

I squint my eyes at him, thoroughly devoid of trust in the man, as I polish off my drink and hail Enrico to fulfill my now dire need for a refill.

"Completely innocent? Just two friends reuniting after many years?"

"Scout's honor."

"You were never a scout. However, I will take you on your word. But understand, I've got plans for this weekend, so I can't make any promises about spending any more time with you than this. Got it?"

"I'll take what I can get."

By the time dinner is over and my fourth mojito arrives, my aim is off, and I poke myself in the eye with the decorative spear of sugarcane garnish that is sticking out of my drink. It's hard to maintain one's dignity when your eye is smarting from the pain of such an injury.

"Claire, I think we'd better get you back to your hotel room before you really hurt yourself."

"Oh, no, I'm jusht fine, Toddshter. Toddshter. What an e-mail name. Toddshter. Ha! Why don't you come on back with me, shleep in my hotel room, Toddshter?"

"I don't think you'll be very happy with that decision in the morning."

"Morning, schmorning, Toddshter. Let'sh live it up a little."

"Come on, Claire." He grabs me by the arm and pulls me out of my seat.

We hail a taxi for the few short blocks. At the hotel we're greeted by another sexy Latin-looking doorman, whose bottom I would have reached over and pinched if Todd hadn't stopped me. Over my loud protests Todd escorts me, wobbling on my heels, to my room.

"Where do you plan to shleep?"

"I'll figure something out, Claire."

"Oh, shtop it. It's one thirty in the morning. Shtay here, Toddshter, or I'll scream and wake up the neighbors."

"Whatever you do, don't do that. How about I just sleep on the couch, okay?"

I'm about to answer him but instead fall down on the bed, shoes still on, and fall asleep immediately, without even brushing my teeth or remembering my hundred strokes on my hair.

I wake at dawn, an unfamiliar thrumming in my head denying me much-needed sleep. Aneurysm. My God, I have an aneurysm. I'm about to die in my beautiful, comfortable, feathered bed at the Four Seasons in Miami. Alone. No kids, no dog, no parrot, no cat. No Jack.

I get up out of bed to look for the telephone, in case I have to call 911. I feel like Wile E. Coyote after the Roadrunner pushes a boulder on top of his head. Then I notice someone asleep on the sofa. Someone naked but for a protruding pair of fire-engine red clingy boxer briefs. Oh, Claire, you stupid twit. You don't have an aneurysm. You've got a goddamned hangover headache.

I fumble in the dark in my purse for two Advil. I know there are some random pills somewhere in the abyss of my purse. I feel around for them. My heart palpitates: the disks of salvation are at my fingertips. Enough of my poetic ode to the miracle drug ibuprofen; I tiptoe to the bathroom, fill a glass with water, and down it in one gulp along with my pills. I chug two more glasses of water and return to the relative comfort of the bed, my head throbbing relentlessly, reminding me with each pulse of blood to my brain what a goddamned fool I am sometimes.

Christ, this is no way to start my relaxing little getaway weekend.

Chapter Nineteen

Alas, sleep is to me what a cock-tease is to a horny guy. I'm never gonna get the satisfaction I need. I lie awake in my luxurious room, unable to stir, wondering what the hell I'm going to do with my unintended guest. My God, what would Jack say if he knew that I shared my hotel room with Todd Sterodnik, of all people? I don't think he could forgive me. I don't think *I* could forgive me, either!

I listen as Todd snorts once violently and settles into a soft breathing pattern again. I think about the many nights I've been deprived of sleep due to Jack's sonorous, rumbling earthquake snores. And how I've so resented that, what with the perpetual state of sleep denial that comes with parenthood, sleep to me being more precious than perhaps it should be. Then I think about how many times my own snoring may have kept Jack awake, and yet he never complained.

As dawn breaks through the windows I neglected to cover with curtains, thanks to my drunken stupor, I glance over at Todd, whose face appears a little roughened by time. I try to imagine how my life would have turned out had I ended up with Todd, had he never ditched me for Vanna Black.

But I can't even conceive of a life with Todd. My world is with Jack: the highs—and there have been many—as well as the lows, which, alas, seem to be the trend. I'm so lucky that I found Jack, despite his current shortcomings. I'm afraid that somewhere along in our marriage, our paths diverted. But perhaps it was just that—a little jog in the road, and our paths are meant to again meet up. Or maybe it's up to me to retrace my steps and rejoin Jack on the way.

"You're certainly lost in thought," Todd says quietly. "Any chance you're fantasizing about me?"

I jump, unaware that Todd had woken up.

"Sorry, buddy, you lost that opportunity long ago."

"Nothing like a disappointed lover." He chuckles.

"You're not my lover," I correct him in case still there's any confusion.

"A man can dream, can't he?"

"You can dream all you want, but my heart belongs to another."

"Even if that other doesn't want it anymore?"

"I don't think we know that's the case for certain. That's what I'm about to find out."

"So that means I'm left out in the cold?"

"I'm not one to hold a grudge, but I would like to point out that you certainly honed the art of leaving a lover in the cold, lest you forget."

"Touché."

"Look, Todd, I'm happy to be friends with you; really I am. But I will not entertain the idea of becoming your lover, your wife, your pet buffalo, or your flavor of the month. So if those are the only cards you're bringing to the table, I'm afraid the game is over."

But then I look at him as an idea dawns on me.

"But, if you're willing to partake in a little espionage with an old friend, well, then, I'm happy to bring you into my plan. But first, please put some clothes on."

Todd cocks his eyebrow. "Ooh, talk dirty to me, Claire Bear."

"I said put some clothes *on*, not take some clothes *off*. By the way, no more Claire Bear, okay?"

"Geez, sensitive, aren't we?" He acts hurt, his lower lip thrusting out in a pout. "So, what's this scheme you're concocting?"

"Jack's secretary indicated that she made reservations for him at some elegant restaurant for this evening. I've made a reservation there as well—I requested a quiet table a little bit out of the way. I'm hoping to figure out who Jack's dinner playmate might be—whether it's a real working dinner, or if he's dining with the strumpet. I'll be much less obtrusive if I am dining *à deux* than dining on my own. So, are you game?"

"It's the least I can do for having left you high and dry those many years ago." Todd sighs. "And if we can snare that husband of yours in his web of deception, well, then, I'll be there to catch you when you fall!"

"Don't sound so gleeful." I smack him lightly, and he smacks the back of my head, which now feels like macerated meat, thanks to my exercise in self-pickling last night.

"Back off, sonny boy—hands off the merchandise." I cradle my skull gingerly, massaging the throbbing pulse points at my temples, hoping that salvation for the pain in my head and my heart are both imminent.

I manage to get rid of Todd and dive in the shower, savoring the curative nature of the hot water sluicing down on me. You really can't say enough about how restorative a good shower can be.

I dry my hair, apply makeup, and pull on a sort of slinky lime green–and-yellow sundress I got last summer on sale at Nordstrom. I slip on my heeled mules and take a long look in the mirror. I should be a little more charitable toward myself, I think, because really, I don't look *that* bad, despite my hangover bloat. Granted, a diet could do wonders for me, but the same holds true for half of America, right? And yeah, some firming up of my biceps, tightening up that pooch of a tummy could do me good. Maybe toning my butt some. Nothing three or four months at a fat farm couldn't rectify. Ah, all things that are not the domain of a mother of five, I'm afraid.

But then again, maybe that's something I should make the time for. Make Jack *grant* me that time. Why should he be the only one to engage in regular self-indulgence?

I check my watch to see if I'm going to be too late. The good thing is, between my hangover and the invasive daylight beaming into my room, it's not even seven yet and I'm ready to go: I think I've got a decent chance of catching old Jacko on his way back from his long run. After all, the early bird catches the worm. Or in this case, perhaps the snake.

I hop in the elevator, ride down to the lobby. Confidently I click across the marble floors, amazed at how little activity is going on at this hour on a gorgeous Miami morning. Outside I get the doorman to hail a cab, and take the short ride over to Jack's hotel.

Luckily, there's a coffee shop nearby. I run in, grab a harsh cup of Cuban coffee and a pastry, and settle in at a cute little wrought-iron outdoor table with a copy of the *Miami Herald* to obscure my covert mission, straw hat and dark shades further bolstering my goal. It's hot enough already that I'm thankful for the umbrella overhead as I wait. And wait. And wait.

Two cups of coffee, another pastry, and the onset of

some serious caffeine/hangover jitters later, I notice some joggers on the horizon. Note I said *joggers*, plural. I tip my sunglasses down in the hopes of getting a better look, still holding the paper up to mostly hide me from prying eyes.

As the runners approach I realize one of them is Jack, the morning sun reflecting off his glistening limbs, his hair slicked back by sweat. He's still going at a fairly good clip—surprising, considering he's probably run six or seven miles.

I stop assessing my husband to settle my gaze on the interloper keeping pace with him. Honey blond hair pulled back into a sexy, girlish ponytail. Heart-shaped lips pursed in determination. Legs. Oh, fuck. Those legs. Long, lithe, muscled. Tanned. I can only imagine that Jack has spent the past hour or so imagining those legs entwined around his waist as he pumps himself into her. His mouth covering her heart-shaped lips, silencing her moans of pleasure. Or maybe he's remembering, not imagining. Oh, Lord help me.

Christ. How can I compete with this gamine gazelle of a woman before me? In my heyday I never looked that good. And I certainly never looked that good covered in sweat.

She looks over at him and says something, and he laughs. They are sharing witticisms. Jack never laughs at anything I say, and I make a pretty good joke, if I do say so myself. Sad thing is that right now, *I'm* the joke.

Imagine Jack, completely oblivious to his wife, Claire, who in his mind is at home doing whatever little wifeys do, while he's off marathon training (and possibly having marathon sex) in sexy Miami with fucking Cameron Diaz's evil twin. Just going on about his happy little life, fantasizing about (or fondly recalling) fucking this girl's lights out, while Claire minds the home front.

The joggers are slowing down nearby. I can't let him see me. I pull the *Miami Herald* up over my eyebrows, feigning interest in a story about Elian Gonzalez's cousin's uncle's mother-in-law or something equally compelling. Didn't that boy go back to Cuba already?

They're actually jogging in place on the street corner not fifteen feet away from me. I hear Julia giggling at some clever nonsense Jack blathers at her. They come to a slow stop and begin to stretch each other out. I kid you not. On the street corner, before my unbelieving eyes, Jack is holding Julia's extended and very lissome leg—no doubt freshly shorn, so it's smooth—against his hard thigh as she bends forward to stretch her quads and hamstrings. His hands gently clutch her delicate doelike ankles. Doelike, yeah. More like cloven-hoofed, being the instrument of Satan that I'm pretty sure she is. Next the interloper places her hands on Jack's shoulders—his strong, well-muscled shoulders—and leans forward, stretching her arms and her back.

Jack reaches down and gives her back a quickie massage while she's bent over. I'm stupefied, watching this public foreplay between my husband and the homebuilding home wrecker. Stupified, but unable to intervene. I mean, yeah, it sure does look like foreplay. But still, is this enough evidence to launch an all-out inquisition?

They look to me like a happy little couple in the throes of budding young love. Young, despite my husband's age. I mean, they look like Jack and I once looked together, long, long ago. If we ever looked that perfect together.

Now they're both stretching their calves, leaning forward, legs extended, heels on the sidewalk, toes up, facing each other and giggling. Don't they look silly together, these young lovers? I can feel my TMJ flaring up as I clench my molars in lockjaw mode.

I take a few deep breaths and try to quell my fears. After all, I'm not yet ready to jump out from behind my newspaper and hurl accusations at them. Besides, here, now, what good would it do? I remind myself that I couldn't fawn over Jack the way that girl wonder is fawning over him if you paid me. Too many latent hostilities brewing for a jovial little jog down the street and an exchange of jollities. In fact, if Jack touched me the way he's fondling her, I'd recoil, suspicious that all he wanted to do was get laid anyhow. All the more reason for me to suspect that's exactly what's on his groin-centric mind.

Watching them now, looking so lovey-dovey and so, well, happy, I realize that it's all about the foreplay, isn't it? The act of sexual gratification—at least for me—can come about only with the act of mutual daily gratification. By this I mean simple daily kindnesses. *Honey—how 'bout I help you with that? Oh, sweetie, you look beautiful. Claire, why don't you treat yourself to a day at the spa? Babe, I'd love to talk with you on the phone right now. Tell me about your day.*

Jack's manner of ordering me around: *Claire, do this; Claire, don't do that.* Snapping at me if I dare call him at work and, God forbid, interrupt him—even though I'm sure Julia Julliard is constantly popping her gilded head into his office and derailing his train of thought. Jack actively practices the ham-handed art of antiforeplay. The Jack that I know thinks foreplay means tweaking my tits for two minutes before he sticks it in me. Somehow he lost the art of gentle kindness toward me, lost that ability to turn me on by his actions, not by his lackluster precoital maneuvers.

So, how is Claire supposed to ever get that revelation through the man's thick skull? By telling him the truth? No way. All that would trigger in Jack would be major defensiveness.

Jack and the barely postpubescent Julia emerge from the coffee shop. I'm sure whatever Julia's biting into contains less than ten carbs, zero grams of fat, and will help her to achieve world peace, being the chosen one that she must be. I think I'm going to be sick when I see her reach over and offer some of it to Jack, who readily indulges. This is Jack, who doesn't even share drinks with me because he doesn't want to get sick. The happy couple stops to pet a dog tied up to a lamppost; damn, I think a little pet poodle would complete their family picture. When Julia brushes pastry crumbs from Jack's lips, I have to get up and leave or I will be physically ill right here not thirty feet away from them. I slip past the cordoned off rope in the outdoor dining area, out of view of the architectural lovebirds who are building their love nest right here in hot-hot-hot Miami Beach. Dejected, I remove my cute little shoes and walk a block or so before hailing a cab back to the hotel. The only thing I can do now is go back and wait for my scheduled massage, hoping that it will at least temporarily erase this episode from my mind long enough to achieve that relaxation Kat said I needed so desperately.

I'm not prepared to indict Jack for unforgivable crimes against our marriage yet. However, one thing's become quite apparent: Jack Doolittle is leading some sort of double life—my current Jack has somehow magically transformed himself back to the old Jack for the benefit of Julia Julliard, homebuilding home wrecker extraordinaire. I gotta hand it to her, though. Somehow she's been able to achieve what I haven't. And truth be told, if given the chance, I'd kill her because of it. Either that or take some lessons from her.

Chapter Twenty

"Oh, this is the life." I can't imagine much more that I could ask for than a massage on my balcony overlooking the gorgeous swimming pool below. Well, I could probably ask for a massage minus the thoughts of Jack and Julia's foray into foreplay dancing in my head. But since I can't do anything about that yet, I'll settle for what is hovering above me. Or make that who. Or is it whom?

Above me Giancarlo, a painfully handsome Italian masseur, is working the knots out of my tense trapezius muscles, and I can feel at least some of my morning's stress and anxiety seeping away into his magical fingers.

"Signora, you are too tense," Giancarlo scolds me.

"You're preaching to the choir, big boy." I close my eyes and think only of Giancarlo's warm, suggestive eyes; his hair the dark of a Tuscan midnight, with a soft wave like a gentle curve in the road; his body expressly designed for the fantasies of sexually repressed middle-aged women. Like me.

"You need to do something about the tension or you're going to give yourself a heart attack." His nimble digits are gently working down my spine. If he keeps doing that in the direction he's heading, he's liable to give me an orgasm.

I'm so relaxed I might just slip off the table. I feel like a slab of raw chicken.

"Or at the very least, agita," I mumble through the face hole in the massage table.

"Signora, who is Tabitha?"

"Oh, never mind." These language gaps can sometimes get on your nerves. "Giancarlo, tell me something."

"Anything, signora." He's exerting more pressure on my back now. It's the sort of pleasure/pain you feel when you floss your teeth a little too hard. I can't decide whether to tell him to ease up a bit or bring it on and let me suffer the consequences.

"You're a man. Well, that's obvious. A gorgeous one, at that. Anyhow, what is it about men and their inability to remain faithful to one woman?"

Giancarlo's hands feel like hot daggers penetrating my butt muscles.

"No, no, no. Signora, you are looking at it all wrong. We remain faithful to one woman, but sometimes there are many other women we want to sample. But we always come back to the one we are bound to."

Well, if that's not a typical bullshit man response, nothing is. I roll my eyes in disgust, but he can't see, what with me looking through a hole in the table at the floor below. "You can't just *sample* someone else!"

"But why not?"

"It's against the rules!"

"Ah, but, signora, rules are merely guidelines. Don't you see?" He is kneading my ass right now so hard it feels as if I've just been charley-horsed in the butt by a linebacker for the Pittsburgh Steelers. I'm getting annoyed enough at his answers to want to return the pain to him.

"The rules are guidelines? The rules are set in god-damned bloody stone! You can't diddle anyone once you're married!"

"Ah, but, signora, don't be so *pazzo* about this. There are many circumstances to consider."

"Circumstances? Tell me, what circumstances make it okay to betray your wife?" My thighs are having the best workout they've had in ages, thanks to this man's miraculous hands; I wonder if this is burning calories.

"Well, signora, what if your wife no longer agrees to have sex with you?"

This hits a little too close to home. I'm silent for a moment.

"Well, what if your husband has turned into Ward Cleaver?"

Giancarlo stops his massage and I turn around and look up at him. He looks puzzled.

"Who is this Ward Cleaver you are talking about?"

What? Do they not show reruns of *Leave It to Beaver* in Salerno? Oh, those poor, deprived Italians.

"Ooooh, never mind. What if your husband changes? What if he used to be sexy and doting and indulgent and sensual, and now he's become more like your father?"

Giancarlo clucks his tongue. "This is not good, if he is like your father. There is no . . . how you say . . . sex appeal in that."

"You can say that again." I'm facedown again, mumbling into my table hole. "Would *you* want to have sex with someone who has turned into your mother?"

Giancarlo pauses again, and I look up to see him making the sign of the cross. I forgot these Italian men think their mothers are saints.

"Signora, I love my mother with all of my heart. But I would not love my wife as my mother."

"Case closed. So he's wrong to be conducting this affair with the home-wrecking homebuilder, then, right?"

"Signora, you are confusing me."

"Oh, never mind."

I close my eyes and drift off to sleep with visions of a younger version of Jack and me lounging on the beach, applying suntan lotion to each other, totally focused on each other. I wake up wondering if we ever really were that way, or if I'm just dreaming that things were once better.

chapter Twenty-one

I've ignored more than four cell phone calls from Mr. Happy in the past three hours. I guess he's wondering where his little hausfrau has gone off to. As they say Down Undah, "Good on him." Let's let old Jack Doolittle stew in his juices for a while; let him squirm. Why should I be the only one suffering here? Besides, I told him I was going somewhere. I told him it might even be Miami. He just chose, once again, to completely ignore me. Serves him right to be sweating some bullets now. Not like he'll do a thing about it—that would mean he'd actually put a whole lot of thought into my whereabouts, which he wouldn't.

Despite Jack's early morning ministrations to that slutty colleague of his, I've had a decent day. The pool was divine, the massage out of this world. I read three chapters of a book I started five years ago, so that was progress. Yes, I think my good friend Kat will agree that Claire is relaxing. While preparing to ensnare her husband in her trap.

* * *

I've got my key in the door just as my cell phone rings yet again. I've had to go to the bathroom since my late-afternoon stroll down Ocean Drive, and throw open the door to my room in a hurry to get to the bathroom. I grab the phone from my purse and notice that instead of Jack, it's my mother calling.

I grab it as I pull down my undies and sit down. Ah, blessed relief.

"Claire? Is that you?" my mother calls out loudly.

"Mom? It's me, Claire," I say.

"I can't hear you—there's noise in the background!"

"Hold on a second, Mom." The sound of my going to the bathroom must be amplified on the cell phone. That's embarrassing.

Finished, I stand up and lean forward to flush, and the phone slips from my hand.

"Stop!" I yell out loud as the phone ricochets off the toilet seat and splashes into the bowl, which has, luckily, just finished flushing.

Dammit. I gingerly retrieve my phone from the toilet and rinse it off with soap and water in the sink. Well, guess that's not going to work for a while. I fleetingly wonder what my mother was calling for, but I don't have time to talk to her now anyhow. I'll call her back later.

I'm putting the finishing touches on my makeup, getting ready for dinner, when I hear Todd knock at the door. I open it to see him standing before me, dressed in a lovely dark suit, a dark button-down shirt, and a lavender tie, with a bouquet of tropical-looking flowers.

"Todd, they're lovely, but you shouldn't have!"

"It can't match your beauty, Claire Bear."

"That's very sweet of you, but remember—flattery will get you nowhere. And lose the Bear, remember?"

"Oops. A slip of the tongue. I'm sorry; truly I am."

"All right, I'll forgive you. But no more tongue-slipping, got it? You're sure you're clear on the situation tonight?" I ask him, anxious that he doesn't screw anything up.

"I've got it all right here." He points to his thinning pate. "We go to dinner at the Blue Door. It's *the* place to dine in Miami—"

"Stop mocking me. It is—"

"All right, all right, so it's hip and trendy. Anyhow, we keep our heads low so as not to be detected by the enemy—"

"Jack is not the enemy. Julia is." I keep wrestling with whom to hate: Jack or Julia. I guess it's like a child who still clings to her abusive parent, avoiding blaming the culprit.

"Ah-ah-ah, you don't *know* that." Todd raises his finger as if to make a point.

"Precisely. That is what we will find out tonight."

"So, to the restaurant, we'll enjoy a lovely meal, and pretend that we are a happily married couple enjoying a romantic dinner together. Very simple. But if we find out Jack's up to no good?"

"I haven't gotten that far along in the plan. We'll have to improvise."

"Oh, great, I love improvising. Just as long as it doesn't involve fists flying."

"We'll be perfectly civil about this. After all, we *are* grown-ups, right?"

"I think that's the problem, Claire. We are grown-ups." Todd's face looks suddenly sad.

"Something wrong?" The last thing I need right now is to have to nurture Todd's emotional wounds. I've got enough festering wounds of my own, thank you.

"Oh, nothing." I can tell he's lying.

"What is it, Todd?" My voice betrays my impatience.

"It's just that Vanna's giving me a hard time about seeing my son."

"You talked to her today?"

"She left me a curt message on my voice mail. Something to the effect that she doesn't want her son's heart to be bruised any more than it already has been."

"Ouch."

"Ouch is right. I don't know what to do."

"You're just going to have to tough it out. No one said it was going to be easy, you know. You've got a lot of years of neglect to undo." Todd avoids making eye contact with me, instead rolling his cell phone between his fingers. "You're ready to do this now, and eventually Vanna Black and her Promise Keeper will see that." I pat him on the back. "After all, she does want what's best for her son, and in the long run a healthy relationship with his father will benefit him."

"Do you think so?"

"Well, that's a stupid question. Of course it will."

"What if he doesn't like me?"

"Todd, chances are right now he hates you. But give him time to come around. Kill him—and her—with kindness. After a while your charm will prevail."

I don't want to remind him that his charm hadn't worked on me. Hate to kick someone when they're down.

"Okay, so let's get out of here."

"Wait." Todd holds up his hand like a crossing guard. "Synchronize our watches." I think he thinks we're preparing to invade another country.

"I don't even have a watch on." I drag him by the arm toward the elevator. "Come on!"

"I'm coming, I'm coming!"

As I enter the starkly chic elegance of the Delano Hotel, I'm beginning to be a bit put off by the fact that my husband chose not to have his lovely bride join him for his obviously top-shelf Miami weekend. I mean, this place is no humble shack, and I don't think most people would come here with just *anybody*.

In fact, this place is the Taj freaking Mahal of Miami. And if he's coming to dine here with Julia Julliard, of all people, well, then, he's gonna have me to answer to. Leave it to the damned architect to find this Miami hot spot.

As the host beckons us through the wide doors to a lovely terrace seat, I ask him to switch us so that I can be cloistered behind a potted palm that will afford me a decent view of the rest of the terrace while keeping me out of view. The night air is already heavy with moisture, and the tang of the ocean is just barely discernible above the gentle smells drifting from the kitchen. If I weren't on a mission to uncover my husband's potentially adulterous deception, I'd almost be enjoying the atmosphere.

I scan around me to see a cadre of beautiful people, which unnerves me. I am so not of that ilk: tan and teeny as hummingbirds, looking capable of ingesting only small amounts of nectar, never actual food.

"Thank goodness we got here early enough so I could scout out the territory before he arrives," I whisper to Todd. "It's bad enough that I have to sit amidst all of these lollipop women and watch-checker men."

Todd knits his eyebrows like I am a lunatic. "Claire, stop speaking in code. What the hell are you saying to me?"

"You know, lollipop women. They're so frightfully thin that their heads are disproportionately enormous atop their stick-figure bodies, so they look like lollipops."

Todd starts to laugh loudly. "Honestly, you are certifiable. You know that, don't you?"

I stomp on his foot beneath the table.

"Ow! What?"

"Be quiet," I whisper-shriek at him. "Do you want to draw attention to us?"

"Okay, okay. You don't have to hurt me! So now that I know who the lollipop women are, would you mind explaining the watch-checker thing?"

"Duh! You know. The big beefy guys on the beach. The ones with the narrow hips, the scary tight butts, the steroid-inflated biceps that are so large their arms suspend at an angle from their shoulders, like a pendulum in midswing."

"Would you mind telling me why they are called 'watch-checkers'?"

"Geez, Todd. Don't you know anything? These are the guys who strut down the beach in creepy Speedos—or worse yet, thongs—and every couple of hundred feet they pause and slowly hoist their wrist up toward their line of vision, as if checking their watch, when really we know they are simply trying to show off their unnatural muscle mass."

"Uh, waiter!" Todd motions to someone nearby with a tray of drinks. "Can you *please* get us a couple of martinis, bone-dry, two olives in mine. Pronto!" He points toward me, rolls his eyes, and says, "I think this is gonna be a long night."

The waiter, a thin-lipped, pretentious Frenchman named Guy—as in Tuskee*gee*—turns on his heel and departs before I have a chance to either decline the drink or defend myself.

"I can't drink that stuff! It tastes like jet fuel! Are you crazy?"

"It's the only way we are going to get through this night. Just drink up when it gets here."

"After last night's drinking debacle, the last thing I need is top-shelf moonshine."

"You're lucky I didn't take advantage of you, you know." Todd has a mischievous look in his eye.

"The good thing is, if you had, I probably would have been oblivious to it."

"I'm trying to decide if I should be insulted by that comment."

"You know what I mean. I was not exactly in mint condition. I mean, I wouldn't have known if Colin Farrell had had his way with me." Or Ward Cleaver, I think, looking at Todd's watch and wondering where the hell the man of the hour is.

As our waiter arrives with our martinis, I get the sense he too thinks I'm a little bit nuts. Not that I care what Guy—or Gee, hard G, or however the hell you say it—thinks of me. The guy's name sounds like the noise you'd make when you clear your sinuses.

He hands us the menu, pauses to give me a dubious look, then recites the chef's special; some weird fish I've never heard of that will be presented in a histrionic manner, perfect for those hummingbird women who deny the existence of an appetite but love to have things look hip and stylish on the plate. Food for thought only, I guess.

Twilight has settled in, and the exquisite sapphire night sky deceptively hides that the warm breezes are beginning to transform into a smothering, muggy chokehold. The terrace is resplendent with hibiscus and frangipani, lending a sensually tropical feel to the place. It's nice that I am hidden by the palm; otherwise I would be head-down, staring at my reflection in the dinner plate all night, avoiding detection. But hidden from view I have a wonderful perspective.

Todd clears his throat.

"Is this your perp?" he asks. I look up as he keeps directing his eyes leftward. My gaze follows his lead; then I look down quickly. There's Jack, his hand comfortably at the base of his dining companion's spine, none other than Julia Julliard. He's guiding her to a table set for three. Jack looks carefree and something else—almost proud—as he escorts the home-wrecking homebuilder in her diaphanous lavender bias-cut designer knockoff, which has settled like a shroud of Brigadoon fog just above her shapely knees. The bitch.

"That bastard!" I mutter through clenched teeth, reluctant to look up for fear that he'll notice me. "What is he doing?"

"He's leaning over and whispering something in her ear. She's laughing. Now he's waiting until the waiter seats her. Okay, she's seated. He's smiling at her as he sits. He's unfolding his napkin and placing it in his lap—"

"I don't need a fucking play-by-play."

"Well, you asked!"

"Ha. Waiting until she's seated. I think the last time he waited politely for me to sit down was at our wedding luncheon." I grab the martini and sip vigorously, if you can do such a thing with a drink like this. It tastes like some sort of chemical compound designed to kill cancer cells. "How can you drink this stuff? Flag the waiter. I need something stiff but not deadly."

I order a Pimm's with champagne—a bit of an improvement over the previous drink: palatable enough that I can actually imbibe, yet strong enough that I'll not be tempted to get drunk on it, given how things might unfold around here.

Guy's returned, tapping his foot, ready for us to order. I haven't even paid attention to the menu, and can't help but continue to look over at Jack wooing that woman who looks so damned good I can't stand it.

"Ummm, go ahead and get his order; then I'll tell you mine," I tell Guy, who clearly prefers to follow protocol but yields to my wishes.

"I'll have the tilapia with balsamic reduction, served

over a bed of saffron risotto, but can you please substitute the sauteed shallots for the pan-seared baby spinach, and I'd like the tomato concassé, but can you please not use basil—I break out in a rash with basil—"

"Christ, Todd, the guy's a waiter, not a miracle worker. Can't you just order whatever the chef's offering and be done with it?"

"Claire, you know that I'm selective."

"Selective? No, *selective* is choosing an item from the menu and saying, 'I'll take this.' *You* are not selective. You are anal-retentive."

Guy is looking back and forth between us, clearly wishing he'd been given the four-top table across the aisle instead.

"I'll just have the special," I say, not really caring right now what my meal will be.

"That's it? You're only having the special?" Todd was never one to make a restaurant experience simple, and at this point I'm not here for the food. "You know, I read in a restaurant insider's book one time that the special is often something the chef is trying to get rid of—"

"Guy, I tell you what. Surprise me. Bring me whatever you think I would like."

Guy looks confused. "Madam, I cannot know what you would prefer."

"Look, Guy, really, just bring me an appetizer and an entrée. I'm sure it will be what I'm looking for." I hand him the menu and motion for him to leave with my hand, as if waving away a gnat.

"So, still have your little food issues, eh?" Dining out with Todd was often an exercise in indecision. No matter what he finally ordered—after painful deliberation—it was rarely to his stringent specifications.

"Claire, they're not 'food issues.' I just happen to know what I want. So sue me."

I look over at Jack, who hasn't appeared this relaxed since . . . well, since . . . well, since I can't even remember, it's been so long. He and Julia are freely chatting. Their drinks are delivered, and I see her offer a taste of her little tropical-looking concoction to Jack, who willingly partakes.

I cannot believe I am watching my husband—*my husband*, for God's sake—sharing fucking tiki cocktails with this chick. I want to kill him. Or her. Kill her and club him. Then grab him by his still luxuriant hair back to the past, back to a time when he would have chuckled at some witty repartee of *mine*, then sipped from *my* drink. Or sipped my drink from my mouth as he kissed me. Jesus, did he ever do something as sensual as that with me? Surely that's how we once were. That's when it hits me: I am here dining with the man who holds the key to my memory bank. It's time to crack open the vault.

"So, Todd. Where else did we have sex that was bold and bawdy besides an elevator?"

Todd, politely sipping his martini, spits his drink out. "Claire, did you just ask me what I thought you asked me?"

"Todd. I have to know whether there's something wrong with me or if it's Jack. You see, I think I *used* to love sex. I think it *used* to be something I looked forward to. But honestly, I can't remember one good fuck I've had in my whole life anymore, and it scares me."

I stare at my champagne flute and spin the stem between my fingers out of nervous habit.

"I'm approaching forty years of age, and I'm married to a man who is gleefully engaging in clever conversation with a woman who obviously has designs on him, while I surreptitiously dine around the corner from him, feigning that I am having a wonderful time in this painfully romantic restaurant with a man I once thought I would marry, and I'm really very confused." I feel tears hovering behind my eyeballs, but I'm damned if I'll let them surface.

"So you see, Todd, I feel like I'm an amnesiac. Like I'm Gilligan, and I got hit on the head with a coconut, and now I'm trying to piece together what the hell happened, and somehow I have decided that you are my Skipper and *you* are going to be a vital tool in my figuring out whether I am doomed to be a sexless middle-aged hag, left to hover anxiously over my brood of needy children, or whether I am going to rediscover that I am a woman with needs and wants and desires and . . . and . . . and—"

"Claire Mooney. Doolittle." He covers his mouth, recognizing the lapse in neglecting to use my married name. "I cannot believe that sex to you has become this thing of the past, like teenage acne, or pulling all-nighters to study for exams. Claire, baby, that's not good!"

"I know, I know," I moan. "It's just that something happened along the way, and I missed out on the whole thing, and I don't know how it happened because didn't I used to be a horny little thing?"

Guy arrives with our appetizers just in time to hear that last sentence. He looks at me with renewed interest, now that he knows I used to be horny, I guess. I want to ask him for a magnifying glass, as I'm having a hard time finding the actual food on my plate, but I don't think he'd be amused. I tap my glass for round two, and Guy slips away with my empty.

"Okay, Claire. I'm gonna give this to you fast, because if I start really thinking about it, I may just ravage you over the dinner table, and that might draw the attention of Jack and Julia over there, which I know would be a bad thing. So here goes. We did it on the

beach. In broad daylight. Now, granted, it was a se-
cluded little half-moon of sand in Costa Rica, and
even if we did get caught we wouldn't know a soul, so
we figured it wasn't that big a deal. We did it in my office, with my secretary outside the door obliviously
typing away. We did it in a baggage area at Dulles airport, just before one of your Washington-to-Paris
flights—I didn't want you to arrive in gay Paree with
your mind on anyone but me. We did it in Rock Creek
Park, both day and night. We did it just before closing
time at the National Zoo. We did it on the fifty-yard line
of the stadium at school. We did it in your car. In my
car. In a rental car. In a barn. In a field. In the woods—
the poison ivy was worth it, by the way. Oh, and we
did it in a glassed-in elevator on Capitol Hill. Twice.

"So . . . tell me about this sexless life you've led?" he
finishes.

I am speechless. Truly speechless. The last time I
was left without words was when my tonsils were ex-
tracted back in 1975.

"Jesus, Todd. I didn't really think I was a slut! I just
thought—"

"You weren't a slut! We were in love. We were adventuresome. We were experimental. We were having *fun*!"

I look at him, pondering this notion. Sex, fun. Sex,
fun. After all this time I've learned to equate sex with
work. Sex, chore. Sex, chore.

"Claire—do you honestly not remember any of
those times?"

I'm starting to wonder if maybe I did a little too
much partying in my youth. Maybe my brain cells
were embalmed in too much grain alcohol or Jell-O
shooters from all of those fraternity parties. But no, I
think it's more than that.

"You know what? Slowly but surely I think I am figuring it all out. And one of the things I have deduced

is that you really hurt me when you left me the way you did."

Guy is back with my drink (thank goodness) and some soup he decided I would enjoy. It looks a bit murky. I nod my appreciation and continue, swatting a determined mosquito away from my face. Guy looks like he doesn't want to leave as he reaches his ear toward our conversation, trying to glean more information about this once-horny woman with the broken heart. My blistering look dismisses him readily.

"So, I'm starting to figure out what happened in my mind. It must have been how I responded to such unadulterated rejection. By you! The person I thought loved me so much!"

"Claire, I did love you—"

"Zip it, Todd. I'm trying to make my point here," I say as I drag my clasped index finger and thumb across my lips. "So after that, I felt this enormous sense of rejection."

I take a sip of the soup. It tastes interesting, in an I-didn't-choose-this kind of way. I can't help but wonder what strange ingredients might be in it. At that thought I put my soupspoon down. "And so by the time Jack came along, I had completely altered how I approached relationships. No longer was I just sweet old innocent Claire. Well, judging by your descriptions of our behavior, perhaps innocent is stretching things a bit. But anyhow, I took a new approach.

"With Jack, I didn't want to give him a chance to reject me. I yielded to him whenever I had to, sometimes in such subtle ways I didn't even realize I was doing it. But eventually it became the way things were. Jack over Claire. Claire subsumed by Jack's needs. And, of course, Jack had a lot of emotional needs. There were things that happened—"

I look over at Jack, having briefly forgotten why we were there. He is now—honestly, I kid you not—cupping Julia's hands in his across the dinner table. Cupping her fucking French-manicured fingernails. She looks like she's crying or something. Crying. At the Blue Door, a way too expensive restaurant in Miami Beach at which my husband is footing the bill! And she's crying, and he's cupping her hands to comfort her.

That bitch! I know a calculated manipulation when I see one.

Todd notices what has distracted me from our gut-flaying conversation. "Claire, don't say a thing. Just let it play out."

But I'm getting agitated. It was bad enough when Jack was just sitting across the table from her, engrossed in conversation. But now there's been physical contact. Hand-to-hand contact. Which had better change, before there's some plain old-fashioned hand-to-hand combat.

"So, Claire, to switch the subject a little bit. You mean to tell me that you and old Jacko haven't had sex in a lot of unusual places?"

My face must be turning ten shades of crimson at that question, judging by the heat emanating from my cheeks; I feel as if my privacy is being invaded. Somehow, how Jack and I have had sex seems to be my business, not Todd's. Of course, the sad truth of it is, I'm really taxing my memory in order to tap into that obscure corner of it that houses the information about my and Jack's mutual sex life.

Why is that? I wonder. Why is there this enormous lump of gray matter that has been taken up by mundane bullshit that consumes our lives? Who drives whom to soccer. Who takes so-and-so to the doctor.

Who attends back-to-school night for one while the other attends a parent-teacher conference. Who fed the dog. Who am I supposed to bake brownies for—the kindergarten or the fourth grade? Come to think of it, I can remember the vivid minutiae of Madonna's Scottish Highlands wedding—courtesy of *People* magazine—and I don't even know the woman, yet I can't remember intimate details about my relationship with my husband. What the hell is wrong with me?

Now I am thinking so hard I'm practically inducing an aneurysm on myself in order to try to reclaim memories of something that must—at the time—have been fun, must have gotten my pulse going. Now about the only thing throbbing is my aching head.

Guy shows up with our entrées. The tilapia smells wonderful; too late, I wish I'd just ordered that. Guy presents me with some Brazilian-Indian-fusion lamb dish with basmati polenta or something equally mushy-looking that certainly is a dish I would never have chosen myself; I'll give old Guy that much.

I've no real appetite for my dinner now. I'm concentrating so hard on trying to remember good times with Jack. But the good times are not surfacing. Instead I'm recalling a night not long ago in which Jack nagged me ceaselessly for sex, and I flatly refused—I was furious with him after he'd criticized my managerial skills for the umpteenth time. Easy for him to fault, because it's not up to him to organize five children's complex lives.

I remember drifting off to sleep. Jack had the television on, the Weather Channel's *Storm Stories*. As some weather victim droned on about the tornado that nearly killed him, I felt the bed come to life. Gradually at first came the faint vibrations. Initially I did not know what was happening, but the shaking motion was actually making me feel seasick. Then I realized what was going on. I was being lulled to sleep (more like rocked awake) by the uneasy rhythm of Jack's deliberate expression of "punishment": he was servicing himself right next to me, causing the bed to rattle as if he'd inserted a quarter in a cheap motel bed to start the magic-fingers machine. Nothing like rubbing my nose in what he viewed as my own inadequacies, or frigidity, or whatever his misconception was.

I look over at him now and feel my rage igniting, as he looks downright lovey-dovey with Julia. I think of the last time he gazed admiringly toward me, and again, the only thing that comes to mind is our wedding day. For me, Jack's rare recent proclamations of love smack as all too duplicitous, considering they're proffered only under the preorgasmic duress in which most every man's brain is temporarily poisoned by overly ambitious emotions.

But what I see in the way he's acting toward Julia Juilliard certainly isn't that preorgasmic lip service. Now, maybe it's *pre*-preorgasmic. Maybe his look is designed to get him in the door—or down her pants, as the case may be—so that he can be orgasmic. With her. Or worse yet, maybe it's *post*orgasmic. My stomach curdles at the thought.

"Why is it I care about this when I can barely muster up even a feigned interest in sex with the man?" I blurt out.

"You say something, Claire?" Todd is busily munching away at his meal, separating out flecks of spices he finds objectionable before enthusiastically thrusting his fork into his mouth.

Oh, man, did I say that out loud?

Luckily, Todd is so wrapped up in his basil-free tomato concassé—whatever the hell that is—that he doesn't pick up on my little slip. I bite my lip to suppress the tears that are lying in wait like a burglar lurking in the shadows, waiting for the best moment to strike.

I notice some movement over by Jack's table. He's standing up, as is she. How strange—they haven't even been served their entrées yet. He's moving toward her, his arms outstretched. I can see the reflection of tears in her eyes just as Jack's body envelops hers, his arms wrapped tightly around her, stroking her back with one hand, her hair with the other.

My God! Does he have no sense of propriety? Right here, on the terrace of this restaurant, fondling the woman?

Julia sobs—loudly enough for other patrons to turn and stare—and Jack bends his head down and whispers gently into her ear. The man is whispering sweet nothings into her ear. That's it. I cannot take another second of this betrayal.

Guy scurries by with a Bloody Mary on a tray. Without thinking I stand up, reach for it, and march over to where the lovers are entwined.

"Jack Doolittle, how *dare* you, you miserable fucking two-timing sneaky little bastard!"

With that, I dump the drink over his head and reach forward to land a slap across his face, the crack of which can readily be heard throughout the now-silent restaurant.

A busboy walking nearby with a pitcher of water sets it on the table and rushes away.

"Claire?" The look on Jack's sneaky face reminds me of Tripod's guilty mug when I catch him eating out of the cat litter. He knows beyond a question of a doubt that I have busted his sorry tight marathon-man butt.

chapter Twenty-two

The next thing I know, Todd is next to me. Through the blunted curtain of tears in my eyes, I can barely make out what is happening, but Todd is wrapping his arms around me, whispering indecipherables, something about always taking care of me, as I sob in racking, heaving, publicly embarrassing sobs just outside of the restaurant, where we were readily escorted by the restaurant manager following my little outburst.

The manager appears to be talking with Jack, offering up a towel to wipe off the Bloody Mary (ha! They should rename it Bloody Jack), which has stained his crisp white shirt. I don't know what's happened to Julia; nor do I care.

"There, there, Claire, it's okay." Todd is gently scratching my head in a way I used to love. "*I'll* be there for you, baby."

"Hey, buddy, get your hands off my wife!"

Jack is picking a strange time to be proprietary toward me.

"Excuse me?" Todd is clearly ready to pick a fight, despite his proclaimed aversion to belligerence.

"I said, get your hands off my wife. Now."

I can feel Todd tense up, and I sense that those flying fists he'd wanted to avoid are on the immediate horizon.

"Todd, wait, no." I hold him back and turn to look at Jack, the corrosive pain of knowing my husband is in love with another woman now beginning to eat away at my logical mind.

I turn to face Jack, getting my face right up into his.

"And *you*. I thought we took a vow to love, honor, and respect each other. You call that respect, conducting an affair with that woman? Taking her out to eat at one of the finest restaurants in Miami, safe in the knowledge that your clueless wife was home taking care of the monotonies of your existence so that you could get some nooky on the side? Is that how little you regard me? After all that we've been through together? You don't even think you owe me the decency of the truth?"

Jack looks bewildered.

"What in the hell are you talking about, Claire? And just who is this man who's got his hands all over you?"

"This man happens to be Todd. My old fiancé. Well, sort of. And I'm talking about you holding hands, hugging that . . . that . . . that trollop—"

"Trollop? Are you referring to Julia Julliard?"

"No, I'm talking about Janet Jackson. Of course I'm talking about her. There was no mistaking your feelings toward her and vice versa back there. Don't play stupid on my account, because I know now what's been going on. Ooooh, wait'll I tell Kat how wrong she was about you."

"If you know what's been going on, then maybe you can tell me, because I haven't the slightest notion."

It really burns me up that Jack is still pretending he's the picture of innocence, even though he was caught with his hands lovingly fondling the merchandise.

"You wouldn't let me join you on this business trip because you'd intended to have a romantic lovers' tryst with that home-wrecking homebuilder—"

"Claire, Claire, Claire. You've got it all wrong." Jack really looks exasperated. "I'm here on business."

"Oh, yeah, I saw what kind of business you were up to. Monkey business."

"Claire, we've been *working* all weekend. In fact, dinner tonight was here only because we were supposed to meet a client. But he canceled at the last minute."

I remember the empty place setting at their table. Shit.

"We decided to go ahead and enjoy a dinner paid for by the firm anyhow. I wasn't exactly holding hands with Julia, Claire. I was comforting her as she related to me a touching story that I could tell was very painful to her—"

"Touching, my ass. The only thing that was touching was your skin to hers. I saw it with my own eyes. And the hand touching led to the hug, and we all know what that was leading up to—"

"I have to warn you that you have made a complete fool of yourself, and you're digging yourself deeper into a hole now."

Jack tries to put his hand on my shoulder, but I flinch and shrug it away.

"The reason I got up to hug Julia was to *comfort* her. She was explaining to me why she'd taken off time from work. Because her twin sister died unexpectedly in a car accident, and it had left her shaken to her core. Julia had learned about Colin's death—"

I can't believe I'm hearing Jack even mention Colin's name. He's said nothing of him in so many years, it's as if a ghost has been hovering over us all this time and only now is revealing himself.

"So Julia knew I could understand her grief. It's the first time she's been able to bring herself to talk about it with anyone. Even her parents are still too heartbroken to discuss her sister's death. I hugged Julia because not only am I her boss, but also her friend. And friends lend comfort to each other in times of need."

I am beginning to feel a little bit foolish for leaping to the conclusion I'd leaped to, but that last line of his doesn't sit well with me.

"They do, do they? So, friends comfort friends in times of need? Well, what about husbands comforting wives? Or wives who try to comfort husbands, but get rejected? And after a while the rejection has left a heavily calloused veneer, covering up any feelings of goodwill that might have once existed. What about that?"

I look around me, a handful of those beautiful people milling about, all without a care or an extra pound among them, and suddenly I feel so tired and so out of the energy to fight.

Then I glance at Jack, and for the first time in ages I see a glimmer of an emotion other than anger trying to reveal itself behind his usual poker face.

"Claire . . ." Jack's face has turned ashen. His hands are suddenly clutching his chest. "Claire, I think I'm—"

"Are you okay?"

"I think I'm having a heart attack." He barely breathes the words as he slumps to the floor.

"Oh, my God, somebody, is there a doctor here? We need an ambulance, hurry!" Instinctually I scream out for help.

Suddenly I see Jack as the vulnerable young man who long ago lost his father prematurely to a heart attack. The notion of my losing Jack, of the kids losing their father, has me frozen in fear. Meanwhile, Todd is pacing nearby, muttering something about only know-ing the Heimlich maneuver or to *stop, drop and roll* when a woman, a doctor, dining nearby, comes over to help.

Within minutes an emergency crew has arrived, and Jack and I are rushed to the hospital in an ambu-lance, leaving Todd and Julia to awkwardly follow.

Please, please, please, let Jack be okay. If anything's going to kill him, it's got to be me, not his heart, I whisper.

I wait in the ER as various tests are administered to Jack. He's hooked up to monitors and they're drawing blood and he looks so weak, so vulnerable, com-pared to how he looked just a few hours earlier. It's certainly a humbling moment when someone you love is facing what could be death. Someone you love but haven't particularly liked in a long time, I remind myself.

The nurse finally beckons me into Jack's cubicle. I hold his hand and stroke his forehead, which is still sticky from the drink I tossed on him, and listen to the steady *beep-beep-beep* of the heart monitor.

"Claire, we need to talk." Jack's raspy voice sounds weary.

I hold my finger to his lips. "Shhh, not now. We'll have plenty of time to talk later. Right now just rest."

I realize that this is the first time that Jack has let his guard down in front of me since we learned of Colin's illness. I haven't seen this overtly vulnerable side to Jack in so long, I barely recognize it.

Eventually the attending physician comes in with the diagnosis.

The doctor—I squint to read his hospital ID, which says, MIGUEL RODRIGUEZ—is old and stumpy, with big bushy gray eyebrows that curl over into his line of vi-sion. I want to take some personal grooming scissors to him, but then I remember why he's here and suppress the urge.

"Mr. Doolittle, you're a very lucky man."

"What is it?"

"Well, despite your family history of heart problems, your heart is in great shape. I'd say you're healthy as a horse."

"Then what happened to him tonight?" I ask.

"Mrs. Doolittle, it appears your husband simply had an anxiety attack. He's going to be fine."

My legs are weak as relief floods over me.

"I'd suggest, Mr. Doolittle, that you take it easy and maybe seek out some counseling, try to work out whatever stress is affecting you so severely. But you're free to go now."

The doctor hands us a pile of paperwork we'll need in order to be released from the hospital. The nurse comes in and detaches Jack from all the things he's hooked up to. He gets dressed, and we settle up the paperwork.

"Look, we obviously have some talking to do." Jack looks worn out.

"It can wait."

Jack takes my hand in his and fixes his gaze directly on mine. "No, it can't. But first let me see Julia off in a cab. This has probably been one night she'd like to forget about. Where are you staying?"

"I'm at the Four Seasons. Room eight-fourteen."

"I'll meet you there in half an hour."

In front of the hospital, Todd says, "Geez, we didn't even get to have dessert." So like him to make light of the situation. "Although I'm glad your husband's all right. I guess. Fact is, I suppose I gave up the chance for dessert a long, long time ago."

I give a small laugh, wiped out from the drama of

the evening. "Yes, I'm afraid you did. But look at it this way—at least we're friends now, right?"

"Yeah, friends. And if it weren't for you, I wouldn't be trying to grow up and become a father, finally."

"You might want to consider working on your role as husband while you're at it. For that matter, I guess we all have some spousal relationships to improve upon."

"Well, thanks, anyhow, for putting up with me. And for forgiving me for being such a selfish bastard with you."

"You know, maybe this will work out well for both of us, eventually. You might just reclaim that missing son of yours, and maybe I'll find out that there is sex—and friendship—after Ward Cleaver." Todd looks at me inquisitively. "Oh, nothing. Just a little inside joke of mine," I clarify.

"Good-bye, Claire Bear."

"Good-bye, Todd. Stay in touch, would ya? And remember, ix-nay with the 'Bear.' "

We hug for a moment; my cab pulls up and I hop in. As the taxi pulls away, I don't dare look back at him. I'm tired of looking backward.

Chapter Twenty-three

I arrive at my room before Jack gets there. I turn on the television, scanning the channels till I get to Lifetime, my favorite channel when I'm feeling maudlin. I'm not sure what to expect when Jack gets here, but I'm half hoping that finally we will put all of our cards on the table to play the next hand.

I step into my spacious bathroom—the Four Seasons knows that a nice bathroom can make all the difference—aghast at the face staring back at me from the mirror. My mascara-smudged eyes, my face puffy from crying. Why do faces get bloated from excessive tears? Do the tears backlog in your sinuses, making them swell up? Hmmm. One of life's great mysteries.

As I survey the damage, I notice that my hair sort of resembles the pile of hair accrued when I clean out the brushes at home. I at least have to do something about that, so I resort to my hundred strokes, which I've neglected lately anyhow. Clearly that hundred-stroke thing isn't doing much good for my hair, but at least it's soothing, and right now I need something to calm my jangled nerves.

I hear a soft knock on the door. Through the peephole I see Jack, my view of him distorted, which is nothing new, as it's been that way for quite a while now anyhow. The contrast between Jack as I see him—still handsome, with just a hint of gray at the temples, and those earnest eyes, his youthful physique nicely emphasized in a Brooks Brothers suit and a crisp oxford shirt (albeit stained now)—and as I *perceive* him, as sort of a stern disciplinarian killjoy, is striking. I will say I always liked Jack in a suit, though. It lends him an air of authority—in a good way, not a Ward way—and manliness.

I open the door, and we stand there looking at each other, unable to find words to suit the moment.

"Claire, I . . . I—"

"Jack—"

"Claire, I feel I owe you some sort of apology."

"No, Jack, I do—"

He puts his finger to my lips to quiet me, then takes a deep breath.

In the background on Lifetime, the violin music swells as some star-crossed lovers finally find each other. It seems silly, those strains playing against the backdrop of our own melodrama.

"I know that things looked suspicious to you from your perspective, Claire, but I want you to know that *nothing* has ever happened between me and Julia. Our relationship is purely professional. We are colleagues, and, well, yes, we're friends, too, but that's it. Nothing else. I promise."

"So, why were you so adamant about my not joining you for this trip, unless you wanted to get away from me—"

"To tell you the truth, yes, I did kind of want to get away from you. You haven't been very pleasant company lately, you know."

"*I* haven't? Are you kidding me? What about *you*?"

Jack stares at the ground as he traces a pattern in the rug with the toe of his shoe. "What do you mean?"

"Jesus, haven't you noticed what a grouchy middle-aged curmudgeon you've become? Haven't you ever noticed that the kids and I are the only ones laughing in the house? I think the last time you laughed at anything was the 'The Sponge' episode of *Seinfeld*, and that was, what, a decade ago? There's something to that old adage, 'All work and no play makes Jack a dull boy.' Not only are you no fun, but you make life no fun for the rest of us."

I bend over a little, looking up into his face to try to catch his eye. He's still focused on whatever he's got going on with the carpet. Or uninterested in hearing what I feel compelled to finally say to him.

"Jack, whatever happened to your passion for life? Whatever happened to that man who could have fun while still taking care of his life's responsibilities? Whatever happened to that great sexual tension we once enjoyed, when even if we were to have a little spat, we'd compensate for it afterward in bed? Somewhere along the line we traded in that sexual tension for just plain old tension. And now there is always an undercurrent of friction. It's not fun. It's stressful. For me, for us, for the kids. There's no longer any fun when it comes to you."

Jack opens his mouth to talk, but his voice falters. "Wow. I didn't know I was that bad. I didn't know how miserable you were—"

"Miserable isn't the right word. Well, maybe it is. Well, how about unhappy? Or disappointed? Or confused? But understand, Jack, if this is all there is left, then I'll settle for it. Because I love you. But the thing is, I know there used to be so much more, and I can't believe we can't somehow reclaim that in our lives. I can't quite say how things came to be like this, but I have my theories—"

"You have your *theories*? Well, then, Mrs. Guru, why don't you give me your armchair psychologist's view of what is wrong," he says, his face pinched. Jack's definitely on the defensive.

"Okay, I will, as long as we're putting everything out in the open. Here goes: you never came back to me after Colin died. When your brother died, the Jack I knew and loved died as well. Not all of you. But a big part of you. The part of you that was funny and frisky and adventuresome and forgiving and gentle and loving and . . . and thoughtful. And alive."

Dammit, my eyes are once again filling with tears. Is this what I should be telling a man who just left the hospital after suffering an anxiety attack?

"Go on." Jack lies down on the bed, still in his suit. He even has his shoes on the bed—something Jack would yell at the kids for doing.

"When Colin died, you were like a wounded animal who retreats into a cave to heal. When you tucked away into your cave, I thought I was doing you a favor by giving you a broad swath of space. I yielded to you at every turn. I tried so hard, Jack—I tried so hard to ease your pain. But you wouldn't let me. So since I couldn't do that, I just did what I thought you wanted me to do. I didn't want to make any waves, create any more hardship for you.

"And remember, I already had a huge fear of loss, having been so hurt by Todd when he abruptly dumped me. I felt so inadequate after that. And I simply could not take losing someone I loved so madly, so passionately, again."

I pace the floor between the bed and the wardrobe, not knowing what else to do with myself as I spill my guts. "I worked hard to mold myself to your needs. And by yielding to you as I did, I enabled you to burrow into your grief and become entrenched in it. So rather than seeking solace from me, you rejected me, and I foolishly allowed this to continue unabated until it became the status quo in our relationship. As time went on, I just never let you know what I needed, what was important to me. And I guess you weren't paying attention to it, so we fell into a bad habit. All along I kept fooling myself that my old Jack would return one day. Then, by the time the kids came, I could barely cope with getting through the *day*, let alone try to rectify our worsening problems."

Jack looks at me, his brow knitted intensely, unable to disguise the pain he feels at hearing my words.

"Maybe some of what you're saying is true, Claire. Maybe I did let Colin's death drag me down. And maybe my fear of losing yet another loved one—first my dad, then my brother—created in me an impenetrable barrier, to save me from ever feeling that anguish of lost love again. But I think you have to take some credit, here, too."

I sit down at the foot of the bed as I listen to him speak, my own eyebrows knitted with worry, wondering where he's going with his point.

"For a long time, Claire, I have felt invisible to you, used by you. Like I was there to serve as your source of income, and maybe the needed tool with which to reproduce children, but nothing more. I really started to think that I was worth more to you dead than alive."

"That's not true—"

"Think about it. You rarely express any positive emotions toward me. How many times have you told me you loved me in the past five years?"

"Wait a second, buster. That goes both ways. How many times have you told me *you* loved *me*?"

"I always tell you that when we make love—"

"Oh, please. Give me a break. Declarations of love under the influence of testosterone do not count. Did you ever tell me you loved me after I gave birth to any of your children? Have you ever told me you loved me when I've had a bad day? Have you ever told me you loved me just because it's lunchtime and you thought you'd call to tell me you loved me? That's when the words 'I love you' count. Not when you're horny and think those platitudes will turn me on. Because you know what? The biggest turn-on is when you are who you used to be—that kind, fun, happy-go-lucky kind of guy who *did* do those things."

Neither of us is looking at the other. Instead, I'm staring blankly at the television. There's a commercial for herpes medicine featuring a wholesome, happy man smiling because he can suppress his disease with just one pill a day.

I wish there were a pill to make our problems go away so easily.

Jack sits up and turns off the TV. Silence permeates every molecule in the room.

"Come here." He motions for me to sit on his lap. Oh, God, I am not built for sitting in laps anymore. I might cause him bodily harm. I hesitate, but he insists.

I settle into Jack's lap with my back toward him; he wraps his arms around me and begins to cry silently. So softly it's almost imperceptible.

My heart aches knowing how much pain he must be in. I want to say something to make it all better, but I think his tears are more therapeutic than my words could ever be. We sit in silence, his forehead pressed up against the back of my head, my hair absorbing his copious tears.

Finally, he speaks. "Claire, how did we let this happen? How did we grow to take each other for granted like this?"

I shake my head. "I don't know, Jack. All I know is that somewhere along the line, the assertive, self-confident woman I was became overshadowed by the subsumed version of me who just let you be the guide. But you were in no condition to be the guide; that's the thing. I needed to lead you then, and I didn't. I was so afraid of your withdrawing your love from me, so I just went along trying to fit my puzzle piece exactly into yours, making sure there were no jagged edges that would not correspond, thus giving you the chance to try to fit your piece elsewhere. Excuse the pun. And eventually I grew to resent you for it. I know that makes so little sense in retrospect—"

"And I in turn shut you out of the most important part of my life. And by shutting you out, I shut everyone, including myself, out. I guess I thought the pain would be less intense; I don't know. And maybe it was. But maybe I've needed to get through the pain to be able to feel again. Only I didn't let myself. And maybe at some point I just became a hardened version of me. Not exactly the man you fell in love with, I suppose."

"No, more like the man June fell in love with."

"Who's June?"

"Oh, nothing, nothing at all."

I look at Jack for the first time in years with something akin to real love in my eyes.

"You know, they said it was for better or for worse, didn't they?"

He laughs. "Who'd have thought it would get this bad?"

I scooch next to Jack on the bed and lean over, facing him, to really hug him.

"I love you, Claire Doolittle. And I always have, ever

since that night we met and you did tequila shots and kept up with me. You know that, don't you?"

"We've come a long way since then, haven't we?"

"It's not too late to fix things, is it?"

"It's never too late. Maybe this is what we've needed to be doing all along—talking *with* each other, not *at* each other."

"Claire?"

"Huh?"

"Do you still love me?"

"I very much love Jack Doolittle. Now, Ward Cleaver, that's another story altogether."

"What are you talking about with June and Ward?"

"Oh, never mind, I'll tell you another time. How about we just hold each other tight?"

"I thought you'd never ask."

"Are you gonna leave your jacket and shoes on?"

He laughs and kicks off his shoes and settles in, with me safely in the harbor of his embrace, drifting off to the deepest sleep I've had in ages.

Chapter Twenty-four

Dawn invades the room very early, since once again I neglected to draw the curtains last night. For a woman who rarely gets to sleep in, I sure don't take the necessary precautions when the opportunity arises.

I wake to the feeling of Jack's warm hands working their way beneath my dress, his unmistakable desire pressed insistently against me from behind.

I turn my head toward him, and we kiss, tenderly, with actual feeling behind it, not the rote chore of old. I reach behind to unbuckle Jack's belt and shift down his pants. Wordlessly he slips inside of me, and finally the rhythm of old takes hold of us, and I'm overwhelmed with such emotion, such raw feeling, so elated not to be sleeping with Ward Cleaver, but making love with Jack Doolittle, the true love of my life.

Now, the old me—of a few short hours ago, as opposed to the *old, old* me, when I was young and sexy and full of vitality—would cynically question Jack's motives.

I mean, come on. What is it about men that triggers

this knee-jerk (or make that an appendage a little to the north) response that invariably elicits the same emotional response: the need for immediate sexual gratification? It could be the queen's Diamond Jubilee celebration on TV and they'd want to fuck. Hell, it could be a midnight clearance sale at Mattress Discounters and they'd want to wham-bam it. So that Jack wants to celebrate our little breakthrough collaborative in this way is to be expected, I guess. Me, I'd probably be more wont to crack a bottle of champagne and shout to the mountains: *Halle-fucking-lujah! Ding, dong, the witch is dead!*

I guess these are cultural differences between men and women, though. Nevertheless, joy of joys, for the first time in a long time I don't find the act even remotely off-putting.

We drift back to sleep, only to be woken by a pounding at the door. Christ, doesn't anyone sleep around here?

I jump out of bed and run to the door, peering through the peephole at the distorted view of two policemen. I immediately open the door, completely forgetting that Jack's lying half-naked in the bed five feet away.

"Christ, Claire, what the hell are you doing?" Jack yells at me.

Oh, my God, is that Ward I hear barking at me? I can see he's going to need some long-term conditioning if we're to fix his character flaws. I throw him a severe look and he turns sheepish.

"I'm sorry, honey," he says. "What's going on?"

"Ma'am." Officer Number One, a José Lopez, tips his hat at me. "We're looking for Claire Doolittle."

I blanch, completely clueless about what they'd want from me.

"I'm Claire Doolittle," I say nervously.

"Ma'am, we received a call yesterday evening reporting Claire Doolittle missing," Officer Lopez says. He glances over at Jack suspiciously.

I look at him, perplexed. "I'm not missing! I'm right here. Who on earth reported me missing?"

Officer Number Two, whose badge indicates he goes by the name of Raul Sandovar, rifles through his notepad. "It says here that someone by the name of Mariah Mooney placed a call at nine forty-one last evening, claiming that her daughter disappeared suddenly while in Miami, that she did not answer her mobile phone, that she was certain her daughter ran into foul play; she was someone who never left home and was very inexperienced in the ways of the world. She said she tried to reach her daughter on her mobile for several hours after hearing her screaming at someone to stop, but to no avail."

I close my eyes in complete denial that my mother would do something so incredibly stupid. And embarrassing. Someone who never leaves home? Inexperienced in the ways of the world? Clearly she's forgotten that I spent my youth flying all over the damned world.

"Officer Sandovar, I must apologize for my mother's impulsivity. She has a vivid imagination sometimes. I've been here the whole time! My battery died on my mobile phone and I got, uh, caught up in things with my husband here." I motion to Jack, who's now yanking his pants up.

"Can you show me some identification, Mrs. Doolittle?" Officer Sandover asks.

I rifle through my purse to find my wallet and show the cops proof of my existence. Officer Lopez radios in to dispatch that he has indeed found his missing person.

By now Jack has gotten up and is standing by my side. "I'm curious, officers," he says. "Doesn't it take, like, forty-eight hours to trigger a search for a missing person?"

But then it dawns on me. "Jack, I know what must have happened."

I briefly relate what occurred to my phone yesterday, complete with my screaming out for the phone to stop falling.

"So Daddy was in the air force with some guy who's some big muckety-muck in the police department here," I say. "Mother must've made him call this guy last night, and when she still couldn't reach me this morning, he felt they'd better track me down."

"I'm so sorry they sent you on a wild-goose chase," Jack says, escorting the cops to the door, showing them out.

He hangs the DO NOT DISTURB sign on the outside doorknob and closes it behind him, making certain to lock it.

"You trying to protect me or something, Mr. Doolittle?" I ask mischievously.

"Do you need protecting, Mrs. Doolittle?" He smiles, biting me on the nose.

"Oh, I don't know," I tease him. "Maybe I need saving, though."

"Jack Doolittle, to the rescue," he says as he pulls my dress over my head and walks me backward to the bed.

The next time we wake up I realize we forgot one crucial little measure: to take precautions and use birth control.

"Fuck, Jack!" I sit up in bed with a start, amazed at my unbelievable stupidity.

"You want to, again?" Jack says blearily.

"No, Jack—we didn't use anything!"

Jack sits up next to me. "We didn't, did we?"

"Oh, my God. We can't have another baby," I moan. "I'm already enough of a mess with the five kids we've got!"

I start to think back to my last period, hoping there's been plenty of lag time to get me over the fertility hump. Okay, it started on a Friday afternoon, I remember that, because I was out for drinks with Kat before heading home. It was long before Kat started doing my boss. Before I knew about this Miami thing. Hmm, according to my calculations it's been slightly more than three weeks. Oh, Lord, let's hope my fertility is on the low end of the bell curve, because if so, I should be okay.

"We may have just dodged a major bullet here," I tell Jack.

"Well, the damage has been done, hasn't it?" he asks curiously, hoping that the rest of his weekend won't be vexed by a lack of birth control.

I look at him warily. "At the very least we need to get something. I don't want to take any more chances."

Jack gets up and starts getting dressed.

"So what's going on now?" I ask him.

He looks at his watch. "I guess it's too late to fit a run in this morning. I need to get back and get changed. I have a client I've got to meet with at lunch," he says. "You want to meet back here this afternoon?"

"Sure," I say. "But we still have more to talk about, you know."

I hate to reintroduce the ghost of marriage past, but if things truly are going to improve with us, we're going to need to straighten some important things out.

"I know, Claire." He leans over and kisses me on the forehead. "But in the meantime, why don't you go and maybe get a massage or something, unwind a little bit, okay?"

I surreptitiously look around me to be sure that I'm still planted on terra firma, because I don't think I've ever had my husband suggest something so indulgent for me in the past fifteen years. Of course, I don't dare tell him that I did the room service special already yesterday, and that it cost as much as dinner last night.

"That's a great idea." I smile. There are gonna be plenty more massages where that came from, if I have anything to say about it.

I call my mother as soon as Jack's left.

"Claire, my baby, thank God you're all right," my mother gushes into the phone.

"Mother, don't you think you overreacted a bit?"

"Overreacted? First I hear these loud noises and I can't understand what you're saying; then I hear you scream, 'Stop,' and the phone line goes dead. What else would a mother think?"

I ponder that for a second, and think how I'd react if I were calling one of my own girls and something like that happened. As much as I hate to admit it, I'd probably be equally paranoid.

"Well, I guess you've got a point, Mom," I say reluctantly.

"So, did Jack ever get hold of you?" she asks. "I thought you were with him already? What in the world have you been up to?"

"Yes, Mother, Jack and I found each other," I say. And we have found each other, in more ways than one, I think.

"You never even mentioned you were going away, Claire! I told you we were coming for a quick visit while we were in town, and imagine my surprise when I show up to find your in-laws there and you gallivanting around Miami! I have to find this out from virtual strangers?" She sniffs.

It completely escaped me that my parents had planned on stopping over.

"Oh, Mother, I'm sorry about that. I just totally forgot about your visit. Come off it, though, Candy and Dick are hardly strangers!"

"And you didn't even think to ask *me* to watch the kids?" she asks, wounded.

"Honestly, Mother, you never offered, and I didn't get the impression you wanted to," I say.

My mother mutters something about being more than happy to help out with the kids, why don't I ever ask her, blah, blah, blah. I'm not sure that she means it, but maybe I ought to just take her up on the offer sometime anyhow. I mean, how much could go wrong?

I get off the phone with Mother and get ready to go to the pool for a while. I test my cell phone, which amazingly has started working again. Must remember to clean with alcohol! Finally I head out for that R & R that Jack and Kat had urged on me.

Jack calls me after lunch and asks if I'd like to take a run with him. The honest answer is that I'd sooner have a root canal than run in ninety-degree heat, but then again, maybe it'll be good for me to work up a little sweat. Plus it's been fifteen years since I've gone running with Jack. I'm not so sure I have it in me.

"I don't think I can keep up with you," I say.

"I'll go slowly," he promises. "And we won't run very far."

Well, I did pack gym clothes in the unlikely event that I would have the time and desire to use the hotel's facilities, so I really have no excuse. Plus, I haven't bought any souvenirs to wrap with them as an alternative.

"Meet you out front in half an hour," I say.

* * *

I haven't run—except after very fast toddlers—in a long, long time. Before we start off, we spend about ten minutes stretching. I can't help but think of Jack yesterday with Julia and their stretch foreplay.

"You really don't think that Julia's got a thing for you?" I ask.

I haven't been a woman on the prowl since around the time of DC Mayor Marion Barry's famous crack bust (Remember that? "Bitch set me up!" Now *that* was a line for the ages), but I can still remember what it was like to set your crosshairs on a man, and unless I was sorely mistaken, Julia's AK-47 was aiming right at Jack's chest. Or lower.

Jack looks a little bit embarrassed.

"What?" I ask him.

"Well, uh, Julia tendered her resignation today," Jack tells me.

"She quit?" I can't believe my good fortune! Unless she's now planning to make it a full-time job to try to land my husband.

"Apparently Julia's intentions with me went a little beyond the professional," he says. "With her letter of resignation was a personal note to me declaring her feelings and explaining that she simply couldn't go on working for me knowing that I was apparently unattainable."

I'm outraged. "That little two-bit hussy!" I exclaim. "What on Earth gave her the impression that you were attainable before? You were married then; you're married now."

Jack shrugs, ever the clueless man. "I guess she read the handwriting on the wall after last night's scene?"

Hard to believe it was only last night that things between Jack and me erupted into such volcanic outrage. And here we are, about to go on a friendly jog together.

Jack holds up my leg as I stretch my quads and hamstrings, just like he did with Julia Julliard yesterday. I hesitate to admit that I spied on them, but I think it's better to get it all out in the open if we're going to pursue this newfound policy of honesty and all.

We start to run and I start to talk.

"I saw you two yesterday morning," I admit.

"Huh?"

"Running," I say. "I saw you running, then stretching, then sharing a little breakfast."

He looks at me, stunned. "And where else did you spy on me?"

"Nowhere else. That was my maiden voyage," I say, then pause for a moment, gathering my thoughts.

"You know, that killed me, watching you two. It reminded me of you and me, way back when. Before things, um, changed. Before our relationship became so stale. I was so jealous of how much you were enjoying her company. Because you haven't enjoyed my company in forever."

I wipe the hint of a tear away from the corner of my eye, and go on.

"I got to the point in our relationship where I felt like to you I was just an annoying little gnat flitting about your life, being not much more than a nuisance at which you swatted occasionally, but grew to simply ignore," I say. "So eventually this little gnat just started hating you for that. It wasn't till I saw you so happy and engaged with Julia that I realized how much we'd lost along the way. If I'm going to be completely honest, I didn't know if I could ever love you again—no, make that *like* you again—because you seemed to hate this gnat so much." I point at myself.

"Sweetie," Jack begins, "I never saw you like you were a gnat. I think it's just that I was very caught up in other things, and I knew you didn't need me to hold your hand, that you were perfectly capable of taking care of yourself, so I left you to it. Then you became so bitchy toward me that I really didn't enjoy being around you if I didn't have to."

"And that's when the charms of Julia Julliard became so tempting?"

"You *do* believe that I never did anything with her, don't you?"

"Well, yeah, but I also think you were tempted. I mean, here you are, this handsome, powerful man, almost an icon to a young woman in the workforce. And she looks up to you like you're something special—"

"Something you certainly didn't do," he interrupts.

"You got me there. But you sure didn't give me much reason to look at you as if you were something special. You were bogged down in your own swamp of misery; then you became so bossy and boring. You were like—"

"Oh, so this is where the Ward Cleaver thing comes in?" He starts to laugh. We're running through a crowd of people and he's laughing very loudly.

"Well, what I was going to say is that you were like my father instead of my husband," I say defensively. "But truthfully, yes, you did remind me a bit of, uh, Ward Cleaver."

I guess I don't have to tell him how very much.

We run in silence for a while, and I can't believe I'm actually running. It feels good employing my muscles in some form of physical exertion.

Jack stops and I stop next to him.

"Claire Doolittle," he says. "You're a nut, you know that?"

He leans forward and grabs me and kisses me in front of all of these strangers on the street.

Jack lifts his head up and looks me in the eye, his hands on my shoulders, arms outstretched. "So, we'll fix things, Claire, okay? And I promise I'll try to get rid of Ward Cleaver. Deal?"

That's all I ever wanted out of this, anyhow—to get rid of Ward and get Jack back.

chapter Twenty-five

The close of the weekend comes far too soon, and I find myself seated next to Jack in business class on the flight back home. He was able to change my flight and upgrade me. I think I'm now sitting in the seat meant to be occupied by Julia Julliard.

The flight attendant, a slight, Demi Moore look-alike whose glossy mahogany hair is eliciting all sorts of jealous feelings from me, seems to have more than a passing interest in my husband. She keeps asking if he needs anything; she even wiped at an invisible drip of something on his lapel a few minutes ago. Jack seems blissfully oblivious to her ministrations, though, as we're busy playing cards. How funny is that, that we're playing cards together? If someone had told me my weekend would resolve itself in so civil a manner I would have denied it vigorously. But here it is.

"Go fish," I say when Jack asks if I have any aces. I'm not a particularly good cardplayer, so I stick to the basics. "Got any queens?" I ask him.

"I'm looking at mine," he says. Oh, my God. Is this

my husband, being so kind and thoughtful toward me? It's like we've been propelled back to our dating days. Bring it on, baby!

I smile and lean forward to give Jack a quick kiss on the lips. I know how hard he's trying, so I appreciate it all the more. It can't be easy undoing years of surliness.

We return home to a scene of domestic serenity. The children are all in their rooms doing their homework. Candy and Dick (snicker, snicker) are playing canasta (who plays that game?) in the dining room. Even Tripod is sleeping soundly in his crate in the kitchen.

Okay, so who drugged my children and killed the dog?

"Claire, Jack! We didn't expect you back so soon!" Candy says, standing up and coming over to give us hugs.

It is weird, actually, that we've remained virtually incommunicado with our real lives this entire weekend (but for the bizarre incident with my mother), especially after I've been so obsessed with thinking I couldn't safely leave the kids with someone else for the past decade.

"So, did you have a great weekend?" Candy asks with a twinkle in her eyes. I wonder if she knew how desperately we needed some marital rehabilitation.

"It was wonderful," Jack says. "Thanks for holding down the fort, Mom."

"It was our pleasure," Dick pipes in.

"Were you surprised by Claire?" his mother asks.

"Like you can't imagine." Jack laughs warmly and smiles at me. "Can't say I've been taken quite that off guard in a good long while."

"We really enjoyed spending the weekend with the kids," Candy adds. "Now, granted, I'd say their lives are a bit chaotic for us old folks, but we sort of got our system down."

System? What does she mean by that? I wouldn't even know what a system was, let alone how to implement one.

"So you had the kids working on the charts, just like you did when we were kids—" Jack halts in midsentence, realizing he's talking about himself and his brother.

"Yes, just like I did with you and Colin." Candy smiles wistfully. I see Jack flinch just a touch. It pains him to hear Colin's name, even after all of these years.

"Someone want to clue me into the system?" I ask, not sure I really want to know.

"Oh, it's all here in this book, dear." She hands me a ledger of sorts.

I open it and see pages and pages of chores, duties, and expectations, all organized according to child. There's a page for making beds, a page for doing homework, a page for helping with the dishes, a page for packing lunches—and remembering to take them to school.

Whoa. I'm blown away by this degree of organization. That someone could come in for a long weekend and whip into shape my chaotic world is quite a feat.

"And this actually *worked* with the kids?" I ask incredulously.

"Oh, sure. Like a charm. The kids love to do it. It's sort of like a game."

Since when has doing chores been a fun thing? Though, who am I to argue with success?

"I'll be happy to go over everything with you, if you're interested in trying it out, Claire. I found it was the only way I could keep things running when the boys were little."

I'm skeptical but desperate. "I guess we could give it a try."

I always used to think that if I could have anticipated the level of chaos that would enter my life with children, I could have planned to be ready for it a little bit more. The demands on my organizational skills prekids amounted to little more than remembering to coordinate my bra and panties when I got dressed. I could never have imagined the extent to which I'd be in over my head from the get-go. I truly believed that the only hard developmental time with children was those "terrible twos." Wasn't I in for a surprise when the terrible twos morphed like a clever virus into all sorts of other terribles—fours, sixes, eights? Teens?

I started out parenthood in a state of disorganization, and I've been careening down the oil-slicked path into what I now recognize as unsalvageable disequilibrium ever since. So it does unsettle me—while providing a (false?) sense of hope that perhaps even I, Claire "Juggle-Six-Plates-in-the-Air-and-Hope-None-Shatter -on-the-floor-'Cause-When-the-Hell-Am-I-Ever-Going-to-Vacuum" Doolittle, can reform my jaded ways. Is it possible to find salvation in one little black ledger?

Just as I mull over this imponderable, I hear an avalanche of children thundering down the steps.

"Mommyyyyyyyyyy!" Matthew wraps his arms around my waist so tightly I have to pee. "I missed you!"

"Matthew, honey, I think you've grown three inches since Thursday!" I exclaim.

The girls come up behind Bubba and reach up for hugs. Even Cam moves in for a squeeze.

"It sure seems like a long time that I've been gone, doesn't it?" I ask. I really am so happy to see them, and feel so energized having been able to recharge my battery—which must have been seeping acid all over my life, now that I think about it in hindsight.

"We had lots of fun with Grandma and Daddy Dick," Lindsay says. "We went to the zoo, and to the movies, and we all did a sleepover in the basement on Thursday night."

"A sleepover in the basement on a school night?" Jack asks with a hint of irritation in his voice. I throw him a look that reminds him I'll be happy to rake through his pile of dead leaves in order to find the new leaf he's supposed to have turned over.

He smiles instead. "Lucky you, Lindsay. It sounds like you had a better weekend than we did." He winks at me.

Looks like both Lindsay and Jack got lucky this weekend. And Claire, for that matter. I look around at my family, happily chattering about our weekend, and for the first time in a while a peaceful smile of contentment spreads over my face. It feels as if a burden that's been strapped to my back for a long time has finally been lifted, dismantled, and packed away for good.

It's Sunday night. We've (notice the plural *we* there) gotten all the kids to bed. Not a word from any of them yet. Jack even helped with the dishes tonight.

I'm in the bathroom, wondering if Sunday night counts this time, considering we took care of Sunday night about ten times over the past two days. Then I remember that Jack is of the male species, so I get out the old prep kit and make myself ready, knowing as I do that, for men, any occasion for sex is a viable one. But that's okay, because I'm starting to get used to the idea that that's a *good* thing.

I slip into bed next to Jack, who—believe it or not—is not wearing his usual pin-striped pajamas.

"Well, this is a switch," I say, looking over at his broad, bare chest. "Going without, are we?"

Jack laughs. "You noticed, eh? I guess I sort of enjoyed playing skins versus shirts this weekend."

"Oh, yeah? Does that mean I'm supposed to be the one in the shirt?"

He looks over and notices that for once I'm not wearing my usual raggedy nightshirt, and instead have dug out an actual silky nightgown from the bowels of my dresser drawers. I think it was one of those failed attempts at a gift for Valentine's Day from Jack a few years back. Not to appear ungrateful, but really, how many women honestly want lacy underthings for Valentine's Day? I'd bet plenty of women would be far happier with a pat on the back and a night off from cooking rather than those thinly veiled sexual aids that are really for their spouses' own fantasy-driven benefit. But then again, it does feel nice against my skin.

"You dressed up for me?"

I didn't think he'd notice, actually. "You know, when you make an effort, it makes me want to try harder, too."

"Funny how that works," he says, snuggling in next to me. "I've been thinking about something, Claire."

"Something good, I hope?"

"Oh, yeah, really good, I think," he says. "Why don't you start training with me, and maybe you and I can run the marathon together?"

Christ, this man must have a hell of a lot more faith in me than I have in myself. Me? Run a freaking marathon? Wait a second. Me. Running a marathon. What's so crazy about that idea? I mean, I've birthed five fairly large children with no epidurals. What can be harder than that?

"You really think I can do it?"

"Claire, one thing I know is that if you put your mind to something, you can do it," he says, scruffing my hair.

Just knowing that he has faith in me is enough for me to blithely agree to this folly.

I dream of being deathly thirsty and having legs made of rubber. Not a good sign. The alarm goes off at five o'clock, and instead of my nudging Jack to get up and turn off the alarm, Jack is nudging me to drag my lazy butt out of bed.

"Rise and shine, lazybones!" he says as he pulls at my arm that's comfortably clutching my pillow.

"I don't wanna," I mumble.

"Come on, Claire, get up. You'll be glad I made you," he says, and tugs a bit harder, lifting my head and shoulders off the bed.

I open my eyes into slits no wider than a millimeter. "Are you sure about this? I mean, you could run a whole lot longer and faster without me slowing you down." Nothing like the self-serving tack to getting out of an undesirable obligation.

"I'm sure, baby. Let's go." Jack hoists me up and forces me onto my feet, then escorts me, zombielike, to the brightly lit bathroom.

Eventually I rally and we dress for our run. I'm starting to view this run in much the same way I had been viewing my Sunday-night obligation.

Since Jack's folks are still visiting, I'm not worried about leaving early in the morning without having warned the kids we'd be out. They'll be fine in an emergency. We step out into the predawn air, and whatever wasn't lucid in me a few minutes ago is jarred awake abruptly by the nip in the air. We stretch for a few minutes and take off slowly.

I don't think I've ever seen my neighborhood this

early before. It's actually quite peaceful hearing only the *clap-clap-clap* of our shoes on pavement and the huff of our breath. Even the birds are still asleep. Heck, the newspaper hasn't been delivered yet. I struggle at first to get a pace going, but eventually I'm able to pick it up and stay close enough to Jack to feel as if he and I are actually running together.

"So? What do you think?" he asks me.

"Running?" I assume that's what he means.

"Yeah. Does it feel good?"

I have to think about that for a moment. After all, altering my precious sleep schedule theoretically would not bode well for me. But this feels so right, sort of like what my body has been waiting for me to discover all this time.

"It feels great," I say. "Really great."

When we get back home we wake the children for school.

Chrissy lifts a sleepy eye to see me sweaty and tuckered. "Mommy—what's wrong?"

"Nothing's wrong, honey," I assure her. "I just joined Daddy today on his run."

Charlotte rolls out of bed. "But you don't run. You're the mom."

"Yeah, well, moms can be moms and do other things, like run in marathons," I say. "Sometimes moms get to do the fun stuff, too."

Of course I laugh to myself, because I never before viewed training for a marathon as fun. But I'm beginning to see things in a whole different light, so why not this? After all, working toward an athletic goal is empowering.

At the breakfast table Candy asks us about the marathon.

"So, you decided to just up and run this thing?"

"It's not quite that simple," I say. "There's an intensive

training schedule I'm going to follow. But I do plan to do it. I think it'll be a good thing for me to show the kids—and me—that I'm more than just Mom, that there's a whole other dimension to me."

"Man, I hope you can do it," Cameron says, rolling his eyes.

"Thanks for that vote of confidence. You don't think I can finish?"

"Don't worry, Cam," Jack said. "Your mother will run it, and she'll probably surprise you at how fast she does."

"Yeah," I say half under my breath, not necessarily believing myself, but hoping Jack's right.

Candy and Dick depart as the kids leave for school. Jack kisses me and leaves for work, and as I walk back into the house I look around and notice something most unusual. The breakfast dishes are all rinsed and loaded into the dishwasher; the milk's been put away. The coffeepot is turned off. And no lunch boxes are sitting on the counter. I wonder fleetingly if I've entered the Twilight Zone.

I'm just about to head off to work when I hear my computer ding. I take a quick glance at my in-box and see that it's from Todd.

My Dearest Claire, it begins.

Hmmm, that seems a little intimate, all things considered. But I read on.

I just wanted to touch base after this weekend's fiasco to find out how things turned out. I was very worried about you Friday night, and while I hated to let you go back to your room alone, I know that you would never have considered me as your escort ☺.

It was great seeing you after so many years.

Claire, you look fantastic. But, of course, it made me sad to know that you weren't terribly happy. Maybe you and Jack have had a chance to hash things out.

I wanted to let you know I got an e-mail from Vanna last night. She says that this summer she'll let Sam come out to see me in Indiana. She mentioned something about armed bodyguards, though. Just joking. She said that she and the Promise Keeper are going to some convention in Indianapolis and maybe they could drop Sam off and then go there.

Tina's not sure what to think about having him come to visit, but she's willing to give it a try. Says she'd much rather it be a girl so they could go have manicures together or something.

Claire, I'm sorry if I presumed too much by showing up at your hotel like that. I know it was irresponsible of me. I guess it was too tempting to try to get back what I once had.

I think about that: how hard it is to reclaim something you once had and lost. Damn near impossible. Can Jack and I really keep up this pace, this level of thoughtfulness toward each other? Is it unrealistic to expect that this is how married life should have been all along? The stuff of fairy tales?

Well, Claire, they're calling final boarding call to San Francisco, so I have to run. Please let me know you're doing all right, and would you please stay in touch?

With love always (can't blame a guy for trying!),
Todd

I take a deep breath, savoring the flattery. It's funny; somehow I became in Todd's mind something more than I probably was. While back when we were together I became stale and undesirable to Todd, in the long run even the fresh-baked goods—his new little Twinkie, Vanna—also became old and tasteless, and instead he retreated to the stuff he'd stuck away in the freezer for safekeeping. What does that make me: his cryogenically preserved ex-girlfriend or something?

But I know that Todd and I would have been a bad combination for a lifetime. Todd is . . . well, Todd. He's just not my cup of tea. And as much as I've wanted to kill Jack for his many transgressions, there's just something about Claire and Jack that feels right. Like that old pair of shoes that you'll never get rid of—the ones that were as close to perfect as you'd ever get. After all, everyone knows that even a good pair of shoes can give you blisters if not worn the right way.

Chapter Twenty-Six

I walk into work exactly five minutes early this morning. As I saunter to my office, ready to close the door, Robert and Kat happen by, arm in arm and grinning.

"Claire!" Kat says. She appears to be physically merged to Robert, like two paper dolls that someone has ironed or hermetically sealed together or something.

"Kat! Robert!" I look back and forth from one face to the other, trying to decipher their facial hieroglyphics.

"We've got some great news for you!" Kat is stroking Robert's hands with her well-manicured nails.

"You're pregnant!" I say, hoping I'm only joking.

Kat waggles her finger at me. "Silly Claire! We'll wait until we're married for that," she reprimands. She will? I can't imagine Kat attempting parenthood at this late age.

"But that *would* be good news, wouldn't it, honey?" Kat asks Robert while scratching beneath his chin.

I feel a bad case of diabetes coming on, what with my glucose intolerance kicking in. The amount of syrupy love goo in here is excessive.

"How was the trip?" Kat asks, and I really want to fill her in, but I don't exactly want Robert to be privy to my most private experience.

"It was fantastic," I say. "Got off to a grim start, had a little trouble in the middle, but things ended up going swimmingly." I grin.

Kat winks. "Like first-time-in-the-water, learning-to-swim, swimmingly? Or more like deep-sea-diving swimmingly?"

"I'd say, ready-to-explore-the-wreck-of-the-*Titanic*-in-a-few-weeks swimmingly."

"See, Claire, didn't I tell you to take Auntie Kat's advice?"

Robert's hands are inching—no, more like they're footing, or yarding—up her body.

"I know, I know. I sort of did, sort of didn't," I say. "I can't tell you how much of your advice or how much of my intuition did the trick, but—"

"So, you did the trick then?" she teases.

"Yeah, the trick. Not The Chore."

Robert is looking at us both like we're speaking Portuguese.

Kat claps. "Brava, Claire! I'm so proud of you! You found it again!"

I blush, because Robert surely must be deciphering our Portuguese.

Kat grabs me for a tight hug and whispers into my ear, "See, I told you you'd want to fuck the man under the right circumstances."

I splutter something incoherent back to her, because I'm still embarrassed that she's saying this in front of my boss, of all people.

"The good news I wanted to tell you is this," Kat says. "The French embassy had a cancellation!"

"For?" I ask.

"For our wedding, of course!"

I look at her, a little surprised. "You're going ahead with it, then?"

"Absolutely," she says. "The embassy has an available date in late October, the thirtieth. You *will* be my matron of honor, right?"

I give Kat a hug. "My best friend, I'd be honored to be your matron of honor. Again." I whisper that last word, hesitant to drag old history into this union.

I learn too late that Kat's wedding date happens to be exactly twenty-four hours after Jack and I will have run the Marine Corps Marathon. How I am going to be able to stand as Kat's matron of honor without some sort of backup support remains to be seen. But I will be there, come hell or high water, to help my dear friend optimistically renew her faith in marriage.

By September, Jack and I are running up to ten miles every few days, alternating cross-training and weights along with shorter runs. We do long runs approaching twenty miles every other Saturday, when Candy can come to spend the morning with the kids. I can't believe how I'm in such better shape in just a few short months. And how much better shape my life is in.

Over the summer all sorts of good things happened. Jack finally had that vasectomy I had been nagging him to do for the past five years. That freed us up a whole lot, and we've certainly been taking advantage of it. We even had a little ceremonial burning-of-the-birth-control celebration, in fact. I can tell you I now know that the bathroom exhaust fan doesn't do a great job of eradicating the smell of burned rubber. I can still smell it on humid days.

Jack also has taken over more responsibility with the children, and I don't mean by being bossy and yelling at them. Instead he does fun things with them:

camping, going to sporting events, that sort of thing. Also, all summer Cam took charge of watching the other kids during a lot of my and Jack's training sessions, which seem to get longer and longer.

The kids have been following along with Grandma Candy's military regimen like champs. Only occasionally do I find them slipping back to their old habits. And now that school's back in session, the kids know that they get only one left-lunch-box retrieval per semester. After that they go hungry at lunch. I probably save ten gallons a week of gas not running to and from school with their meals.

Luckily Jack and I have comfortably slipped back to our old, old habits. He and I have discovered how much we actually like each other again. Jack has been seeing a therapist to help him finally come to grips with the loss of Colin after all these years. It's been wonderful to see him shed the suit of despair he's worn so awkwardly for so long. And it's been fantastic to see me shed the extra weight that seemed to accompany my marital woes.

I'm working at my desk on a press release about a new-and-improved tin can for some manufacturing association—ah, the glamour of PR—when I notice an e-mail has arrived. I click on the name and read on.

> Dear Mrs. Doolittle: My dad says I should send you this e-mail to thank you for reminding him what a "stupid dope" he was (his words). He tells me that you are the one I have to thank for him finally coming to his senses, and that if he hadn't been shamed into action by you, he might never have known the joys of fathering a kid as nice as me. He thought it might be a good thing for us both to e-mail you to let you know how

much we appreciate your intervention on my behalf. My father just hollered something about your "bossiness," but please disregard that.

I spent a few weeks visiting with my father this summer, and since then he's been coming out to see me with all of the frequent-flier points he's collected over the years. At first I thought he was a real jerk, but I finally let myself get to know him a little bit, and I don't think he's half bad.

Thanks again for helping me to get my father back. It's something I've always hoped for.
Respectfully,
Sam Sterodnik

Aww . . . I'm touched by such a sweet note. I'm surprised that he has his father's name. Wonder why he didn't take the name of his stepfather?

I decide to write back before returning to my compelling press release.

Dear Sam: That was the nicest thank-you note I think I've ever received. I'm very happy for you that your father has come around finally. I guess he's just a lot slower than the rest of us, don't you think? I can't take much credit for his transformation—I just gave him the little push I think he knew he needed to collect up the courage to contact you.

I'm sure he's the proudest father to be found, now that he's got you back. Make sure you keep your dad on his toes, okay?
With best wishes,
Claire Doolittle

My computer dings and I see it's from Todd:

Claire—what can I say? You're the best, still.
Lucky for me I decided to track you down when I
did. While my motives may not have been pure,
your advice most certainly was. I finally feel good
that I've righted a few enormous wrongs in my
life: with my son, and with you, of course. It's
good that I'm getting the hang of this fatherhood
gig, because Tina just announced that she's expecting. She's certain it's a girl. Wow, when it
rains it pours. I can honestly say that life is good.
And in large part I have you to thank for lighting
the match underneath my butt. I hope all is well
with your passel of kids and that you and Jack are
on speaking terms. Been in any glassed-in eleva-
tors lately? Take care, Claire, and thanks again.
T

Wow. How nice that I was instrumental in that
father-son reunion. And that Todd was equally instrumental in my little husband-wife reconciliation. I have
to write Todd a quick reply.

Dear Todd: Sam's e-mail was so heartening to read. I'm
so very proud of you for fixing your mistakes. You're a lucky
man that your son wants you back, you know. And a baby
on the way! Wow, you're in for a new adventure. Sounds
like you'd better start saving up for those many manicures
your wife and daughter will be enjoying!

Things are going well here. Yes, Jack and I are talking
again. In fact, we're talking lots. And running lots. Believe it or
not, I, Claire Doolittle, am training to run the Marine Corps
Marathon in just a few weeks. Can you believe it? Me?! I've
been training hard and in my spare time doing some volunteer
work for the free clinic nearby. I'm thinking of leaving my job

sometime soon to get involved in something I really believe in. Kat tells me she hears a PR job might be opening up at the World Wildlife Fund, which I think I'd like. But I'll wait till the marathon is over.

Kat is getting married again the day after the marathon. I hope I won't have to be dragged down the aisle because my legs refuse to work!

Well, Todd, it looks like we helped each other out of quite a mess, didn't we? Let's hope we're both on the straight and narrow now. But if you ever need anything, you know my e-mail address!

Love, C

(P.S. You may have noticed that I signed off with the word "love," and I think I'd better clarify my meaning. Because I do still love you, after all we've been through together. It's not a romantic love, as it once was long ago, but it's a love built on our shared life experiences, respect, and a lifelong friendship. I'm glad we're friends again.)

Chapter Twenty-Seven

I hear noises in my sleep. Ringing, banging, rattling, clanking noises. I reach out with my arm to hammer down the snooze button for a few more blessed minutes of shut-eye, but instead I feel hair. Or fur. Hard to say.

Suddenly the room is bathed with predawn light, and the noises get louder. I squint to see the kids surrounding the bed, pounding on pots and pans with wooden spoons and other pilfered kitchen utensils.

"Wake up, Mommy!" Matthew has a toy drum, too, and he's drumming right next to my ear. "It's marafon day! Come on, wake up, Daddy!"

I feel a tongue laving my face. It smells vaguely like truffles. Or some other woody fungus. Tripod. Blech.

I drag an arm across my face to wipe away the unwelcome coating of slime. The next thing I know the kids and even the dog are jumping up and down on our bed, and I feel like we're lost at sea in a powerful storm. My stomach is lurching with the motion, the aroma of dog breath, and the rattling nerves that began to plague me around bedtime last night and con-

tinue still. Today is the day to see if I can tough it out
for twenty-six long miles traversing the nation's capital.

Bubba springs off the bed at the sound of a nearby
meow. He creeps stealthily toward Dolly Llama and
snatches her, redepositing the cat on top of my face.
Her long calico fur smothers my breathing passages
until she decides instead to stand and poke into my
hair, kneading her paws along my scalp line, giving a
little kitty massage.

All of this activity is a bit overwhelming for me this
morning, especially because I know I need to get up
and get going so that we're there early enough to get
ready for the race. But I'm still so very tired and I'm
not ready to awaken.

Jack is laughing at the chaos in our bedroom.
"Come on, kids. Let's dump your mother out of bed."

At that, the six of them go to Jack's side of the bed
and hoist the mattress up, literally dumping me onto
the floor.

"Hey! I resemble that!" I say, laughing despite myself.

Jack comes around to my side and lends me a hand
to get up.

My mother pokes her head into the bedroom.

"I heard all sorts of commotion coming from here!"
she says with a sly grin. I know my mother put the kids
up to the noisemaking. "Get out of bed, already. You've
got a big day ahead of you!"

She's not kidding there. Twenty-six freaking miles
I'm gonna run today? I've gone only twenty so far. How
I'm going to find the strength to get through that final
six is yet to be determined.

I peer out the window at the bluebird sky we've been
graced with today. Not a cloud in sight, only a con-
stant flow of air traffic headed to and from National
and Dulles airports. The planes above wink at me, the

early morning sunlight reflecting off their metallic exteriors. It's early enough that traffic on the Shirley Highway is still light; no bumper-to-bumper meanie commuters out today, thank goodness. Jack and I decide to drive separately from the rest of the family, leaving my parents to haul the kids down a little closer to race time. We figured any distractions at this point would be detrimental to our game-day mental state.

We park at the Pentagon, stopping at the Runners' Village before taking Metro blue line over to Rosslyn. The Metro is packed with fellow martyrs, all flocking to the Iwo Jima Memorial to begin what may well be the hardest day of many of our lives. Fitting that it's the Marine Corps Marathon, because I almost feel as if I'm bracing for battle.

We collected our numbers—numbers 11,484 and 5 respectively—and secured the chips to our shoes yesterday at the Marathon Expo. All we've got to do now is stash our belongings at the designated location and head to the bathrooms. While I had only a small cup of water and a banana today, I've already peed five times. When I get nervous I'm a veritable river overflowing its banks. It appears that I'm not the only one desperate to use facilities, and the sea of Porta-Johns is teeming with about a thousand others who have equally nervous stomachs, apparently.

At this point we have little else to do but be anxious, so waiting in a bathroom line isn't such torture. My only worry is that I'll finish up and need to keep getting back in line so I can be sure to go one more time before the cannon goes off.

Jack's holding my hand as I pace a step in each direction, back and forth.

"You'll be fine, honey," he says. "You're going to finish in no time."

"I only have two concerns: one, that I finish, and

two, that I beat the bridge. Well, maybe three: that I don't keel over and die along the route."

They reopen the Fourteenth Street Bridge by one forty-five in the afternoon, and that's no time to be stuck running across it, with a million speeding cars whizzing by with their noxious fumes. Plus, it seems sort of symbolic, being able to make it before the race gives you up for gone.

"No problem. You'll beat the bridge by a long shot," Jack says.

There are so many runners that we have been divided into two waves. We're in the first one, so we linger as close to the start as possible so we can hear any relevant announcements. Everywhere I look are handsome marines. Can't get a better-looking group of volunteers, I think. At least if someone has to give me mouth-to-mouth I'll be able to enjoy it, maybe fantasize about a man in uniform a bit.

"Mommy!" I hear Lindsay shouting at me. We told my folks to meet us here; they'll then try to follow us to different points along the race.

My mother and father come up behind the children, and they're holding out shirts emblazoned with our names across them.

"See, I read about this on the Internet," my mother says. "We have your names on the shirts so that while you're running along the race course, people can cheer you on."

I look at the shirts. Mine says, "Claire Bear," and beneath that it says, "I'm with Jack." Jack's shirt says, "Jack," and of course, "I'm with Claire." Cute. Of course, now strangers will be hollering for Claire Bear, which is a touch embarrassing. Plus, who knows how far ahead of me Jack will be? Well, I know my mom means well. It was sweet, really, that she took shirts Jack and I already have run distances in. The last thing

I want right now is a new shirt that will rub me raw in all the wrong places once I'm well into the race.

We don our shirts—I pull my original shirt out from underneath my new one, an old trick we girls learn once we're old enough to not want people to see our boobs—and pose for pictures with the kids. I think they're more excited about this race than we are. They've been talking about it for ages, especially Matthew, excited to watch the "marafon."

We give kisses to the kids and they wish us well. We look at the official clock and see that there are only about twenty minutes left till race time.

"I hate to say it, but I have to pee again before I can't pee for hours," I say. We look around to see enormous lines at the multitude of portable toilets.

"Come on, Claire." Jack grabs my hand and we head up a hill. We get to the top, and he points at something in the distance.

"Hey! You see that building?" he asks me.

I look off in the direction he's pointing. "Where?"

"There—past the building made of white bricks, that redbrick one, with all the balconies?"

"Yeah, I see it," I say.

"That's where it all started, remember, Claire?"

Of course. Jack's apartment, with the obscured view of the Iwo Jima Memorial.

I snort. "How could I forget?" After all, my first time there was certainly a memorable occasion.

He leans over and kisses me. "So, when you get to the point of the race that you can't go on, when your body wants to quit and your legs won't move and you can't breathe and you can't think and you're a complete mess, Claire, I want you to think about us, the first time we were together, and think about how much we've been through, you and I. And you'll know that you have the strength to do it, okay, baby?"

I wipe a tear away from my eye. "That's so romantic, Jack! Thanks, sweetie. The two of us together can do anything, can't we?"

I hug him.

We look down to where the race will be starting in minutes.

"But now you'd better do your business," Jack says. He tries to block me from others' view (no small feat with thirty thousand runners and their supporters milling about); I'm behind some trees, but not many. I pee, then get up and turn, only to see a whole lot of other bare white bottoms exposed nearby. I guess we weren't the only ones who didn't have time to wait for the Porta Potties. Jack and I crack up laughing, and head down the hill.

I can't believe the mass of humanity assembled here. All of us trying to tame a beast that is just out of reach. I can tell by looking around that I'm not the only newbie to this thing. You have the serious runners, those lean, rangy individuals who are akin to human cheetahs. Then you have people like me who run despite our physical disinclination to do so. Lucky for me, I was able to train without serious injury.

We're amassed like an enormous herd of buffalo awaiting the cannon shot, and as soon as we hear it people take off, some just shooting out of the starting line and cutting clear of the masses. We're way back in the crowd, many minutes from the starting line. Jack and I plan to pace ourselves so that we don't use our energy reserves too soon. We're going to stop at every watering station to stay hydrated. I told Jack that he doesn't need to stick by me, because I don't want to hold him back.

The first couple of miles are relatively easy. The hardest part is navigating the other thirty thousand runners: the crowd is still thick and claustrophobic. We run up Lee Highway, then head down Spout Run along the George Washington Parkway, my favorite road in DC.

We cross into Georgetown, and I distract myself imagining the debauchery that will occur here in two nights, when the area is overrun with Halloween revelers. Right now, partying is probably the farthest thing from the minds of the people who have currently overrun the streets of Georgetown. We travel along the Rock Creek Parkway (where there's a great bagpipe band playing for the runners), and by the time we're passing the Kennedy Center and the exquisite monuments—the Lincoln Memorial, the Vietnam Veterans Memorial—I'm starting to feel it. I grab a Powerade at a watering station and go on. Jack isn't too far ahead of me, and occasionally he looks back to be sure he hasn't lost me.

We head up past the Washington Monument, the Capitol. This is the way to tour Washington, I think. No parking, no schlepping backpacks and juice boxes, no kids whining because they wanna go home, or demanding to ride on the carousel on the Mall. Just me, my feet, and a powerful determination to finish the task at hand while reveling in the beautiful scenery.

As I get to East Potomac Park I feel a lump in my shoe that feels like a pebble or something. I'm approaching my favorite statue—*The Awakening*, which appears to be a giant supine man emerging from the earth—and I just have to stop and get this stone out of my shoe. Quickly I remove my sneaker and peel back my saturated sock, only to find out that what I thought was a pebble is actually an enormous blister that has ripped open.

Where's that Drawer of Excess when I need it? No Band-Aids, no scissors to cut the skin off, no tube of

Neosporin like I'd use on the kids. So I just smooth out
the flap of flesh, coax my wet sock back on, and tie up
my shoe. I look up to see Jack headed—backtracking—
toward me. Unable to expend my energy with my voice,
I mouth to him, *I'm okay; I love you*, and give him a
wink. He gives me a thumbs-up and turns back in the
proper direction. Of course, I'm lying to the man. I'm
not okay. I'm dying a slow death. But I can't go this far
and quit, no matter how battered and bruised I'm starting to feel and how devoid of oxygen my lungs are. It
would help if there were more people along the side-
lines cheering here, but the crowd is sparse. I soldier on
like a good marine, though.

Despite my exhaustion, I have to hold my breath at
the point where we cross over to the Jefferson Memorial. It's such a beautiful spot, with the water reflecting
the crisp blue sky and the trees in their autumnal
splendor. The majesty of the monument is truly breath-
taking. It's one of those sites that make you feel that all
is right with the world. Even when gasping for air and
feeling so weak from saline depletion.

At this point I start to notice the many strangers who
are calling out to me: "You can do it, Claire Bear!" "Go,
Bear! Go, Jack!" It's energizing to hear these people encouraging me on. And I realize I need the encouragement now, because this is where the tough part kicks
in. I've never run this far in my life, and these last five
or six miles are going to be nearly impossible.

I beat the bridge, a milestone I needed to achieve
for my own peace of mind. I don't think I could have
continued if I had to deal with the onslaught of auto-
motive emissions. My mind is a miasma of confusion
now. My hands are swelling up, as are my ankles.
Someone along the side of the road hands me a
chicken bouillon cube, and I grab it, pop it into my
mouth. I know I have to get some needed salt in me.

The tang of salt and concentrated processed chicken makes me want to throw up, but honestly, I'm already leaking enough from the other end—having birthed five children, I'm struggling with a little incontinence right now, unfortunately—so I'd rather not have things come out the top as well. I swig a Powerade, knowing it's going to run right through me, literally. Well, all dignity has been dashed at this point anyhow, so what the hell.

The salt helps to clear my muddled head, but still I need a focus, something to keep my brain going and force my legs to move on, one step at a time, especially through Crystal City, which is probably the low point of this run. At least it's pretty flat.

Then I remember Jack's words, about thinking of where we've come from, how far we've gone. Maybe a bit about how far we strayed before veering back on course. I think about that first night on the balcony of his apartment, the amazing amount of love—well, maybe it started out as lust, but still—we held for each other.

I think about the day that we found out about Colin. How stoic Jack was, how strong he was in the face of adversity.

I think about the day each of our children was born: from Cameron, who took two days to arrive, all the way to Bubba, who was almost born while I drove the minivan to the hospital.

It's been a marathon we've been running in all these years, I realize now. Nothing we ever trained for, but something we got into for the long haul, for the duration. We didn't enter for the short race. Granted, perhaps we hadn't anticipated quite so many bumps in the road. Didn't know about those blisters that would get to the point that they felt like stones—make that boulders—in your shoes.

Of course, I didn't know that I'd also have strangers

to cheer us on, and loved ones, too, when we least expected it. Candy and Dick (tee-hee-hee), who would swoop in when I needed it most to help me get through the hard times. Kat, my voice of reason, making sure I didn't succumb to my sometimes irrational suppositions (even though I did. But at least she tried).

My feet are like concrete blocks now. I have sweat blinding my eyes. Each breath feels like I'm inhaling underwater, or like my head is submerged in a goldfish bowl. I worry that I reek of pee, but my head is so oxygen-deprived that my sense of smell has been obliterated and I can't even tell. I don't have the energy to get through this thing. Someone hands me a tube of GU energy gel, and I gladly squirt it into my mouth. I can see Jack off in the distance, but everything is a blur in my head. I'm having tunnel vision. My foot is killing me, but it's nearly numb, so it almost doesn't matter. If I don't stop soon I don't think I'll ever be able to stop running, like I'm on autopilot forever.

Passing the Pentagon is a desolate stretch, as there are no crowds here. The only thing keeping me going is that I know I'm getting close. Hard to believe that just about five hours ago I was full of energy and jitters parking my car nearby, and now I feel like a partial cadaver. What a difference a half a day makes.

Further along Route 110 the crowds are going wild, jangling cowbells, screaming out to those of us who are this far back in the race, encouraging us to keep running: "You're almost done," "You can do it."

I hear someone screaming out my name and I look over to see who it is.

"Pick it up, Sky Slut!" It's Kat, attached to Robert, waving a sign with Jack's and my names on it.

There are a few people who stare over at me to see who—and what—exactly is a sky slut. Then others start rooting for Claire the Sky Slut, and I laugh as best I can under the circumstances. Thank God for Kat, because that was the boost I needed to continue. Sometimes, when I'm reading to the kids at night, my eyes close just a little bit with each word on the page; that's how I was feeling until I heard Kat holler at me: each step was one step slower than the last, and I was fearing I was about to come to a complete stop, short of my destination.

The shimmering reflection off the Potomac has mesmerized me. I'm getting so close to Rosslyn, and I can't even see Jack anymore. I don't know if he's gotten some magical powers and picked up to a near sprint. Or maybe he's fallen by the side of the road and I'm too oblivious to notice. I sort of remember feeling this out-of-it one time in college when Todd's roommate gave us hash brownies to eat before a midterm exam as a joke. Such pressure to succeed, but some strange internal refusal to do so. Like something's pushing me forward and pulling me back all at the same time.

Come to think of it, I think I felt a lot like this after forty-eight hours of labor and my body being pushed inside out. At least then they handed me oxygen to breathe after every time I had to push. Oxygen would be a good thing right about now.

I'm approaching Heartbreak Hill, the final ascent. People are screaming and yelling, and in the near distance I see throngs of people, everyone waiting to see their loved ones as they complete this amazing milestone. I put one foot in front of the other; I think I'm running slower than I could walk it. I feel as if every cell of my being is breaking down. I don't know how I am going to make it.

Just then I hear, "Claire!"

I look up to see Jack running down the hill toward

me. I reach out my hand and he grabs it and guides me up the hill, pulling me just enough to encourage my own forward momentum.

"Claire, you're almost there," he says. Yeah, I remember him telling me that when Cam was being born, and that took two freaking days.

"I can't do it," I say to him. "I'm out of steam."

He tugs at my arm and won't let go. "You *can*, Claire. You've done the hard part. Remember, you and me, baby—together we can do anything."

We chug up the hill, and the finish line is before me. Jack, who already went through it, pushes me across. A marine grabs me and helps me slow down, handing me a blanket to make sure I don't get chills. Then I am set upon by Jack, the kids, my parents. Someone hands me a bottle of Gatorade, which I inhale and promptly throw up. I end up with a cookie in my hand; Lord knows how that got there. I can't decide if I'm hungry or if I want to throw up again, but I know I am so elated I can't begin to describe it. All I know is my skin is coated with salt crystals, my jog bra has rubbed the skin raw beneath my boobs, and I must smell like one of those ten thousand Porta Potties over there.

Jack comes over and just wraps his sweaty arms around my equally drenched body. We support each other like two poles from a teepee. Our breathing is labored; sweat and salt just coats us. I look down at my foot and see that my shoe is completely red.

"Oh, my God, Jack, my foot," I say, pointing down, but I'm unable to bend over to remove my shoe just yet.

My mother comes over and takes my shoe off, peels away the soaked red sock to reveal that where once was a blister is a gash that's probably been bleeding profusely for six miles. My folks have brought along a bag with some warm-ups and fresh socks and shoes for us. I hobble with my family over to the first-aid tent to get my wound cleaned and dressed.

As I'm coming out of the tent I hear Jack saying something to someone, and I turn to see about the last person on the face of the earth I expected to see here: Todd.

"What are you doing here?" I ask him incredulously. I think Jack wants to know the very same thing.

Todd shakes Jack's hand and gives me a hug.

"Claire, I wanted to be here to see you now that you've found yourself," he says. "I wanted to see you as the winner I know you are, the winner *you* needed to know you were."

"How did you know where to find me?" I ask.

"Remember, Claire, you told me you were running this marathon today. I was able to divert my travels through Washington so I could cheer you—and Jack—on. I knew I could find you at the finish line."

"Wow," I say, hardly full of words right now. "How thoughtful."

"Look, Claire, I don't want to disturb your family moment," Todd says. "I just want to say congratulations, and to tell you I'm proud of you: you took charge and fixed things, and that's not an easy thing to do."

I nod my head and reach out to give him one last hug. "Right back at ya, big guy."

Todd takes a few minutes to meet my kids and say hello to my parents (who aren't exactly wild about seeing him, especially since they're not up on all the details); then he walks away.

"Claire?" Jack looks at me. "Is there anything you need to tell me? Is everything okay?"

I sigh and smile at him. "Nope, nothing you need to know about. Everything's just perfect, Jack. Just perfect."

Amid the throng of people at the finish line, we revel in the accomplishment, this amazing achievement; then I wonder: how the hell am I going to be at Kat's wedding tomorrow?

Kat and Robert arrive to find us decompressing. Kat has a bottle of celebratory Veuve Clicquot, which under normal circumstances I'd gladly chug willingly, but now I can take only small sips or else I'll throw it up.

We hang for a while near the finish line, cheering on others, trading stories with those who finished already. One woman told me that during those last arduous six miles, she plotted the detailed murder of her beloved husband. I don't think I'd be inclined to admit that one, however.

I am amazed at the stamina of the many who performed this marathon in wheelchairs, despite the hills, despite the relentless crowds, despite their distinct disadvantage. They are the true victors here. The rest of us are just lucky to have done it on legs.

We work our way over to the Rosslyn Metro, only to find that—surprise, surprise—the escalators are broken down and we have to walk the steep decline into the bowels of the underground subway system. It's a bit funny to see the hundreds of other runners who are struggling to figure out how to get down the escalator steps while experiencing such intense muscle fatigue. Lucky for Jack and me, we have each other for support, as well as my parents and the kids.

When we arrive at the Pentagon station—surprise, surprise—the escalator steps are broken and we have to mount the hundred-plus steps to get back out again. Ah, technology. The many limping runners milling about remind me of lame soldiers heading homeward at the end of the Civil War.

We say our good-byes to Kat and Robert, and my

folks take the kids to their car. Jack and I struggle to get to our car on weakened limbs. I'm so glad that he's driving, because I don't think I have enough strength to depress the accelerator (or the brake, for that matter).

At home, Jack and I sink our battered bodies into separate ice baths, hoping to stave off at least a little of the postmarathon aches and pains. We pop some Advil and each take a couch and lie prostrate, unable to think about moving, at least for a couple of hours.

Chapter TWenty-eight

Though it's Sunday, I don't expect even one child to waft into our room tonight. After what we've been through today, Jack and I made the kids swear they'd give us a good night's sleep. It helps that my folks are staying over to take care of them. Tonight we should sleep the sleep of the near-dead.

I finish brushing my teeth, and the hundred strokes on my hair, and I open the Drawer of Excess in search of lip gloss, only to see one of those old condoms staring up at me. For a moment I wonder if Sunday night will be business as usual, but then I think better of it. Even my Jack isn't going to be up for anything more amorous than a good-night kiss tonight; I'm sure of it. Not that I'd mind under normal circumstances, but tonight I do think it would be too much like corpse sex.

Sure enough, I go back into the bedroom and Jack is sound asleep, despite the news still blaring in the background. I turn off the television, take two more ibuprofen, slip beneath the comforter, and snuggle in next to Jack, every bone, muscle, tendon, and fascia hurting so badly that I worry how I'll get out of bed to go to the bathroom in the middle of the night. It feels so indescribably good.

My parents take care of getting the children off to school in the morning, mercifully letting us sleep off the exertion of the day before. I wake up feeling as stiff as a granny, and creak delicately into the bathroom. I am so thrilled that we've got massages scheduled today. Our wedding gift to Kat: a his-and-hers spa day for the four of us. Perhaps a little self-serving, but that's okay. My parents are taking the kids until tomorrow, and we're going to the Four Seasons (fast becoming my favorite hotel) in Georgetown for pampering, and to stay the night after Kat's nuptial extravaganza.

We pile our formal wear and suitcase into the car and head off to Georgetown. I've always wanted to stay at this Four Seasons, where until now I've gone only for cocktails, but never had a good reason to, since we live just across the river. But since Kat's wedding is on a Monday night at the French embassy, we thought this was a perfect excuse to stay nearby.

We pull up by the entrance and hand the keys to the valet while we check into our room and leave our bags.

We head to the spa for our eleven a.m. appointments for the works, and find Kat and Robert making googly eyes at each other in their spa robes.

"Claire, Jack!" Kat calls to us. "Finally you get here." She's got a bottle of Cristal champagne nearby, and Robert pours some into flutes for Jack and me.

"I honestly thought you two would call and try to poop out on us," Kat says.

"We wouldn't dream of it," I say. Of course, I don't bother mentioning that this massage is the one thing that might keep me alive today, and thus guaranteed my attendance. Well, that and maybe this champagne. Kat always has great taste in champagne.

A spa attendant greets us and sets Jack and me up with robes and slippers; then we girls are taken off for manicures and pedicures while the guys do whatever guys do at spas.

As I sit with my feet soaking in the hot Jacuzzi foot-bath, those amazing jets of water pounding away the pain in them, I moan with pleasure. Despite the gash on my foot.

"God, Kat, that feels orgasmic," I say, and I mean it.

"And isn't it good that you remember what orgasmic feels like?" Kat teases. "I am so very proud of you that you managed to run that marathon. And I'm even prouder of you that you fixed all the problems with Jack. So much easier than getting a divorce."

"You are the expert there," I tease Kat. "But no more. This is the real one, right?"

Kat pauses to think about that.

"Well, the difference this time is how much Robert wants it, I think," she says. "In the past I think *I've* been the motivating force behind getting married. But now it's good. Robert wants it. Badly, if I do say so myself. But I want it too. I've done both sides; I'm older, more mature. I know what I'm looking for."

"You *were* kidding about a baby, weren't you?"

"Oh, God, yes, Claire." She smiles. "No babies to muddy up these marital waters. I have my Tallulah; that's all I need."

The aesthetician is performing a deep-tissue massage on my feet, and I think I'm going to have to tip her my entire bank account—it feels that good.

"So, everything's fine with you and Jack, then?" Kat asks.

Now it's my turn to think. "You know, Kat, everything's pretty close to perfect. Couldn't be better."

After lunch, Jack and I get his-and-hers massages together, and I'm not sure which of us passes out first. I hardly remember my masseur (I think his name was Alex) telling me to flip over, I was so out-of-it.

I feel like a new woman (well, maybe half of a new woman) after that, and we both retreat to our room for a good long soak in our sunken tub before it's time to get dressed for the wedding.

We take a short nap and wake up with barely enough time to shower and dress and get over to the French embassy. I have to be there early as Kat's lady-in-waiting or whatever I am. Luckily, Kat left it to me to wear whatever I wanted as matron of honor. "As long as it's black," she said.

I have a sparkly black strapless ballerina-style dress with layers of tulle that cascade from the waistline. I've pulled my (recently highlighted) hair back in a bun. I apply makeup, put on my diamond necklace—Jack gave it to me for our anniversary last month—and do a double take when I glance back into the mirror. I hardly recognize myself.

Jack is tying his bow tie when I finish up in the bathroom and join him.

Since it's Halloween tomorrow, Jack chose a black tie with an orange cummerbund covered in pumpkins. Kat will probably kill him for Halloween-izing her wedding, but I think it's funny.

"You look like a princess," Jack says, kissing me on the nose.

"In that case, you must be my handsome prince," I reply. I size him up with a scrutinizing eye. Jack looks fantastic. And I look pretty damn good too. Of course, we're both moving awfully slowly today, but all things considered, we're doing just fine.

The embassy, a colossal contemporary marble structure, is bathed in colored lights, which adds to the festive feel of the night. We enter the embassy and are guided to the reception room, which is draped in soft pastel silks to make it feel like we're in an intimate bedouin tent somewhere in the middle of the desert. A string quartet is warming up for the actual wedding ceremony, which is to be held in one end of the room, where chairs covered in linen with bows on the backs are lined up. Kat and Robert will stand beneath the floral canopy set up in the front of the room by the wall of windows.

"Kat, this is amazing," I say. Only an event planner would be able to throw together something so sumptuous in a few short months. And during the high party season in Washington, no less.

Caterers are buzzing about, setting up the bars and the food stations.

Kat and I go back into a private room, where I help her put on her gown. You'd think after three marriages, one would shy away from a white wedding gown, but Kat has a flair for the dramatic, and couldn't pass up yet one more.

Her gown is a formfitting, high-necked, featherlight satin, with a sexy vee slashed all the way to the base of her spine. The train follows subtly behind her, like a shy friend behind the popular girl at school. Kat's sleek dark hair has been slicked back in a chignon, and she honestly looks like she's just stepped from the pages of a bridal magazine. Maybe *Re-Brides*.

"You're magnificent," I tell her. "I've never seen a more blushing bride."

"Thank you," she says. "I think perhaps marriage agrees with me."

We both get a good laugh out of that line, but deep down I hope this time she's right.

Tallulah manages to thoroughly upstage the bride by walking down the aisle first, tossing rose petals along the way, looking like a pink tulle angel sent from above. I help Kat with her train and get her situated before the makeshift altar, then take my cue to sit down in front with Jack. The female minister begins her spiel and I wonder if Kat really takes to heart the words she's saying, words she's heard a few times before.

Kat and Robert do look very smitten with each other, perhaps more so than the last three guys did with her on their wedding days. I start thinking about how tough it must be in some ways to buck up and attempt marriage yet one more time. Marriage is an institution, they say, yet some institutions can be mighty confining.

But then I realize that what's so beautiful about Kat trying this again *is* her boundless optimism, her faith in the possibility of marriage, her belief yet again that this time it will be better.

Sitting on the other end of the aisle from us are my sister Sydney and Philip, of e-mail fame, whom we've grown to adore over the past several months. He treats Syndey as if he really loves her, and she so deserves that. Of course I did make Jack threaten him with bodily harm if he hurt her. (Well, I asked Jack to do that but for some reason he refused.) I watch Syd and Phil's interaction as they focus on the ceremony unfolding. As the minister expounds upon the meaning of love, Philip leans toward Syd's ear and whispers something, eliciting the type of broad, comfortable smile I haven't seen it my sister since her Howdy days.

I look over at Jack to see he's been staring at me. I wonder what he's thinking, wonder if he's reflecting back to our wedding day, so happy, yet so sad. Jack grabs my hand and places it in his lap, holding tightly. He turns it over and traces his finger across my palm. I think he's just doing a random pattern, but then I realize that he's tracing out letters.

I love you, he's writing in my hand.

And I, with my own restored faith in love and marriage and the power of two, reply. "I love you, Jack," I whisper in his ear.

The minister pronounces Kat and Robert man and wife. They kiss, and kiss, and kiss again. Finally they come up for air, and everyone claps. I stand and help Kat with her train, and she and Robert walk up the aisle, looking blissfully content.

Throughout the reception I enjoy watching Kat's furtive glances toward Robert. It's hard to believe that I once viewed Robert as my miserable, pain-in-the-butt boss, but now I look at him in such a different light. He's the one who brought joy back to my dear friend's heart.

Kat has pulled out all the stops for the reception: top-notch food prepared by several of her favorite local chefs and served by the caterer she works most closely with, and an orchestra best known for playing the premier parties in Washington.

It's only fitting that when Kat tosses her bouquet, it lands, unbidden, in Sydney's lap. We all laugh, and Philip and Sydney exchange knowing glances that suggest her being next to the altar might not be such a bad idea after all. Another wedding in the family would be a welcome event. Then maybe Sydney can provide my kids with a few much-needed cousins.

Jack and I are dancing to "The Way You Look To-night," one of my favorite songs. We probably look pretty funny dancing under our current state of physical duress. Nevertheless, I pull him tighter as we glide across the dance floor, and it seems that it's only the two of us, feeling pretty creaky but so happy to be together. Life is good.

After sending Kat and Robert off in fine style, Jack and I hop a cab back to the Four Seasons. We both struggle to get out of the taxi; Jack holds my hand to assist me, and we manage successfully, then limp through the hotel lobby arm in arm. It's late—after midnight—when I hit the button on the elevator. The doors open, and Jack and I get on.

When the doors close, I look at Jack mischievously, and he looks back at me.

"You ever do it in an elevator?" I ask him suggestively.

"Not with you I haven't," he teases. "How 'bout you?"

"Oh, maybe in another life. But never with the likes of you."

Jack quickly looks at the control panel, then finds and flips the stop switch. "There's a first for everything, you know," he growls sexily, pulling me into his arms.

"Jack, we could get caught." I wink at him as he leans over to kiss me.

"That's half the fun of it," he reassures me, reaching up underneath my dress and running his hands up and down my back.

"Oh, I think there's more than that that makes it fun."

Jack's running kisses down my neck.

The alarm starts to ring. He flips the switch on to stop the noise, then flips it off to stop the elevator again.

"We've gotta make it quick," he says as he unzips his tux pants and I step out of my panties.

Jack lifts me up and holds me tightly as I wrap my legs around him. God, his poor legs: first a marathon, and now he's gotta hold me up. He presses me against the elevator wall and slides seamlessly into me. Perfect. The zipless fuck. For a minute we're all hands and mouths and groping and moaning, and I feel Jack tense as I do, and at once we're in sync with each other and we come together in a perfect moment of warmth and love and release.

The alarm begins anew, and we quickly disengage and straighten our clothes before anyone comes to see what's wrong with the elevator.

We get off on our floor and walk arm in arm to our room. I marvel at the knowledge that I know now we've truly left Ward Cleaver behind for good, relegated to maybe an occasional viewing on late-night television. No longer sleeping with Ward Cleaver, instead I'll be happily sleeping next to Jack Doolittle. And the only time I might refer to Jack as Ward in the future is to say with a mischievous grin and a twinkle in my eye, "Ward, I don't think you were hard enough on the Beaver last night!"